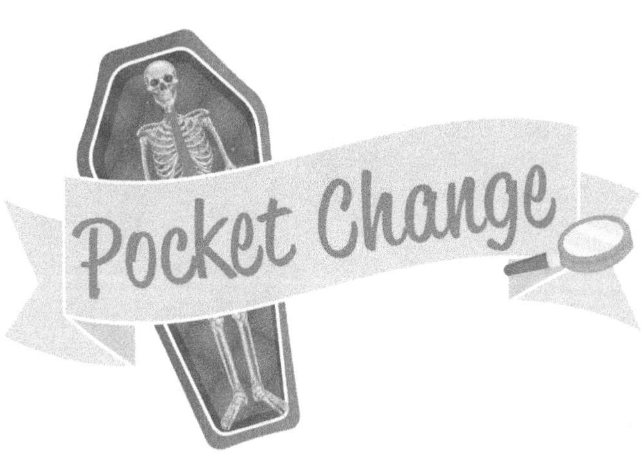

Debbie Archer

Published by Scrivenings Press LLC
15 Lucky Lane
Morrilton, Arkansas 72110
https://ScriveningsPress.com

Printed in the United States of America

Paperback ISBN 978-1-64917-040-8
eBook ISBN 978-1-64917-041-5

Library of Congress Control Number: 2020940033

Cover by Diane Turpin, www.dianeturpindesigns.com

(Note: This book was previously published by Mantle Rock Publishing LLC and was re-published when MRP was acquired by Scrivenings Press LLC in 2020.)

ACKNOWLEDGMENTS

I could never have written without Jesus. He plants the seeds, and I pray my work will glorify Him in every way. Thank you, Lord, for placing the following people in my life to encourage and love me.

Mack, my best friend and love. You never gave up on me. I love you.

To Mom for telling me I could write, and to Daddy who taught me art comes in many forms. To my big brother, Richard, who caught my engineering goof and fixed it and who demanded more of Uncle Ardmore. For Carma and Pete who loved me, and to Aunt Teen for her precious family scrapbook and for being the matriarch of our wonderful family.

To my friends across the years and to Linda, a best friend throughout all the years.

To the Mantle Rock Publishing folks for believing in me. Kathy and Jerry, Diane, my phenomenal cover artist, and Pam and Kathy, editors who go above and beyond. I adore you all. To my entire Mantle Rock author family, what a fun and exquisite group you are. Regina and Candance, you are the icing on the cake! Thanks, also, to Shannon and Linda of Scrivenings Press.

To Penny Sloan, owner of Spider's Webb Bookstore and promotion queen extraordinaire. What would I do without you?

To my friends at Barnes and Noble, ACFW Arkansas, and Writers' Ink. To Arkansas writing cohorts Tara Johnson, Candance West Posey, Dorothy Johnson, Talya Tate Boerner, Ann Cooper McCauley, Rosie Baldwin, Shannon Taylor Vannatter, Martha Rodriguez, and web designer Linda Nixon Fulkerson. There are so many more, including my beta readers. While space prohibits me from listing everyone, know that you are in my heart.

For critique partners near and far, thank you for your honesty. Know that my appreciation is beyond measure. Joy Avery Melville, you are a light unto this world and a pure blessing in my life. I'm so honored to be your friend and blessed to have you in my life. We're releasing the same month! Wouldn't our Kate, who championed both of us, be thrilled?

For my Street and Review Teams, you're all the bomb diggity! To librarians everywhere—our hearts beat as one. To Rhonda Potter for your prayers and pure love of God, and to all my praying soul sisters and brothers. Prayers were answered.

To my guardian animals who stick with me in my office when I'm holed up writing. A special thank you to my students for being excited for me and to my church family for celebrating this blessing with me.

John and Renee Bland, thank you for all you've done to support and encourage me. Joyce Rose, thanks to you I am enjoying a life filled with joy and fulfillment. Had you not cared all those years ago, this writer would never have made it to college. Thank you for being my friend.

To the two Bonnie's in my life, both teachers: One taught me to English and French; one taught me strength and journalism. I love you both dearly and am so honored to now call you friend.

To Shel who always listens to my plot lines and to Claudia for your true-blue friendship. Deb Blalock, you are God's gift to everyone around you. God bless you for your goodness and for your support.

To my teacher friends throughout the years and those involved in Teachers as Writers. What fun we had. Thank you, Alexandria LaFaye. You. Are. Remarkable.

Finally, to my Facebook friends and encouragers: Thank you for caring and sharing, for posting and commenting. You have my loving appreciation.

Blessings to you all.

To Mack...Always

CHAPTER ONE

"The twinkle lights are perfect. Let's get the coffin and put Bo in it." I shouted to make myself heard. From the parking lot, I cocked my head and examined the two sparkling bay display windows of Pocket Change, my brand-spanking-new business. The glittery cob-webbed scarecrow nestled nicely in the antique rocker. I rubbed my arms and fussed for not grabbing my jacket before coming outside. For mid-October, the wind had a bite. The thermometer strained its little mercury to stay on thirty-nine. Touching forty was evidently out of the question. My gaze shifted to the bay window to the left side of the front door. It screamed "perfect spot for Bonesie!", our resident skeleton. I gave Mama an okay sign through the window then headed for the door, slowing when a movement to my right caught my attention.

With a sideways glance, I stopped in my tracks. All thoughts of the brisk cold disappeared when a pair of broad shoulders and a head of dark brown hair stepped out of a pea-green Chevy truck parked in the next lot. Had a tropical front moved through? The temperature was on the rise. I quit rubbing my arms and squinted. Multi-tasking is not my strong point. Applying mascara and forming an O with my mouth at the same time is about all I can handle.

I moved to the privacy of the big oak tree in front of our new shop. Mama had named the tree Mabel. When asked how she knew it was a female, she told me she thought all oaks were female. They were strong, protective, and loved to reach for the sky. Couldn't argue with that.

"Oh, Mabel, would you look at that?" I muttered, praying Mabel's crimson autumn splendor would camouflage my own red hair and freckles. From my vantage point, I could view the new arrival walking around to the other side of his truck, where he pulled a green toolbox from the front floorboard and sauntered into the back of the old building next to mine. Once a bait store, the rustic clapboard structure sat lonely and locked up.

Until today. Now a muscled-up man tromped around inside. I aimed my phone, focused, and snapped two pics. My private Businesses Around Town board was kinda skimpy. Truth be told, there weren't many businesses of any kind in my little hometown anymore. I hoped to change that.

Still spying on broad-shouldered, brown-haired-cute guy, my ears picked up a persistent tapping noise. Mama stood in the window and pecked on the glass. That crimp in her brow was a good indicator she was aggravated. Even with reinforced storm windows between us, I could clearly hear her voice. "Mary Clare, what are you doing?"

I hurried back inside. The tropical breeze passed, and I was pretty sure the goose bumps made my freckles look 3-D. "Okay, let's go to the storage building, Mama." If I could get her sidetracked, maybe she wouldn't ask me about my mini-spying expedition.

She pushed her sleeves up higher on her arms, which meant a heavy-duty tug job was inevitable. "Wait just a minute." She blew a few wisps of chestnut hair out of her eyes. "Let me put the finishing touch on that armoire with a few more sparkles, and we'll tackle the coffin." She scurried off to the other side of the store, a glittery spider web in hand.

"The casket will set just the right tone." I sidestepped over to the area where we would park the casket and looked at the lettering for the display. R.I.P., which stood for Read in Peace, had been Mama's idea. Cozy little crannies made up of gadgets, puzzles, and puffy pillows gave the store a homey feel.

I don't know who was more excited about our new business venture, Mama or me. I'd named the shop Pocket Change as a play on words, but it meant much more. I needed to succeed at this. Lord knows there's a whole list of things I'm not good at, but maybe I could do something to help our town. Pocket Change stood for the changes we hoped to set in motion in our tiny metropolis of 1,235. People would be employed because of our little venture, and while it wouldn't change international economic forecasts, it might boost the little municipality of Pocket. I stuck my phone in my bra and breathed a sigh of satisfaction.

Every item in the store had a story all its own. Each odd antique held its own mystique. Every book contained that elusive smell of paper, ink, and inspiration. I realized paper books might soon be considered vintage, but I didn't care. I mean, I like my e-reader, but I like cuddly paper-printed books too. It's important to preserve some things.

Like books. Traditions. Friendships. Recipes.

The pride of a little town.

That was a biggie. We wanted to make Pocket, Arkansas a town of delight again and not the place known only for its ten-mile-long monthly yard sale.

For now, though, getting the shop ready ranked as top priority, so everything had to be right.

The shop glistened. We'd shopped right up until last night, when we'd attended an auction in Mountain Home. Our haul from the night before, Fenton glassware, now sparkled in the mirrored cases. The vast collection sparkled beneath the cases' spotlights. Ruby red vases, milky white birds, and creamy pastels of the ornate pieces took my breath away. Bling at its best.

We scarfed up everything the auction offered. When the evening sun shone through the leaded glass side windows, the display of Fenton flashed with flare and brilliance. Their prisms of color saturated the nearby primitive church pew and threw shards of color everywhere.

However, the skeleton and coffin in the window would cap everything off and steal hearts from the street, luring them to partake of the store's boundless offerings. The plan included Bonesie, Bo to his friends, to sit propped up in the coffin, a book in one hand and an old magnifying glass in the other. Somewhere Mama located a tattered Sherlock-looking hat that would be his crowning glory.

"Ready?" Mama slid into her jacket.

"Actually, I thought a break might be nice." My stomach rumbled. After all, a girl can only slave so long without a Coke and a Snickers. We'd been working since sunup. I pulled out my phone and checked the time. Most of the morning had vanished. I took a step toward the kitchen. You'd have thought I wanted to pierce my knees.

"Mary Clare Casteel, we don't have time for a break. The UPS guy will be here any minute with that big shipment of books for the Children's Chamber." Mama yanked a nubby scarf around her neck. Its thickness matched her tone. "We have to get Bo settled and the rest of this display finished, so we can tackle that tonight. If we're going to open Pocket Change on schedule, we have to get the lead out!"

I opened my mouth to argue but realized it would be useless. One simply doesn't do that with Lilly Casteel when she's on a roll. So, being a good daughter, I muttered my O.S.P. (old standby prayer), put all thoughts of sugar out of my mind, stashed my phone, and sashayed out behind Mama.

I peeked next door. No sign of broad shoulders. We passed Uncle Ardmore. From the looks of it, he was planting a dollar bill at the side of the shop. "Mama." I jerked my head in Uncle Ardmore's direction. "He's doing it again." I'd long ago figured out money did not grow on trees as my Uncle Ardmore insisted it did. He is my uncle on my daddy's side and was never "quite right," according to Mama. Something about a bolt of lightning and the steel plate in his head. To this day, Uncle Ardmore plants at least one dollar bill in the back yard of every family member. He tends to them faithfully and feeds them Miracle Grow every month. He once grew a handsome cocklebur plant that reached five feet tall. The local paper came and took pictures, but the only thing he got for all his effort was a mess of cockleburs the size of Pittsburgh.

"Honey, he plants dollar bills all over town. You know that."

"What's he doing now?" I squinted into the morning sun.

"Watering it."

"Oh, my goodness!" I yelped, hearing the tell-tale *zip*. I opened my mouth for a second yelp when he turned and loped off across the yard, shaking his left leg. "Was Daddy like that?" I stared at my uncle's retreating back, a little worried about my daddy's side of the family. Everyone said I remind them of him.

"No. Your daddy was just about perfect." A wistfulness in her voice made me sorry I'd asked. "Ardmore wasn't like this until that lightning storm." She shook her head. "He'll be back in a few minutes to put Miracle Grow on it. Just go with it, honey. Think of it as his house warming gift to you."

I huffed out a quiet sigh. There were worse gifts.

Maybe.

"He means well, Mary Clare."

I glanced back at the corner of the structure and shrugged. Uncle Ardmore ran a rake over the damp ground and sang. How do you stay miffed at a guy who hums "This Little Light of Mine?"

Mama's soft spot for Uncle Ardmore began when she was twenty-four, when Daddy died. I was four. Uncle Ardmore stood beside Mama and me as they lowered my daddy into the ground. He saluted him then held both our hands all the way through the service and never left our sides until we got home. He took one look at all the food people had brought and started to cry.

At age four, I didn't understand why people brought cake at birthdays and when someone died too. I don't think Uncle Ardmore did either. But the array of cakes, pies, and casseroles that ended up in our kitchen boggled my mind. People tried to get us to try a bite of whatever goodie they brought.

Sometimes having an above-average memory isn't a good thing. I wish I didn't remember biting Pearlie Washburn's finger when she tried to stuff a piece of her raisin pie in my mouth. Pearlie just wanted to make me feel better. To this day, when I smell cooked raisins, I think of Pearlie sticking her bitten finger in her mouth and trying to suck the hurt out. I chomped down pretty hard. But Pearlie should have known the same thing Uncle Ardmore and I knew. No pie or cake or casserole can fill up that part of our heart that's hurting.

I glanced back at Uncle Ardmore, who dipped the rake like a skinny dance partner then went back to drawing it over the ground then blew a kiss our way and trotted off. By some miracle, I wished just one time he could have a good bumper crop of dollars pop out of the ground. He deserved that much.

We hurried to the large storage shed, and I flung the door wide. Mama marched over to Bo and lifted him carefully from his partially bubble-wrapped cocoon. "Mary Clare, let's go ahead and put Bo inside now. I don't think I can steer this casket and carry him at the same time."

I nodded, turned, and admired the coffin. Not that I am in the habit of admiring caskets, but this one couldn't be ignored.

It was one of the rare Victorian types with a breathing tube inside. Evidently, back in the day, it was common for some poor souls to be accidentally buried alive, and these caskets came along before embalming. Anyway, there was a small breathing tube which doubled as a passageway for a bell string. The loved one's family would attach a string to the finger of the person in the casket. In theory, should the departed not actually be departed, he or she would awaken and ring the bell. Guards were posted in the cemeteries to listen for ringing, although they couldn't pay me enough money for that job or that of a rescue team that would exhume the casket, hopefully before the person actually died of fright.

In any event, the caskets were difficult to come by. Yet here I was, getting ready to tuck Bo inside one. Fingers chilled to the bone, I carefully pried the top open and lifted it with a loud grunt while Mama hurried to retrieve Bo from his plastic-wrapped home. A gasp shot from my lips as the air sealed my throat as tightly as any steel-girded coffin.

"Uh, Mama." The chill in my body no longer sprang from the cold. "I don't think he's gonna fit."

"Of course, he will. We measured." She scowled over her shoulder to the rattle of bones.

"No. Trust me on this." I was quite sure the rattle of Bo's bones had nothing on my own, because everybody in the South knows you don't put two in a casket.

And this casket was already occupied.

CHAPTER TWO

I wanted people to expect the unexpected from my business. Let's face it. There weren't many shops like mine around. Books, Bling, and Memories. Wasn't that slogan, painted in gold script font, showcased on my brand-new shingle?

This was a little too unexpected. I thought about what to do. I'd almost made up my mind when I heard a huge thud behind me. Mama sprawled on the floor, out cold, with Bo on top. It was hard to tell who was paler, Mama or the skeleton.

I was open to the idea of mini shock therapy sessions. Sometimes people needed a little shaking up to help get their ducks back in a row. There were benefits to being shocked, whether with an actual electrical current (as my Uncle Ardmore swore by) or in beholding something bizarre, like a new dead body in my new old casket. The benefit in this instance was finding out I could hold my breath for an extended period and not lose consciousness. I simply forgot to breathe. Mama, on the other hand, not only breathed, she snored. Obviously, we dealt with distress in different ways. She napped. I went into a breathless stupor.

Once I'd checked to make sure she wasn't gagging and no

bones were broken, I plucked a soft leather-bound copy of Agatha Christie's *Curtains* from a stack of nearby books and tucked it under her head. I relocated Bo and put him atop the bundle of bubble wrap next to Mama.

A quick reach into my bra produced my cell. But finding a body has an effect on a girl. While I wasn't on the floor like Mama, my hands found it impossible to hang on to the phone. My fumble resulted in Gertie, my phone, plopping into the recesses of satin. Now I had no choice but to reach in and fish it out. Okay. This was awkward. Especially since the phone had landed in the nether regions between the occupant's legs. Oy.

Maybe it was a joke from the guy who had sold us the coffin. Deep down, however, it didn't feel like a joke. From the teeny flash of flesh I'd seen when I opened the lid, I knew it was a body. A real body. Deciding not to look at the face, I readied myself. Nowhere in my being was there a deep desire to see who occupied my coffin. Being a true believer that familiarity breeds contempt, I also believe anonymity dictates detachment. Oh, well. I had to gawk at the face before I could grope among the satin. I threw back my shoulders and with one eye closed, ogled the occupant of my window display.

As I stared at that swollen countenance, all detachment flew out the window. The man lying in the coffin was my contractor, Smitty Small. I hadn't seen him since yesterday when he'd told me he planned to return last night and work on caulking our upstairs bath and a display piece in the Children's Chamber. I glanced at his hands and frowned. They were bloated, too, but no sign of caulking appeared on his fingers.

It was high time to locate the phone and alert the powers that be. How in the world was I going to explain Smitty being in my casket? He was supposed to be finishing up last minute details like tightening bolts, caulking seams, and figuring up his bill. My hands fumbled around for my techie lifeline.

Thank goodness for the glow from the screen. I reached in

and hauled out the contraption, ready to punch in those three glorious little numbers. 901. No, wait. That wasn't right. 119. 019. Was I having a stroke? I was too young to have a stroke. Or was I? Okay. Think. It was 9 something, something! With a deep breath and a quick prayer, it occurred to me that 911 were the numbers my mind couldn't grasp. I poked the digits into my phone and waited for a competent person to pick up on the other end. I needed to calm down. Spotting a half-eaten Snickers sticking out of Mama's pocket, I popped it into my mouth and listened to the ringing on the other end.

"911 operator. What is your emergency?"

I recognized this voice. It used to sit behind me in Miss O'Malley's math class. Gum smacking really should be prohibited while answering emergency calls. Far be it from me to cast stones, however.

"I need help." I tried not to sound like my mouth was full of caramel and nougats.

"Mac, is that you? Oh. Excuse me. I guess you prefer Mary Clare now that you're a millionaire. Girl, I haven't heard from you since you won all that money. Somebody said you went off to one of them fat farms. That so?"

I thought about the sinful confection in my mouth and winced. "Um." I gulped. "I need you to send—"

"Mac, are those places real expensive? My husband's been after me to go, but I don't know. I could spend that kind of money on bigger clothes."

"I need you to send the police over here right away." Gritting one's teeth is only one step away from biting one's tongue.

"Well, honey, why didn't you say so? Have you lost those two greyhounds again? They are the cutest things I ever did lay eyes on. To think people would put those little darlins down, just because they can't run fast enough at the track. You did a noble thing adopting 'em. Why just the other day–"

"The dogs are fine! My mother's passed out! There's a dead

guy in my display casket, and I think I'm having an insulin rush!"

"Oh, my gosh! You hold tight. Let me see what I'm supposed to say." The sound of shuffling papers crinkled in my ear. "Wait a minute. I'm gonna put you on hold. I've got to check the manual. I'm just standin' in for Betty. She had to run to the bathroom."

There was one more gum smack before she disconnected us. I decided to do what any well-heeled Southern girl would do in a crisis. I finished chewing my Snickers and checked on Mama.

I knew for a fact the 911 chick had never mastered speed reading or geometry. There was plenty of time to ponder the situation. I shook my head, rolled my eyes and looked at Mama. Rolling one's eyes, according to her, was an absolute sign of bad breeding. The only time it became acceptable was if a person suffered from a bothersome contact. I don't wear contacts. Yanking my ponytail tighter, I slid to the floor and blew stubborn red bangs out of my face.

Sirens blared. Mama moaned. I reached over and swabbed the drool off her chin then remembered my own chin and wiped away the Snickers evidence. The shed door opened wider. The Pocket cavalry arrived.

When the EMTs began checking Mama, she looked up and patted one of them on the head. The sheriff jumped out of his car about the same time Mama decided to wake up. She staggered toward the shop, carrying Bo under one arm, then got her wits about her and made a beeline for the Snickers stash. Trotting alongside her, I hurried to keep up.

"Mama, what are you doing?"

"There's a body in our casket, Mary Clare. Sugar fortifies after being startled. Care for a candy bar?" She studied the crumbs on my chest and rolled her eyes. She doesn't wear contacts either.

"Mama, you rolled your eyes."

"Did not. I must have a concussion."

She looked stricken for about five seconds then proceeded to unwrap the candy while offering the retreating EMT squad a treat. After she slid Bo into a chair at the kitchen table, she unveiled the candy and sank her happy teeth into the chocolate. She was still licking her fingers when Sheriff George Boomer strode in. At one time, Boomer worked as the Schwan's Man, delivering frozen meats and other treats to homes around the area. Then his wife left him, his dog died, and he decided he needed more excitement in his life. Everyone in town knew him, liked him, and trusted his judgment. He became our new sheriff by a landslide. Now, he cruised around town in an old black and white car with no air conditioning. I wondered if he ever missed his big ol' refrigerated truck. Amazing how one's mind wanders when it's going into shock. Mine wandered right to the big arch between the kitchen and the main showroom.

There, in all his broad-shouldered, brown-haired glory, stood the guy from next door. I'd never seen shamrock green eyes before. Maybe it was the light playing tricks. I'd need to get closer to make sure. Oh, wait. Snicker breath. Checking his peepers would have to wait. Instead, I offered a shy smile and slapped at any tidbits of candy I might have missed earlier. As he moved closer, his mouth opened, but the words that followed came from someone else.

"I'm sorry, sir, but you'll have to leave. Mac and Lilly appreciate your concern, but you need to vacate the premises." Boomer fairly growled as he pointed at the door.

Our visitor acknowledged Boomer with a nod and, for the briefest moment, we stared at each other. I had just been outside. The sky couldn't have turned any bluer if it tried, so there simply was no explanation for the jolt of lightning that struck me. I may have swayed. Two strides put him at my side, and sure enough, I felt lightning accompanied by some sizzle. I tried to tell him I felt fine, but all I could do was smile.

I'm sure he thought I was addled in some way.

He opened his mouth again. I couldn't wait to find out if his voice matched the rest of him. I wasn't disappointed. Cultured, but rugged. Rich, creamy, and oh, so baritone.

"I apologize. I was next door working when I saw the ambulance pull in. I was worried someone might be hurt." He glanced at Boomer but offered his hand to me. Now wasn't the time to be rude. I took it. Ah. Large, strong and incredibly welcome. "Looks like we're going to be neighbors. I'm taking over the shop next door. My name is Mick Walker." He dipped his head once and offered up a lazy smile that showed every gleaming tooth. Oh my. Snow white teeth and those eyes…definitely shamrock green. My fingers itched to snap a selfie with him.

"I apologize for all the commotion. My mother and I just found a dead body in our shed." If looks could wither, Boomer's would have left me fifty pounds lighter.

Boomer turned to our visitor. "Mick Walker?" Boomer inserted his voice smack dab into my daydream. "Not Joe Walker's son?"

Mick turned to the sheriff and extended his hand.

"I haven't seen you since you were a little tot." Boomer grinned. "You're moving back?"

"I am. I've decided to reopen my uncle's shop. Some work needs to be done before it's ready for business. I figured today was a good day to start." His left hand rested at the small of my back. When he removed it, a scorch mark would no doubt be visible. "I'll be next door, if I can help."

"Hold up a minute, Mick. I have a few questions for you, but first I need to ask Lilly about something." He turned back to Mama. "Lilly, did you remove an item from the crime scene?" My own blue eyes darted back to Mama. Boomer gave her a positively thunderous look. Okay. I needed to focus now.

Mama held up both hands.

"The EMT boys said you carried a skeleton in here with

you." He paused and looked at Bo sitting at the table. "Would that be the one?"

"Boomer." Mama waved her hand in dismissal. "This is our display skeleton. We were trying to put him in the casket, but we couldn't because that other guy's lounging around in there."

"It's Smitty Small, Mama."

"Smitty. What in the world is he doing in our casket? He was supposed to caulk our bathroom last night."

"I'd like to know the answer to that myself, Lilly." Boomer's eyes sparked like a struck match. "How did Smitty get in the casket, and why did you bring the skeleton in here?"

"I don't know, and I didn't want his body parts to get stepped on." Mama pulled Bo to her.

"Huh?" The sheriff scratched his head.

"I don't know how Smitty got in our casket. I brought Bo in here because he is very expensive. I didn't want some nincompoop stepping on him." Mama placed a protective hand on Bo's shoulder. She reached over and crossed his bony legs. She was getting way too friendly with that skeleton. This woman needed to get out more. I realized Boomer's questions were now directed at me.

"What did you say?" I turned to face him.

Boomer tapped his foot. "Is Bo the skeleton's name?"

"Yes, sir." My neighbor moved back to the counter beside the pantry. He leaned on it in a male-model fashion: arms crossed, ankles crossed, brown locks flaunting themselves near long dark lashes. Those luscious eyes nailed me.

"Mary Clare, what do you know about Smitty Small being in that casket?"

I pulled my gaze back to the sheriff. "Nothing more than what Mama just told you. We were trying to get the front display set up. When we went to the shed to get Bo and the casket, there he was." I'd almost said, "big as life." Given poor Smitty's small stature (He couldn't have measured much over five feet) and his current condition, I would have to be more careful. A slip of the tongue would be considered poor taste.

My nerves were doing a rousing routine of calisthenics. Something about the way Boomer kept looking at me set off alarms in my muddled mind. I inched toward the candy stash. Where was the harm in having another Snickers? Mama saw me. Besides, Mick Walker watched my every move. I couldn't inhale a calorie-laden confection with him standing there.

"You don't know if he came inside the shop?"

"No, Boomer. I don't. He kept his tools out in the shed. He was supposed to work last night."

He turned to my neighbor. "What about you, Mick? Did you see anything suspicious?"

Mick shoved away from the counter and shook his head. "I didn't work yesterday and only arrived at the shop a little while ago. Sorry, Sheriff. I'm not much help." He shrugged and looked my way again. "This is going to be unsettling for the town and especially for you two ladies. You okay?" His gaze searched my face. What could I say? I was having difficulty breathing, but it had nothing to do with poor old Smitty.

"I'm fine." I kept waiting for something brilliant to tumble out of my mouth, but moments passed without one stunning word. His gaze roamed over my lips. Watching for signs of intelligence, no doubt.

With a slow smile, he turned to Mama and Boomer. "Is there anything else, Sheriff?" Boomer shook his head. "I'll be next door for a while if you need me." With a lingering look in my direction, he headed out the back door, his large frame filling the doorway.

Mama craned her slender neck and studied Mick as he closed the door. "Mary Clare, that is one fine looking young man." Never one to disagree with my elders, I nodded, hurried to the back window, and peeked out. His fine parts strode across the yard, his brown hair blowing a bit in the wind. It fell just a tad past the collar of his camouflage jacket. When he stopped abruptly and turned to look back, I dropped the kitchen curtain and ducked. Had he seen me? Why had he turned around? I grabbed a vintage church fan from a stack by the door and began fanning myself.

"Boomer." Mama gritted her teeth. "We certainly didn't have anything to do with Smitty's, um, problem. Everything was in order when we left yesterday for the auction. The doors were locked. I double-checked them myself. Besides, what are you doing poking around on his body? Don't you have to wait until the coroner comes or something?"

I glanced at Boomer and wondered what they served in jail by way of food. Surely Brother Everett would visit her while she was incarcerated.

"Lilly, for your information, the coroner is out there now. It didn't take him long to declare Smitty dead." The dryness in his voice could have sopped up Lake Jesup. "Are you trying to tell me how to investigate this murder?"

"Murder?" She fell into a chair beside Bo. Her fair complexion teetered on Cadaver Pale #21. I'd seen a compact of it on clearance at the novelty shop just last week.

"Surely you didn't think he crawled into the casket and then strangled himself, Lilly."

Mama pulled herself up from the chair and tried to look taller than her four feet, twelve inches. She'd painted her fingernails chartreuse the night before. She pointed one of the neon digits at Boomer. As though speaking to one of her fifth graders, she took careful aim and wagged that finger back and forth like a metronome.

"Don't you get feisty, Boomer. Sarcasm has never flattered you. I'm a little rattled. Mary Clare and I are not used to starting our day with dead bodies. It's not our fault Smitty is dead and in our casket. We are victims in this horrible mess. You should be ashamed of yourself." With that Mama marched out. The UPS man marched in.

"Who are you?" asked Boomer.

"I'm delivering a shipment of books for Mary Clare's grand opening." He turned to look at me. "Mercy, Mac. Gossip has it there's a dead guy out there. You haven't even opened for business yet."

I wasn't sure what that had to do with anything unless he thought that was my plan for getting rid of dissatisfied customers.

"You know, this may be great for business. When word gets out about this, folks are gonna pour in here." He rubbed his chapped hands together and did a little jig.

"How did you know anybody was dead?" A tiny tic settled into Boomer's right eye.

"Heard it from Maybelline Huff. I ran a delivery by her place. She said she heard it from her cousin's neighbor who works as the 911 operator."

"She's the one who took my 911 call while ago." Boy, talk about grapevine gossip.

"Those calls are supposed to be confidential. I'll speak to her." If I were a betting woman, I'd bet Boomer's scowls were right up there with Dracula's.

"Don't be too hard on her, Sheriff. This is the most exciting thing to happen around here since the last mosquito festival. You remember those mosquito cookies? Those things weren't half bad. I delivered a whole crate of freeze-dried mosquitoes to the mayor's office. That was a first." He hitched up his belt and studied his nails.

It was time to remove Leroy from the conversation. "Boomer, is it okay for him to put those boxes in the basement for me?"

"It is. I checked that area. Shove them inside the door and leave."

"Sure thing. Say, Sheriff, do you know what happened?"

"That information can't be shared at this time." Boomer scribbled on a note pad cradled in his hand.

"Too early to release the gruesome details. Gotcha." He turned and winked at me. That wink told me either he had something else on his mind or he'd return tomorrow expecting to get the full story. I closed my eyes and thought of Dollie's Money Mart. A little therapeutic shopping might be just the ticket for frayed nerves. I could almost hear the daily specials beckoning from forty miles away.

I stepped closer to the sheriff and watched Leroy saunter toward his truck to retrieve my shipment. He certainly did carry out his family legacy well. Tall, dark, and hopelessly dimwitted. At least he wasn't mean like some of his family. "He's right, you know."

"Right about what?" Boomer rolled up his sleeves and looked at me like I'd sprouted a unicorn horn.

"This is the biggest news to hit Pocket in a while. What do I say when people start calling me?" One look at the road confirmed people were already cruising by.

"My advice is to be unavailable." I could manage unavailable. Then reality punched me on the shoulder. It was Mama.

"What do you mean not be available? Our grand opening is in eight days."

"Your grand opening is whenever we clear this area, Lilly. As of now, your shed is a crime scene and so is the surrounding grounds that I'm having cordoned off. And nobody will be conducting business on these premises until I say so. I've already called the forensic guys from Jonesboro to come in and have a look around. Until they get finished, stay out of the way."

With that, Boomer stomped out the door. He supervised the loading of Smitty and my prized casket into the ambulance. Then he returned with a crew of five men at his heels. Bumps from below reminded me that the delivery man was still on the premises. It would be just like him to eavesdrop if he thought he could pick up an interesting tidbit or two. Boomer came back into the kitchen and reached for Bo.

"What do you think you're doing?" Mama splayed her entire body in front of the skeleton.

"We have to check him, uh, it, for fingerprints, Lilly."

Mama shook her head in pity. "I knew this job would be too stressful for you. Bo doesn't have fingerprints. He's a skeleton."

"I'm not looking for Bo's fingerprints. I'm looking for the killer's." Not having a reply for this, Mama stood down and watched helplessly as Boomer carted Bo through the Art Deco Area and into the front foyer. Within a few minutes, he returned, sans Bo.

"Mac, I need you to take me through the shop. Have you noticed anything missing?"

"No. Nothing looks disturbed. We started locking up about three weeks ago when the first shipment of antiques arrived. Counting the basement entrance, there are three other doors, the front door, the basement entrance, and this back door." I pointed to the kitchen exit. "We've been in and out all of them including Mama's private entrance that's in the garage. It leads to her apartment but not into the shop."

"Would you mind giving me a tour?" He smiled for the first time since his arrival. The weight of the world tumbled off my shoulders. I knew Boomer. He wouldn't be smiling if his immediate plans included hauling me off to jail. I could have twirled and pirouetted, the kind one can only do in dreams or in the virtual version of *Dancing with The Stars*. Instead, I returned his smile and assured him I'd be happy to take him wherever he wanted to go.

We started in the office. When I flipped on the overhead light, my gaze went to the oversized poster board check from Publisher's Clearing House proclaiming my winning amount. My plan was to hang it in the office as a reminder of that blessed day when my bank account went from $15.33 to $21,000,015.33. The real check never made it inside my house. That little jewel was cashed as soon as the prize patrol zoomed away. Their exhaust fumes still hung in the air as I rushed to my ratty Impala and raced for the bank, still in my robe and sock feet. For now, the cardboard replica leaned contentedly against the wall, waiting for its mounting.

Beaming, I started Boomer's tour by explaining the two-way mirrors in the office. The look on his face was somewhere between awe and admiration. Score one for technology.

He ambled around and took in all the angles. One mirror faced the main room. Another faced the room displaying the glassware. From the office, we could assess customers in both areas. When I pulled out the wireless security pad that showed the two of us featured prominently on its display screen, I thought I'd have to whistle for the paramedics to resuscitate him.

"How in the world does that work?" He tapped the screen then jumped when the picture enlarged.

"I like gadgets, Boomer. I confess to being partial to conveniences." I didn't mention that this spiffy piece of technology had cost more than my first car. "It's important that the customers don't feel like we're breathing down their necks. At the same time, we want to cut down on theft, so, this seems like a fun thing to try. We can walk anywhere in the shop and carry this dandy little slate around, and no one is the wiser. They just think we're playing on a tablet. Cool, huh?"

"What happens when somebody walks up and sees you snooping?" One of his eyebrows hitched up. If we'd been playing chess, he'd make a suave little check move. But we weren't playing chess.

"Then," I punched a little button. "I press down on this white control and the display goes back to the preset weather page. It will stay on that most of the time. We'll only engage the snoop button when no one is near enough to us to see what we're doing." I placed the pad back in the office and turned off the light.

"I don't suppose you have a camera outside that's angled toward the shed, do you?"

I hung my head. "No. I'll look into outdoor security." I looked back up. "Okay, you've seen this floor. What would you like to see next?"

He nodded. "Let's start in the basement. If that UPS guy's still there, we can get rid of him. Lilly, if he comes back up here and tries to hide out somewhere, you run him off, okay?"

"I'm on it." She craned her neck to keep an eye on Bo. "You did tell those Jonesboro boys that Bo is an extremely valuable prop, didn't you? You will remind them he's quite expensive, won't you, Boomer?"

"I told them he cost an arm and a leg, Lilly."

It was my turn to raise an eyebrow. What do you know? Driving that freezer on wheels had not frozen Boomer's sense of humor.

CHAPTER THREE

"The blueprints are downstairs, Boomer." We made our way down the extra-wide, padded steps. My mind moseyed on its own merry path. Despite the mess I found myself in, the thoughts dancing through my head had more to do with Mick Walker. My brain told me that Smitty's murder should be front and center, but for the life of me I couldn't get rid of an odd, fluttery feeling in the pit of my stomach that had nothing to do with my deceased contractor. I forced my mind to focus. Scrutinizing the bottom level of my new business, I had to smile. The ringing of Boomer's cell phone gave me a chance to admire the basement room.

The Children's Chamber. An on-duty clerk would supervise the reading centers while keeping a watchful eye on the children's novelty antiques Mama and I purchased. We'd furnished it with an old-fashioned phone booth, complete with a life-size figure of a Christopher Reeves Superman. Smitty was supposed to seal it last night after he worked on the bathrooms, but there was no sign of caulking. I'd have to get someone to do it before the grand opening. Having a hysterical child stuck inside would not bode well for business.

While the booth wasn't actually an antique because it wasn't one hundred years old, it was a great piece as were the toys scattered around the room. Marma Lee Mason, my cousin, located many of them during her last shopping trek.

The rest of the room was arranged in sections for young adult as well as young and intermediate readers. Comfy chairs, bean bags, and twinkle lights brought it all together.

I jumped when my phone began vibrating like crazy in my pocket. The peal of a bell let me know that a voicemail waited for me. Had I given my number to Mick? Not pulling the phone out and checking it was torture, but Boomer trumped the phone.

"Mary Clare." I knew a hedge when I heard it. Boomer was hedging, and he wouldn't make eye contact. This wasn't going to be good.

"Yes?" I sliced the word and stared at him. I could tell his next few words wouldn't be music to my ears.

"I hate to tell you this." He clapped his cell phone closed. "The Jonesboro crew has insisted on impounding that casket of yours for an undetermined amount of time."

"What!" Shrieking is not usually my path of communication. On the upside, I discovered that sound certainly does carry in a basement. Maybe it wasn't such a good idea to put the Children's Chamber down here after all. "What are you talking about? That casket is rare. You simply can't be serious. How long can they hold it?"

"I'm sorry, but with Smitty in it..." He trailed off. "I'll take precautions. But, really, I have no way of knowing. Is it insured?"

The laser look had no effect on Boomer. Mama said I can shame a duck out of its last quack. Boomer was neither a duck nor a lightweight sheriff. He had to take my casket and was only doing his job. "Over here's the door, Boomer." The growl that rumbled out of my mouth wasn't the least bit ladylike, and I kicked the closet door shut on our way to the reading counter.

"Hey, that hurt." The UPS guy came out of the closet rubbing his nose.

"What are you doing in my closet, Leroy? You should have left already." It occurred to me that I liked having hips to put my hands on. It gave a girl quite a power rush. I stomped my foot for further effect.

"I'm trying to help by measuring to see if those boxes will fit in there for you. You know, Mac, I'm good at a lot of things." The man stood straighter, reminding me of those guards in Britain. "If you'd put me on your payroll, I could be a jack-of-all-trades. Plus, I can lift heavy objects with no problem. Let me show you!" Without so much as an inkling of warning, Leroy swung me around like a bag of potatoes.

"Put me down, you buffoon!" I pointed toward the door and ran my hands over my ruffled bangs. If he thought I was going to hire him because he could lift heavy objects, mainly me, he had another think coming! The nerve of some people.

"Well, if you're not going to hire me, then at least consider Roger. He needs the money. Everybody knows he's head over heels for you. If you'd just give him one more chance, Mac, you and him could get hitched just like that." He tried to snap his fingers, but apparently lifting heavy objects had left him lacking in finger coordination.

Ignoring the comment, I stared Leroy right in the eyes. "Why does Roger need money? Last I heard, your no-good cousin was working at the pharmacy. Is he NOT working at the drug store?" That's what I deserved for not keeping up with his profile. Which reminded me, there was another profile I needed to check.

"No. He got caught rearranging a few unmentionables, and the pharmacy guy, well, he let him go."

"You mean he fired him, right?" My ears couldn't believe what they were hearing. The man I'd nearly married was well on his way to breaking the Guinness World Book Record for most jobs lost in a year's time. So why did I feel responsible for him? The man oozed ineptness and flaunted his failures.

"You know, just give the guy a little loan, Mac. It wouldn't have to be much. Fifty thousand would do it. He could finally start that mole catching business he's been trying to get off the ground. You know how many moles live around here? He'd make a fortune and pay you back, Mac."

"Fifty thousand? Is he crazy? No, Leroy. No money now. No money later. He still owes me for the last little 'project' he wanted to get off the ground." Lord help.

Boomer cleared his throat with gusto and pointed toward the door. Leroy sighed, took the hint, and hustled out with another wink. Without a doubt he'd be back tomorrow. He wouldn't find me unless he drove to Jonesboro and shopped at Dollie's Money Mart.

"Mary Clare, where are those blueprints?" Boomer had a pretty good scowl going himself.

"Over here. Sit on a bar stool while I get them for you." I rummaged under the counter. The blueprints were beside the emergency flashlight.

Boomer eyed the stools. "Don't you think you've got those things a little too close to the floor?"

I shook my head and handed him a menu.

"What's this?"

"A book menu. We've arranged this area to resemble an old-fashioned soda counter. It's facing the stairs leading up to the main floor as well as the basement entrance so the clerk can monitor who comes in and out. It's kind of like combining a security and entertainment system. The clerk can monitor the entire room as she's reading to the kids on the bar stools. The best-behaved child gets to 'order' the title he or she would like read. We'll have all the books displayed on this back wall. The mirror behind the books and the twinkle lights will make it entic-ing, I hope."

"Sure wish we'd had this kind of set up when I was little. I might have liked reading more."

He'd given me a tremendous compliment, and I could have hugged the stuffing out of him. Instead, I smiled at the man sitting there with his knees nearly touching his ears and handed him the blueprints. Smitty had used them down here last week to make modifications. When we realized we'd have children in wheelchairs, I'd instructed Smitty to make the restrooms and entry door handicapped accessible.

"Those were the only changes made?"

"The only important ones." I pulled my phone from my pocket and peeked at my missed call.

"What do you mean?"

Rats. The call had just been from Marma Lee. I sighed and started to stick the phone in my bra, then looked at Boomer. Better to just hang onto it and a lot easier to check. "Smitty also built the writer's cottage and the shed. The original plan called for the front of the cottage to be a generous seventy-five feet from the back of the shop with a breezeway between the two buildings. Smitty started digging the footing for it then decided it wasn't far enough away. Something about a city ordinance. Anyway, he told me the cottage needed to set back another twenty-five feet. It wasn't a big deal, but I nixed the breezeway idea. Instead I had him lay cobblestone for a nice walkway. I don't know if that's really considered an alteration to the blueprints or not, but it was a change from my original plan."

"Is the cottage completed?"

"It is now. Smitty had the sheetrock man in last month, and the rock fireplace went in two weeks ago. The only tasks left are the cosmetic things, you know, rugs, pictures, that sort of thing. The drapes are up, and I moved in a few days ago after the wireless network went in. The storage shed was finished first. We built it on the edge of the property. I didn't want it right up against the cottage."

"You're planning on living in that little hut!"

"It's not a hut and it isn't a playhouse, Boomer. It has an upstairs loft with two bedrooms and two full baths. It's more than enough for me. When authors come for signings, I'll stay above the garage with Mama. We built a full apartment up there for her."

"Can I say something to you?"

My breath got hung up and refused to go in or out. Surely the police department couldn't impound a whole business. A lot was riding on the opening of Pocket Change. My hands felt around for the reading bar as I sat down on the storyteller's stool. I even picked up the reader's apron and clutched it the same way I used to clutch Wally, my stuffed bear, after Daddy died. I wondered if Boomer would find it rude if I put my head between my legs.

"I don't think this money thing has changed you one whit."

"What?"

"You don't have an uppity air, Mary Clare. You know how some people get when they marry into money or when somebody's relative dies and leaves them a bundle. You aren't like that. How come?"

I drew in ten gallons of relief and exhaled. "You remember O'Hare's Antique Shop, Boomer?"

He scratched his head. "Yeah. Yeah, I do. I haven't thought about that place in ages. That was the nicest establishment in the state, probably in the country. What's that have to do with you not having an uppity air?"

"A few months after Daddy was laid to rest, Mama and I went window-shopping there." People came from all over to admire the other fine old antique shops in our town, but O'Hare's got the majority of the gawking. It carried unique pieces from all over the world. But, it was the cutting-edge inventions that put it right over the top. It was like seeing the best of the past and the promise of the future.

"I remember easing down the main aisle looking at all the

stuff they had. Mama grabbed on to my hand and rushed us over to the other side of the store. She looked up at an old mantle clock. In my eyes that clock registered a ten on the ugly scale, but Mama started crying and stroking the oak sides of that old clock. As little as I was, I knew Mama needed that clock. That was thirty years ago. I've thought about that clock a lot over the years. I think she needed it to remind her time doesn't stand still. We're all meant to march on, even when the one we've marched with is gone.

"I tugged on her hand and asked her how come she liked that old clock so much? She told me she and Daddy used to have a clock exactly like that one. They had to sell it one winter to buy groceries and pay bills.

"Now remember, Boomer, I was four and still thought Uncle Ardmore knew what he was talking about. I told her not to worry and that I'd buy that clock for her as soon as Uncle Ardmore's tree started putting on leaves.

"That's when she explained money doesn't really grow on trees or in bushes. I guess I accepted that as true when Uncle Ardmore's plant ended up being a giant stinkweed that particular year."

"That's about the time Thelma and I got married. Pocket was a beautiful place." He shook his head.

"Now, Pocket's best known for its monthly ten-mile-long-yard sale along Highway 34." I knew I sounded sarcastic. But thanks to a seedy journalist from Little Rock, Pocket had received bad press. It was almost like the man was determined to grow his readership with a "Kick Pocket While They're Down" campaign. His snide articles and snarky remarks didn't do much to help restore pride in our little town.

It hurt. This was home. This was where Daddy was buried. This is where Uncle Ardmore believed in miracles and Miracle Grow, and this is where determination began for me.

"You're strong, Mary Clare. You've made it through a lot of

things, and you're gonna make it through this too. I'll do what I can to help."

Relief flooded through me from head to toe. "I'm sorry, Boomer. It's just that I thought for a minute you were going to say you needed to impound the business. You're not, are you?" My hand covered my heart. I looked ready to either pass out or pledge allegiance to the flag.

"No, Mary Clare."

The instant he said no, I sent up a silent thank-you-gram. "Sorry, Boomer. I'm a little overwhelmed. To answer you, yes, it's great to have the money. I sure don't miss budgeting on a single woman's paycheck."

"You're a hard worker, Mary Clare. You used to put in a lot of long hours at Mr. Chick-A-Boom's Chicken Palace at night."

I smiled. Sort of. If I never had to cook another chicken liver, that would be fine with me. Working my way through college had been my idea, not Mama's. She wanted to take on a night job in addition to teaching all day and selling Avon. I said no. I got a loan, fried up chicken, and earned my master's degree. It never occurred to me that anybody like Boomer noticed such things. Made me feel kinda proud. Then I remembered why Boomer was here. Knocked the pride right out of me.

"Winning the money was great, but as soon as my name was published, people I didn't even know were asking for money. The landline rang off the hook until I finally got enough and came up with a scheme to put an end to it. It hasn't worked completely, I still have characters like Leroy who bug me about a job, but the phone calls have slowed down."

"What'd you do, if you don't mind my asking? Wait. Was it legal? Maybe you better not tell me."

"Calm down. It was legal, and Mama got a kick out of it. When someone called to ask for money Mama would tell them they would have to talk to me. She explained it might be a few weeks because I was busy looking into buying a circus. She told them I would be delighted to pay them a salary providing they perform in a sideshow. By the time she asked for their name and number, most had hung up. We managed to scare everyone off, except one."

"You mean to tell me someone actually took you up on that offer?"

"Yep. A nineteen-year-old girl. Said she had to have a job to help support her family and didn't care what it was as long as it was something she wouldn't be ashamed to talk about in church. I hired her that afternoon. That girl wanted to work. She's the one who will be in charge of the Children's Chamber and over-seeing our Internet sales. Her name's Molly."

"That's what I mean." Boomer slapped his knee. "Most people would get mad over the calls and bring in legal loonies to run everybody off. You handled it yourself and had fun. Plus, you did a good turn for someone."

"Mama's had a great time with this. She's protective about some things, like Bo. We've never had money. Now that we do, we try not to flaunt it. We do enjoy the comforts it's given us. At least we did, until now." The dismal sigh that phoophed out of my mouth wasn't entirely due to the predicament I was in with Smitty. "I guess you need to see the rest of the shop, huh?"

"I reckon so." Boomer's knees creaked when he stood.

Mama met us at the top of the stairs. Behind her on the floor lay a caulking gun. A light flickered in my head. "The caulking gun. That's what Smitty was supposed to be doing here last night." Boomer nearly slapped my hand as I stretched for it.

"Let me see it." Boomer pulled a pair of latex gloves from his pocket.

As he reached for the tool, his hands strained the latex to their limit. The man had hams for hands. Made me wonder what kind of hands my next-door neighbor had. I'd been too busy admiring his face to take note of much else. A girl could get lost in those green eyes.

"This one looks new." Boomer turned the tool around to examine the back. "No caulking residue anywhere on it. If Smitty used it last night, he did a thorough job of cleaning it. Do you know if he had another one, maybe in the restroom upstairs?"

"I'm sure he did," Mama offered. "He had already caulked the kitchen. He left it on one of the cabinets. His initials were scratched into it, and it had gunk all over it. Looked old too. Maybe it broke and he bought a new one."

"There wasn't any caulking on his fingers, either." My fingers tapped and rolled on the phone screen. My search for Mick was just a tap away. The silence of the room stopped me cold. When I glanced up, Boomer's eyes drilled holes into the top of my head. Mama was looking at the ceiling and scratching her elbow. I stopped my search and put the phone behind my back.

"You searched the body?" Boomer could look downright mean when he put his mind to it.

"Of course not. I happened to notice it when I found Smitty."

"What exactly did you do, Mary Clare?"

"I had to dig my phone out of the casket, Boomer. It slipped out of my grip when I started to call 911." That was the total truth. He needn't know I had butterfingers, and the fact that I used my bra as a phone sling was completely irrelevant.

He turned his head away from me and nailed Mama with what I was quickly recognizing as his just-shy-of-throwing-a-fit look. "Did you notice anything interesting, Lilly?"

"Mama was busy examining the floor of the shed."

"She means I fainted, Boomer. I don't deal well with sudden death when it comes in a box. Guess I'm what you'd call delicate."

I wondered how long law enforcement officers had to train to become truly gifted at showing no signs of shock. Boomer nodded and started to climb to the next level. I offered to continue the tour and knew it wouldn't be long before Mama and I would have to accompany him to his office and give statements. I told Mama to go rest for a while. For once, she didn't argue. One long sigh later, I gave up any hope of looking Mick up online in the next foreseeable hour.

"How do you know that's not the calking gun he used in the restroom?" I asked Boomer. By then we had reached the upstairs landing. Boomer stared but not at me. I followed his gaze. From where we stood, we could see the upstairs restroom. The door was open, and the sink top had been placed in position. It was obvious from the gap between the marble top and the wall no caulking had taken place last night. Interesting. That explained why Smitty's hands were clean and why the phone booth in the Children's Chamber was still a problem.

"How many keys were made?" Boomer asked.

"Only three. One for Smitty, one for Mama, and one for me."

"Your mama still have hers?"

"I'll ask her. Are you thinking someone could have stolen a key? Why would anybody do that? If it was a robbery, they would have taken some of the antique pieces. What about Smitty? Did he have any money on him?"

Boomer stared past me. "I'm sorry. I can't divulge that information."

"This is my business. That has to count for something."

"It does. It means some people might consider you a suspect."

"What!" I realized sound carried pretty well upstairs too. Or maybe I just had an extraordinary set of lungs. Mama had muscle. I had volume. What a team.

"I didn't say I agree. It doesn't make sense to me on several levels."

I relaxed. "Smitty was efficient, and he wasn't all that expensive. He could have tried to gouge me, knowing I'd won all that money, but didn't. As a matter of fact, after he started building, he even talked about a little windfall of his own."

"What kind of windfall?"

"He didn't go into detail. He just came to work whistling one day and announced he was coming into money."

"He was whistling?" Boomer asked.

I nodded. "That man was as happy as a dog with a bone, and it had to do with money. Smitty was not a whistler by nature. He usually passed the day with a nod of his head. Sometimes Mama baked things for him and his crew. He always said thank you, but he wasn't one to go on about things."

"You know anything about his family?"

"No. I don't think he had any. Could you check, Boomer?"

"I'll look into it."

"Boomer."

"Yes, Mary Clare."

"I wouldn't hurt anyone."

"I know. Now show me the rest of the upstairs."

Boomer followed me into the two large rooms. I explained the purpose of each room, beginning with the Writer's Cove. Netbooks were set up in this room for would-be authors to reserve a time to write. This was a trial run to gauge the demand. The remainder of the room held writers' reference books and other nonfiction works. This was the only room that didn't contain antiques. Its purpose was practical and functional.

I peeked out the window, hoping to get a glimpse of my new neighbor. I could see his truck but not Mick. On the downside, I did spot a rusted-up Camry at the stop sign. Why was Roger nosing around? Hadn't I told him in plain English not to come back? Maybe Leroy hadn't delivered my resounding NO to his request for money. I sighed and gave my attention back to the tour.

The upstairs restroom was next door to the writers' room. Boomer glanced inside, frowned, and moved to the remaining room, which happened to be my favorite, filled with old Christmas villages we'd found from all over the United States.

"Marma Lee wanted to call it the Village Idiot's Room. I ignored her." This room held vintage villages, accessories, and an extensive collection of Christmas titles. An idea I'd spotted on Pinterest stood in the corner. The four-foot Christmas tree made of spiraling books offered a happy glow to the room. They were rescue books, ones I'd found outside someone's home, standing forlorn by the trash. When I asked the homeowner if I could have them, she'd helped me load every title into my vehicle and confided it nearly killed her to throw them away, but she simply didn't have room. The strand of big white bulbs offered extra light and a splash of perkiness.

"How're you gonna monitor the upstairs?" Boomer asked. "You've got the perfect solution for the Children's Chamber, but folks are as apt to steal upstairs as down. Does that gadget you showed me work up here too?"

"It does, but we wanted to ramp it up a notch. There will also be floating fictional characters strolling by this room all through the day. The customers will never know when one might pop in. The characters will dispense lemonade in the summer and cider in the fall. There's a hidden camera and mirrors in each room. See the portraits hanging on the walls? We had them made so the eyes actually move. You know, like the old haunted house flicks. Each portrait is stationed in a prime area. All the merchandise is within sight of the portrait, and each portrait is equipped with a surveillance camera. The customers will just think the portraits are props. The security cameras are mounted in my office, which will stay locked so customers can't wander in accidentally. Eventually, we'll have to hire someone to monitor the cameras, as well as the Internet usage in the Writer's Cove, but for now we'll wing it. Pretty nifty, huh?"

Boomer nodded his head. "Maybe I'd better sign you on as

my department's security consultant. You've got some great ideas."

"It helps to have money." I shrugged. "It's nice to be able to splurge."

"Why are you working? Most folks wouldn't with the kind of money you've got."

"Mama's always saying a person needs to be tired at the end of the day. Sitting around being rich isn't exactly strenuous, Boomer. She taught me to work hard and play with any left-over time and energy. I think that's a good philosophy."

"So do I." Boomer stretched. "Speaking of which." He glowered at me and scratched his head. "Mary Clare, that feller you were engaged to, is he bothering you?"

"Roger?" Well, yes, he bothered me. Kind of like a bad case of poison ivy. But I couldn't sic Boomer on him for being brainless.

"Do I need to have a talk with him?"

"He hasn't done anything illegal, at least not that I know of. He's like the rest of the nuts who want money. But it's driving him a little nuttier than the rest because he thinks that money could have been his if we'd gotten married. Lucky for me, I saw the real Roger before I waltzed down that aisle. He's having to deal with being one cherry short of a jackpot. If he becomes too much of a pain, I'll let you know."

"Sometimes those kind are dangerous, Mary Clare. Just stay on your toes, you hear?"

"I'm pretty sure I can handle Roger, but it's nice to know I can call if I need you."

Boomer nodded. "Who did you get to play the fictional characters in the shop? Anybody who might have it in for Smitty?"

"Absolutely not! I've hired some senior citizens to work from nine in the morning to three in the afternoon. Mama's friend, Rennie, wants to help out when she has time. There are a few high school kids who will come in and work until we close at six. The nursing home residents are making all our costumes for us. I bought the material and patterns. Their activity director rounded up some sewing machines. They're having a blast, and they're all coming for the grand opening. Sheila, Louella, and Lisa are coming with them."

"Who are they?"

"Friends of mine from the nursing home. Sheila and Louella are amazing nurses. Lisa works with them as a CNA." I guess my sigh concerned Boomer.

"It'll be okay. We just have to figure out who did this, Mary Clare."

"We?" I perked right up.

"Don't get excited. I meant the police department. I'm not about to let you get involved in this. When you get the urge to play detective, remember how Smitty looked when the killer got finished with him."

The man had a point. Besides, I had other interests to delve into.

"By the way, what did you mean when you said some of your time will be spent in the kitchen?"

"That was probably an exaggeration. Mama has this idea about serving a Country Tea, and I want to integrate some tech time for those who want to learn. Kind of a meet, greet, eat, and play with technology. I thought I'd call it Calories and Clicks. What do you think?"

"Clicks?"

"Yeah, you know. Like clicking a mouse. Clicking on a button." From the vacant stare Boomer gave me, I knew the man was lost. What he lacked in tech knowledge, he made up for in common sense.

"Anyway, I've hired a man called Sam Dawson to act as a facilitator of sorts and kick it off. Among other things, he's a writer and motivational speaker. Supposed to be the best in the South. He specializes in helping small towns pull through tough times. He believes good things can begin from even the humblest of beginnings."

"Uh huh. Where is this Mr. Dawson?"

"He won't arrive for about a month. A small town in Georgia has him booked right now. He spends four to five weeks in a little city heading up town meetings and leading small group gatherings."

Boomer grunted. Apparently, he didn't think much of a town motivational speaker, but I'd heard Sam. More importantly, I'd seen him in action when I'd visited the fat, uh, weight control ranch. He'd realigned their program. In my opinion, he was exactly what Pocket needed right now. Maybe what the whole country needed.

Returning to the main floor, we found Mama reclined in one of the chairs in the Cozy Area. The crackling sound from the gas logs sounded soothing. It soothed her right into another nap. Boomer admired an old trunk as Mama roused with a snort.

"Oh. I had the worst nightmare. I need an aspirin. It was horrible. Smitty was in our casket and that sheriff…" She looked up, saw Boomer, and sank back into her chair. She moaned. "This wasn't a dream, was it?"

Boomer ignored her. He seemed quite taken with the old trunk. "My grandpa used to have one of these old steamers. I haven't seen one in years." He reached down and stroked its old, weathered sides. His actions reminded me of Mama and that old clock.

"Lilly, where is your key to the shop?" When it came to business, Boomer could turn on a dime.

Mama jabbed her hand down in her jeans pocket and pulled out a key chain with a tiny silver turtle on it. Dangling from the turtle was an odd-shaped key.

"Is that a real skeleton key?" Boomer asked.

"No." I fingered my phone and wished for this conversation to be over. "We thought it would be fun to have these made to resemble old skeleton keys. All three of them look the same." I fished mine from my purse and held it up for his inspection. "They don't fit in pockets well, but it's much easier to find in a purse."

"So Smitty's looked like this too?"

"Sure did." Mama yawned.

He nodded and sauntered toward the door talking on his cell phone. Within the hour, he deemed the shop clear and left out the kitchen door. After all the activity, the quiet was deafening.

"Come along, Mary Clare. Let's drive to Pa Daddy's for one of their big ol', juicy cheeseburgers. You care if I call Rennie? She loves their burgers. I may get an extra order of fries for the babies."

"Oh, my gosh." I squealed, raced to the back door, and yanked back the little curtain. In all the excitement I'd forgotten about the greyhounds.

There was nothing to worry about. The "babies" Mama and I had adopted in Memphis snoozed on the cottage steps. One big greyhound cuddle up. I wish we could have taken them all. The Humane Society had rescued them from a nearby racetrack. They were scheduled for euthanasia due to their inadequate speed.

While talking to the attendant in charge, I noticed two small greyhounds, if greyhounds can be small, huddled in a corner away from the other dogs. The girl on duty explained they were not brother and sister, but they rarely separated. They were devoted to each other. My heart melted and before long, both Flash and Blur, as Mama named them, were settled in the back of my new Enclave, headed for home. Flash, a sleek black male, slept with one paw slung protectively over Blur, a slightly smaller pearl-gray female. She nuzzled his chin. I'd once watched an old rerun of *The George and Gracie Burns Show* with Mama. Flash and Blur reminded me a lot of those two loving, funny people.

I heard Mama talking to Rennie on the phone. Her name is really Renesta, but she hates it. So, Mama and everybody else in Pocket call her Rennie.

"We won't be gone long." Mama pulled on her gloves. "Yes, I'll tell you what happened. Bye."

"She's going to meet us?"

"Yep. She said she thought it would settle her stomach."

"What's wrong with her stomach?" If Mama answered, I didn't hear her. I took one more peek at the dogs. Blur's ears were twitching, and Flash looked toward the lot next door. My ears twitched too. Hammering came from next door. In a totally uncharacteristic move, I decided to do something I'd probably regret. Blur turned to look at me through the window. I think she nodded. That was all the encouragement I needed. Slipping out the back door, I headed to the gate at a brisk trot. Both dogs rode the heels of my high-tops.

I was five steps into my plan when the hammering stopped. My heart, however, hammered harder. Exiting the back of the bait shop, Mick had his jacket thrown over one shoulder. Talk about ruggedly handsome. The toolbox I'd seen earlier swung from his other hand. I could see his muscles bulge as he hefted the box into the back of the truck. When he saw me, he waved. Taking a deep breath, I continued. I could feel him watching my every step. I stopped in front of his truck, wishing I'd slapped on a little makeup and maybe glued on a pair of false eyelashes.

"Hello again." How brilliant was that? I wondered if our nearby college offered Witty Repartee 101. The toe of my shoe dug into the dirt.

He slipped his jacket over the t-shirt he wore but left it unzipped. "Hello." There was something about this man that made coherent speech difficult for me. I didn't usually react this way. For heaven sake, I'd grown up with the Barber twins. They were now plastered on billboards across the nation advertising workout equipment, but this man…I sensed he had something more than both Barber twins put together.

"Hello," he repeated. Great. Now he probably thought I was hearing impaired as well as slow-witted.

Totally embarrassed, I blurted out my reason for the impromptu visit. "We're going for a burger. I'd be happy to bring you something to eat. I wasn't sure how long you'd be working, and this place makes great burgers, and I wouldn't mind at all."

Was I babbling? Yes. Was I breathing? No.

His smile broadened, and his eyes were lost in the crinkles. "I appreciate the offer." He wiped his hands on a rag he pulled from his pocket. "But I brought a sandwich with me. Just polished it off a little while ago. Thanks for asking."

I shrugged and tried not to look disappointed…or winded. "No problem. Just wanted to do something to repay you for checking on us earlier." My feet took it upon themselves to start back peddling. "I should be getting back. They'll be waiting on me." When I turned to go, the silly thought crossed my mind he might call to me. He didn't, of course. There was no reason for him to, but somehow, I knew, simply knew, had I turned around, he would still be watching me. Smiling, I jogged back across the lot. My dogs stared at me like they expected details. I patted both of them on the head. "Nothing to report. Sorry," I mumbled. "I just made a complete fool of myself."

Blur cocked her head and woofed. I think it was Dog for "Woohoo! You gave it a shot."

As I stepped back in the door, I saw Mama reaching for her jacket from the front closet. I tried to remember what she'd been saying when I sneaked out. Something about Rennie's upset stomach.

"Tell me again why Rennie needs TLC."

"Her editor is getting antsy. She's running late on her deadline. You know how Rennie is. I told her she better get the lead out. Of course, nobody listens to me."

"I do, Mama."

"Since when?"

"Since you said you wanted to get something to eat. I'm starving, but I don't see how Rennie figures a greasy cheese-burger is going to settle her stomach."

"She meant it will settle her nerves."

"Is she nervous over this new book?" I grabbed my keys.

"Writing children's books is stressful. Fierce competition. I told her with a pen name like Little Miss Bellybutton, she's not going to be forgotten any time soon. Her editor wants three Little Miss Bellybutton books a year. Rennie does real well until the fall. Then she turns into mush. I think she needs hormones."

I didn't say a word, but fifteen minutes later when we walked into Pa Daddy's Café, I was, as always, amazed at how a fifty-six-year-old woman could be in such great shape. I'm twenty-two years younger, and she outcurves me by a mile. Everybody in Pocket knew Rennie was a retired dance instructor from Memphis-turned-children's-author. With a figure that turned every man's head whether he was twenty-five or half dead, she could probably still out shimmy-shake Beyoncé any day of the week. She motioned for us to join her at the back booth and informed us she'd already ordered our burgers and drinks. Notes were scribbled all over her napkin. A writer never rests.

I wrangled my phone from my jeans. Halfway listening to Mama and Rennie, I began my online search for the cutest man on the face of the earth, Mick Walker.

Google search. Images.

Nada.

"Out with it." Rennie looked at Mama and shoved the napkin she'd been scribbling on into her purse. She waited for us to slide into place and then folded her arms.

"Let me catch my breath." Mama fanned herself with her menu. "Did you tell the girl I wanted a glass of water with my

Coke? You know sometimes they get busy, and you can't get a refill of soda."

Twitter account.

Non-existent.

"Yes, Lilly. I've been eating with you for eight years now. I know how you operate. You look a little peaked. You okay?"

Facebook profile.

Zilch.

"Yes, but Mary Clare better tell you all the details."

Rennie turned a questioning glance my way and waited.

I blinked a couple times, cleared my throat, and tried to concentrate on Smitty instead of a certain man with green eyes and shoulders the width of Texas who did not have an online presence. Trying to absorb this monumental disappointment, I faced Rennie and swallowed my distress. "Mama and I were setting up the front display window. When we opened the lid to the casket, there was Smitty Small, big as life."

Mama rolled her eyes.

CHAPTER FOUR

The landline in the office was ringing when Mama, Rennie, and I returned. I glanced at the Caller I.D. Hmmm. Unknown Number. Well, it would be. Mick's new number probably wasn't registered yet. "Pocket Change." I sang the greeting, hoping it was a certain new neighbor.

"Miss Casteel?" It was a male voice. Funny, I didn't remember Mick having a nasal problem.

"Yes?"

"Miss Casteel, my name is Boyd Barlow. I'm Mr. Small's accountant. I'm calling from Westchester, ma'am. A few moments of your time are required."

My blossoming fantasy screeched to a halt.

Westchester was a few minutes' drive from Pocket and considerably smaller. I sorted through my brain to recall a Mr. Barlow. Why in the world was Smitty's accountant calling me?

"Do you have a few moments, Miss Casteel?"

"Certainly."

"I'll get to the point. Mr. Small worked for you." Before I could pucker my lips to confirm, he charged on. "I've been notified Mr. Small has passed away. It is my sincere hope you don't think the remainder of your bill will be dismissed. I handled all of Mr. Small's business and have been asked to continue. His crew must be paid. I would appreciate it if a check for the remainder, I believe it was $10,495.00, be made to Mr. Small's account as soon as possible."

Well, of all the nerve. How had this bozo gotten word so quickly about Smitty's death, and what did he mean he'd been asked to continue handling Smitty's affairs? "I hope you're not insinuating I would shirk my bill, sir." My stiff reply complemented my raised eyebrow.

"No, ma'am. I'm sure you wouldn't. That would result in a lawsuit."

"Why, you rude, little pipsqueak. How dare you." Sputtering wasn't ladylike, but sometimes a girl couldn't help it.

"Have a nice day, Miss Casteel. I'll be in touch, and I will expect that check within the next few days."

The dial tone hummed in my ear. I'll admit I wanted to pray the man would get fleas in his armpits. Maybe other places too. It would serve him right. Instead, I sent up my O.S.P., then climbed the stairs to Mama's apartment and relayed his message to Mama and Rennie. Mama nearly stroked.

"Casteels have always paid their bills. Anyone who knows our family knows that."

Rennie's hands shot to her hips. "Of course, they do. Smitty knew it too. He was a good businessman. The man never was late to pay for his dance lessons. He always paid in advance."

"You knew him in Memphis?" I asked. "He took dance lessons?"

"Sure did. He was a regular weekend member at the All Shook Up Dance Club where I worked. He always signed up for waltz lessons on Friday nights and foxtrot lessons on Saturday afternoons. He never took it seriously, though. Spent most of his time hitting on women. He was a lot more entertaining than the dance classes. Plus, he fancied himself a singer.

He'd belt out tunes while whirling his poor partner around the floor."

"When was this?" I asked.

"Just before I retired and moved here. As a matter of fact, I hadn't been in Pocket too long before I noticed Smitty. It was probably about nine years ago. It surprised me. If he recognized me, he didn't let on. But, like I said, I don't think he ever noticed the dance instructors."

"Did you ever say anything to him about it?" I asked.

"Nope. Didn't see any reason. Sometimes he'd come to the club a little loopy. Everybody said he drank back then. It might have embarrassed him if he'd realized I knew about his past. I mean, I saw how many times he struck out with the women. That's got to be hard on a guy's ego."

"Small world," Mama said. I looked at Mama and frowned.

"You hear that? Sounds like car doors." Rennie paraded to the window and peeled back the curtain.

"What time is it?" Was that hysteria in my voice?

"It's three-thirty. Why are your eyes bugging out like that, Mary Clare?" Before I could answer, a whole herd of people came bounding through the front door. It seemed like a herd. There were six. The local writers' group had arrived. I'd forgotten to tell Mama and Rennie to call and cancel their group's tour.

"Oops," Rennie muttered.

"Hey, cuz." Marma Lee waved. I plastered a smile on my face.

"How did your sister ever come up with a name like Marma Lee?" Rennie leaned in to whisper in Mama's ear.

"The whole time Dovie was pregnant, she craved marmalade," Mama whispered back.

I moved toward the group and extended my hand to the group's leader, Ruby Holly. She was their history buff, genealogist, and founder. One look into her eyes and you knew you were looking at brilliance. She also had a doozie of a handshake. I sincerely hoped I had some Aspercream in the medicine cabinet. I was going to need it.

My mouth was opened and ready to tell the group this wasn't the most opportune time for a tour when my cousin began gushing. She did that a lot. She was the romance writer in the group. Unfortunately, for the lifestyle she'd become accustomed to, she was not very successful. I paid her well to attend auctions in Branson and Nashville as our antique buyer. She called herself an Antique Acquisitions Specialist. There were many names for Marma Lee.

"Mary Clare, I can't believe it. Ralph told us what happened." From the way she splayed her hands over her chest, she looked like she was rehearsing for a heart attack. Ralph was the only one who paid her any attention.

I eyeballed Ralph Perty, owner of the real estate agency across the street. We'd bought the property for Pocket Change from him. Actually, his nephew Newton sold us the lot because Ralph had been on vacation in Greece. Newton told me later he'd nearly been fired when he told his uncle about the sale. The land sat undeveloped for years, but instead of being grateful to Newton, he'd chewed him out for not charging us more because of my recent winnings. He wasn't happy to have an honest nephew, but the papers were already signed by the time he returned. Ralph brought out the worst in me. It wouldn't hurt to repeat my O.S.P.

I nodded my head in his direction and tried to remember his redeeming qualities. He volunteered at the hospital and always bought Girl Scout cookies. That was pretty much it. Mama said he volunteered because he was chasing after one of the nurses, and he only bought cookies because he liked them. Having graduated in the same class, she had a healthy immunity to his suave good looks, athletic build, and quick smile, but they wove a spell over other ladies. He patted his hair into place. I didn't care for men who preen over their hair even on a windy day. "It must have been a harrowing event. Some of the others hadn't heard, so I filled them in." His burrowing brows were a little over the top.

"Yes, harrowing." I glanced at Mama who murmured something polite. Rennie blatantly batted her eyelashes at the man. If I'd been closer, I would have elbowed her.

"We could come back if you prefer." This was Ethel Glacier. Quiet. Reserved. Thoughtful.

This woman needed to sit down. I led them to the Cozy Area and sat Ethel by the fire. The others didn't seem to notice her paling pallor. Maybe she always looked this way. I'd only met her a few weeks ago when Mama and I delivered a basket of goodies to Ethel the day she moved from Little Rock. I'd never met anyone who wrote travel pieces for airline magazines. Mama said she worked full-time as a travel agent in Jonesboro. She needed to book herself an outdoorsy excursion. The woman was in dire need of some sunshine.

"This is nice, Miss Casteel." Ethel gazed around the area with appreciation.

"Thank you. Please, call me Mac. All my friends do."

"Not since you won all that money." Rennie grinned. "Everybody is determined to make you more sophisticated, whether you want to be or not."

"I think she's quite sophisticated. She takes after her mother."

Turning, I smiled at the tallest member of the group, Richard Lorch. He looked at Mama and lit up. Oh, my. Mama had an admirer. I wondered if it bothered her that her suitor wore a bad toupee.

"Other than Ruby," he continued, "I've belonged to this group longer than anyone. I can't remember ever meeting in such a grand establishment." He gazed at his surroundings. "It positively inspires." Richard wrote for the greeting card industry.

"I'm glad you like it." I tried not to notice him straightening his hair. At least he wasn't patting it. I turned to face the stranger in the group. "Welcome to Pocket Change. Are you new to the group?" I extended my hand to the man standing beside Richard.

"Yes, ma'am. I'm Saige Nichols, and for the record, Mr. Lorch is right. This is a beautiful shop. I love antiques, but I've never seen anything like this. It's amazing. You must have an artist's heart."

He had a great voice. Nothing that compared with Mick's but still, a great voice. His Rolex glistened, and the scent of expensive aftershave swirled around what Mama would call a well-developed body. I guessed him to be a year or two older than me and a few inches taller than the six-foot Christmas tree I'd bought on clearance last year. I was rudely brought back to the present when Marma Lee pinched my arm.

"Ouch." I yelped then turned to look into my cousin's face and knew from years of experience she'd tagged Saige as her next mark. Good thing I had my sights set elsewhere.

"Why don't I whip up some hot chocolate? Mama, you and Rennie take everybody on a tour. When you get back, I'll have the cocoa ready." I started for the kitchen, rubbing my arm. I'd have a bruise the size of a bagel by morning.

For the first time, Mama appeared a bit flushed. "Do you think it's okay, Mary Clare? Boomer did say…"

"Boomer cleared the shop, Mama. We just have to avoid the shed and taped off areas."

She perked right up. "Follow me, y'all." She winked at me, and I knew what she was telling me. We'd decided not to share with anyone about our security system. Folks mean well, but they sometimes forget what not to tell.

Marma Lee had Saige by the arm. A year older than me, she'd already had two husbands and one poodle named Toodles and a cat named Dusty Rosie. Only the critters remained.

It was easy to keep up with the group's progress. An occasional "ooh" drifted down the stairs. I turned my attention to the cocoa, turning down the heat. Mama's recipe guaranteed blissful results. A packet of mix, milk, and a splash of vanilla. Top it with a great big spoonful of marshmallow cream, and it's to die for.

I jogged out to the cottage, found mugs, and raced back to the shop with Flash and Blur at my heels. They hustled in the back door with me. If anyone minded, I'd put the pooches out. They immediately went to the Cozy Area and sprawled in front of the fire.

"What beautiful dogs." I thought Ethel had gone with the group. I nearly dumped the tray holding the pot of cocoa and shortbread cookies.

"Thank you." I gave a little skip to try and hide my stumble.

Ethel's face glowed. The magic of animals. More people should own them. Prescriptions for Prozac would go way down. I gestured for Ethel to sit in the wing-back chair she'd vacated earlier. The telephone rang, and I excused myself. Was Mick checking on me? Was he worried? I was disappointed. Verna May Peabody's whiny voice reminded me why I hated to talk on the phone. "No, Verna May. I don't have any details, but I do have guests. Gotta run."

At least it wasn't a repeat call from Boyd Barlow. I returned a few moments later.

"It was a lady who wanted to chat. I'm not much of a chatter on the phone. I'm all for swapping info as long as it doesn't take more than five minutes."

"I'm exactly the same way. My job mandates certain social skills on the phone, but I'm not a phone person by nature." She ducked her head. "Ten minutes is a lengthy phone conversation for me. My friends tell me I have some kind of phobia."

"I must have it too. Tell them we're starting a club."

"When Ruby suggested we hold our meetings in a store, I wasn't sure. We always met in private homes in Little Rock, but this place…" She paused to take it all in. "It feels like a home." She reached over and picked up a mystery novel.

"I think it's the combo of books and antiques. We wanted to furnish and stock it so folks would feel welcome." The rest of the group trudged up from the basement, and I wondered why Ethel hadn't gone with them. Maybe two sets of stairs in one visit were too much. Although she didn't look much over forty, you never knew. Appearances could be deceiving. Look at Rennie.

Soon the couches and easy chairs were full of contented people. The temperature dropped outside, and the sky darkened to a bruised blue. Cocoa hit the spot. No one seemed to mind Flash and Blur, so I left them on the hearthrug to soak up the warmth of the fire. Flash tended to snore, but no one seemed to mind that either. Even the intermittent ringing of the phone didn't wake the dogs, and I decided to ignore it. The reason for the calls was no doubt due to the morning's escapades. Later, I would check the Caller ID, return the important calls, and kick myself if one of the calls happened to be from Mick Walker. My fingers were itching to go online and dig deeper.

"Mac, if you don't mind, we'd love to meet in your beautiful shop." Ruby looked pale but excited. As a matter of fact, she looked worse than Ethel. Learning about Smitty must have taken a toll on these ladies. Ralph should have been more considerate and not announced it to the group on the way over. Mama said he never had been smart. Good looking yes, smart…no.

"We'll be happy to pay you, of course," Ruby finished graciously. Mama looked at me expectantly. She hadn't been a member of the group long. Rennie had talked her into trying her hand at writing mysteries. So far, she refused to let me read a single word.

"We would love for you to meet here, and we wouldn't hear of payment. This will be fun." I was about to offer refills on the cocoa but never got the chance.

"It's settled then." Ralph slapped his hands on his knees and stood. Everyone in the group, including Flash and Blur, jumped.

Tranquility vanished. "I hate to be the one to break this up, but I have to show a house in an hour."

"I thought Newton ran the place on Friday." Richard peered at the realtor.

Ralph scowled before turning on Richard. "Newton doesn't have my experience." He straightened his tie. "I like to take Fridays off, naturally. That's why I was at home today, but a couple from Blytheville wish to see the Weatherly place, and the family up in Chicago who owns the home expects me to show it. It's been sitting empty far too long. So, if everyone's ready…" He made a sweeping motion toward the door. "I need to go home and get my car."

Richard murmured something about wanting to browse for a while, and the others looked around longingly, but each ultimately collected his or her coat and walked to the door.

"We shouldn't leave you with a mess," Ethel fretted. "I'll come back and help you clean up." She leaned over to get her purse which had toppled over on the rug. Ralph helped her scoop up the contents then strode to the door, drumming his fingers on the knob.

"No," Mama declared. "After the kind of day we've had, we need to take our minds off this morning. Cleaning up will be just what the doctor ordered."

Ethel paled. This was one delicate woman.

Richard lagged behind. He approached Mama from the side. She scurried into the kitchen. Can't blindside somebody with eyes in the back of her head and great peripheral vision. He'd have to work on his approach. Maybe Marma Lee could give him some pointers. Sighing, he headed out the door, holding his hair in place.

"Whew." Rennie plopped onto the couch. "What a bunch. We don't have two people in the whole group that write the same kind of stuff."

"Genre." Mama sat straighter.

"What?" Rennie gawked at Mama.

"I've been studying my literary terms. You're the one who got me into this. Genre refers to category. No one in our group writes in the same genre."

"I'm proud of you." Rennie glowed with pride for her fellow writer and friend. "Did Saige ever say what kind of writing he did?"

I winked. "No, but I bet Marma Lee can tell you. She probably knows his shoe size, favorite color, and the names of all his brothers and sisters by now."

Mama chuckled. "Rennie wants to go see the cottage, honey. You want to come?"

"Sure." I loved showing off the house out back. With Flash and Blur in the lead, we headed to the cottage.

Rennie pointed to the maple floors and put her hand over her heart. I could tell she loved it. This is where I would live, vacating it only when author visits were planned. With help from our old co-workers at school, we'd hatched a plan to bring in several authors to make school visits. Education funds are tight. They might eke out one author visit every four or five years, but with the money from the Publisher's Clearinghouse, I planned to host at least one per semester.

Tonight, though, Mama and I would stay here. Her electricity had been turned off in her old apartment, and the garage apartment wasn't ready. I glided over to the thermostat and bumped it up a couple of notches. A leaded, stained-glass cathedral window on the west side captured the evening light and sent warm splashes of turquoise, amber, burnt orange, and emerald green skidding across the room. The cottage was perfect right down to the little country kitchen. Cheery rugs flattered the hardwood floors and red and white chintz curtains hung from wrought-iron rods. Rennie declared it an architectural dream.

I thought it totally rocked.

The sun went down while we were inside. Shivering, I

decided to turn the thermostat up once we got back to the shop too. Mama and Rennie joined the dogs in front of the fire. It was time to take the bull by the horns. Mr. Barlow's rude phone call had bothered me all day. I had a plan.

Marching to the phone, I reached for the business checkbook and wrote out the amount Boyd Barlow had quoted, checking it against my itemization. I used my phone to look up his office number and dialed it, waiting for the man to pick up. He didn't. I left a snappy message instructing him to pick up Smitty's last installment at nine a.m. sharp the next morning. I hung up and took a deep breath. I would, of course, expect a receipt with his signature. In return, he'd be rewarded with a check tucked safely in a travel-sized Bible. On page 618, he'd find Psalm 16:8 high-lighted.

On the way to the kitchen, I whistled a happy tune to myself. Then stopped. Something shifted in my head. Smitty had whis-tled. He'd been a happy, living, vital man, with a windfall of his own. That's what he'd told me. And it hadn't been long ago, maybe eight weeks. Did Boyd Barlow know? I would need a witness when handing Mr. Barlow his check. There was the possibility he couldn't be trusted. I could get Boomer. He needed to know about this guy anyway. Boomer had a lot on his mind, but this could be important information relating to the case. I pulled my cell from my pocket, looked up the number, and dialed the sheriff's office.

"Hello." His bark made me jump.

"Why are you answering the phone? Don't you have a deputy or something to do that for you?"

"What do you want? I'm busy."

Not a nice attitude to have, but I'd forgive him. "I have some information that might shed light on the case."

"I told you to stay out of this. Let the police handle it. You're just a citizen. I don't want you meddling in police affairs."

I'm not sure why, but that rankled me. Snapping my mouth

shut, I decided to keep my suspicions about Mr. Barlow's knowledge of Smitty's windfall to myself. "Could you come by around nine in the morning? I would like you to witness my last payment to Smitty's accountant." That seemed to raise no questions or suspicions in Boomer's head. For some reason, it hurt my feelings that Boomer thought I had the intelligence of an ant. Otherwise, he would at least have asked what I knew about Mr. Barlow. Instead he grunted that he'd be there.

"Thank you," I said sweetly and hung up, with perhaps a tad more zeal than usual. Maybe I needed to brush up on Psalms myself. Flash and Blur followed me into the kitchen to inquire about their dinner. Both dogs sat with heads cocked to the side.

"Honey, you feelin' okay?" Mama asked from the doorway. Rennie peeked over her shoulder. Their expressions looked a lot like Flash and Blur's.

"Nothing a trip to Dollie's Money Mart won't fix. You two up for a day out tomorrow? I'll buy breakfast at Maybelline's and lunch wherever you want." Now that was an enticing offer. Mama cheered immediately. She all but clapped her hands. The woman was a Dollie's Money Mart junkie. After winning the money, Marma Lee asked if Mama and I planned to start shopping somewhere classier. Mama's response was simple. If they didn't run specials over the intercom, she'd pass. Give her a flashing blue light special, and she was in heaven. Guess I came by it naturally.

"Count me out, girls." Rennie sighed. "This book slump is killing me. The only way to get over it is to get over it. I'm going to park myself at that computer and get this book finished if it takes forever. Of course, my agent says I have until next Friday, so, thanks anyway." She yawned and started out the door. "Y'all call me when you get in and tell me about your bargains. Oh rats, it's starting to rain." She pulled the door shut.

I was still fuming about Boomer when Mama suggested we order Chinese for dinner. I didn't have any other plans, and I was always ready for Chinese. We flipped a coin for who would go. She lost.

"That's okay, dear. I need to pick up a few toiletries anyway." I told her I'd finish cleaning the kitchen then meet her back at the cottage. She grabbed her coat and dashed to the car. As she backed out of the drive, I made a mental note to check and lock the doors before leaving for the night. They hadn't been locked since all the brouhaha this morning.

Ten minutes later, I finished cleaning the kitchen in the shop. Dishes were washed, dried, and put away. I swiped the last cookie crumb off the counter when I heard a creak upstairs. I froze. So did Flash and Blur. They heard it too.

Somebody was in the shop.

CHAPTER FIVE

My gaze flitted around for a weapon. The only thing handy was the pan in which I'd heated cocoa. Not ideal, but Paula Deen's cookware has a great bottom. Hearing another creak sent me digging into my pocket for my cell, but it wasn't there. I remembered putting it down after I called Boomer. I inched my way toward the office and the only working landline. Maybe it was another loon wanting money. The last one had been two weeks ago. A man wearing a tuxedo juggling rubber band balls. Mama sent him bouncing right out the door.

The dogs didn't bark, but they began to crouch. I froze. There was nowhere to go. There was no door on the office yet. I'd have no protection once there. Plus, I'd have to pass through the main room to get there. I raised the pan high. A shadow loomed in the doorway.

"What in blue blazes are you doing?" Marma Lee yelled and clutched her sweater. Flash and Blur collapsed onto the floor. They pretended they wanted their bellies rubbed, but I knew it was sheer relief, because I felt like doing the same thing, but first I had to beat my cousin to a pulp with the Paula pot.

"Why are you sneaking around the shop? You scared me half to death," I yelled back.

"I forgot my cell phone upstairs in the Village Idiot's Room. Or, at least I thought I did. It's not up there. You know, that room's starting to look kinda nice." She smoothed her hair as if nothing in the world was wrong. Couldn't she see she'd scared me out of fifteen prime years? "You know, if you're worried about someone coming in, you shouldn't leave your front door open."

"I didn't," I snapped. "It was unlocked but not open."

"It was open when I came in. You were bumping around in the basement, and I hollered to tell you I was going upstairs to look for my sweater. Guess I left it this afternoon. It got kinda warm upstairs. Speaking of warm, what do you think about Saige?"

I'd stopped listening right after the part about her announcing her arrival.

"I wasn't in the basement. I haven't been down there since showing Boomer around this morning. Mama, Rennie, and I have been in the cottage for the last thirty minutes. When Rennie left, she went out the back."

We gaped at each other and darted toward the back door at the same time. Racing to the cottage, she reached the door first. We stopped so short, the dogs bumped into us.

"How do we know someone's not in the cottage?" Marma Lee tugged at my arm.

"We don't, but whoever was in the basement wouldn't take a chance on coming out here with the lights on. You probably scared them off."

"Let's call Boomer." She reached for her phone then remembered it wasn't there. "Use yours. And hurry up."

"No."

"Why not?" Marma Lee's shrieking point was legendary. Good lungs run in the family.

"Because he patronized me." Even I could hear how childish that sounded.

"I'm going to call, Mary Clare. Give me your phone." She opened the door but didn't go in. Bright, wonderful, safe illumination flooded the room. The loft was pooled in soft light as well. The areas not in view were the bath and the space behind the fireplace. We hesitated outside and listened. Nothing but the wind howled around us.

"What are y'all doin'?" Mama asked over our shoulders. Our screams ricocheted off the porch and landed somewhere around the puddled wonton soup at our feet.

Other than Monteen's business and Perty's Realty across the street, the closest neighbor was none other than Mr. Bait Shop Owner. Sure enough, within sixty seconds, he was at the gate heading toward us. Bounding might be the wrong word, but he was definitely moving at a pretty good clip. I wondered if coming to my aid was getting old. One look at his face told me the answer. He wasn't irritated but concerned. It had been a long time since I'd had a male face concerned on my behalf. It was more reassuring than hot buttered toast.

I tried to explain the situation to Mama and Mick. After all, there was a good reason why Marma Lee and I had screamed like a couple of banshees. I looked to Marma Lee for support. She openly gawked at Mick. If I didn't make a tactical move soon, Marma Lee would make moves of her own. I pinched her from behind, right in the soft midriff. Tit for tat. She could set her navigational equipment on Saige if she wanted, but I'd sink her sonar if she set her course for Mick. Jumping, she glared at me. I smiled serenely and refocused my attention on the reason for Marma Lee's smarting skin. He looked at the two of us and waited.

His five o'clock shadow begged to be stroked. I instructed my eyes to move past his chin and concentrate on his eyes, but they never made it past his lips. I tilted my head, kind of the way

Flash did when he wanted a biscuit. Clearing my throat, I found my voice. Marma Lee's concern now centered on her bruising middle.

"We're sorry to have bothered you. Mama startled us when she came back so soon. We're a little on edge."

"That's understandable given the way your day started. Why don't I have a look around?" His eyebrows knit together as he studied Marma Lee. "Did you say you heard noises from the basement, Marma Lee?"

She nodded. An odd look dimmed her enthusiasm. She was not really much of a nodder. She usually seized any opportunity to talk, yet she hadn't said a word since I pinched a plug out of her. She shivered. I hadn't pinched her hard enough to cause a coma.

"Mama." I cut my eyes toward Marma Lee.

"Mary Clare, we need to get her inside. She looks a little faint." Mama took Marma Lee by the elbow.

"You ladies go on in the cottage. I'll look around the shop and make sure everything is okay."

"I don't want to put you in any danger. Why don't we call the police? They can come and check it out." For Mick, I'd swallow my pride.

"Let me have a quick peek around. If I'm not back in fifteen minutes, call Boomer." He took off his jacket and handed it to me. His fingers brushed mine. A taser couldn't have had more zap. From the look on his face, I wasn't the only one tingling.

"Put this around her." He nodded toward Marma Lee. The jacket smelled like Paul Sebastian cologne and sawdust. What a combo. I'd never smelled anything so wonderful. Well, maybe once when I toured Krispy Kreme, but that was a long time ago. I watched him jog across the yard. Once he had disappeared inside the shop, I faced Marma Lee. Definitely not right.

Ever since we were kids, she'd had this delayed reaction

thing. She was fine in the heat of any conflict, then, poof, she went all fuzzy and feather headed. It never lasted long, usually a couple of minutes. Aunt Dovie said it ran in the family.

Within a few minutes, Mama had her in front of the fire in the little cottage. While Mama tucked and clucked, I checked the clock. Five thirty-five p.m.

"Come on, honey," Mama cooed. "Let's get those shoes off and put your feet on this nice cushy footstool."

"Ottoman," Marma Lee corrected.

"She's coming out of it." I tapped my foot and thought about following Mick.

"You want some Szechwan Chicken?" Mama asked. My brow furrowed. That was my dinner she was giving away.

"Where did you get it?" Marma Lee inquired.

Oh, yeah. If she was lucid enough to be picky, she was on her way back.

"Sum Ting Wong," Mama purred. If I hadn't been familiar with the quirky name of the Chinese restaurant, I'd have thought Mama was inquiring as to Marma Lee's condition. She already had a plate ready and was about to spoon-feed my cousin when I took matters into my own hands.

"Marma Lee," I said sweetly.

"Yes?" Her weak voice went perfectly with the gesture she used to accompany it, the old put-the-back-of-her-hand-to-the-forehead pose.

"You want some hot tea with that?" I asked.

"If it isn't too much bother." Her huge sigh ruffled Blur's fur and being the brilliant dog she is, she moved.

"Mama, you want some?"

"No, honey. I'll take iced tea. I got the really hot, hot dishes tonight."

One look at Marma Lee's flaming cheeks attested to the fact.

"Water," she gasped.

"Oh, my goodness." Mama fanned my cousin's face. "Honey, I'm sorry. I thought you knew Szechwan Chicken is hot."

I stuck a glass under the ice dispenser. I didn't get in any hurry pressing it, however.

"Water." Marma Lee croaked again.

"Coming up." I handed her a tall glass of ice water and sat down to watch her gulp. She finished it off in three swigs.

"Better?" I inquired.

"Much, but I'll pass on the chicken, Aunt Lilly. Thanks anyway." She gave smiling a try but failed miserably. "I'll take iced tea."

"That will go better with the little fortune cookies Mr. Wong gave me, honey." She patted Marma Lee's hand. "He always gives me extra cookies and huge servings of the entrées. I think he's flirting. Bless his heart."

I snatched my dinner from Marma Lee's outstretched hand. Glancing at the clock, I noticed it was a quarter to six. No sign of Mick. Not wanting to alarm Mama and Marma Lee, I side-stepped into the kitchen to get the tea. Someone knocked on the door. We all jumped. After I squinted through the peephole, I flung the door wide and ushered in my flannelled-shirted hero.

"Everything okay?" I asked.

"Sort of." I hustled him to the fire. "I'll fix you some coffee."

"Can I do anything to help?" He strode over to the bar which separated the kitchen from the living room and propped himself against the counter. Did the man have no shame? Wait. I tried looking at his face. He wore a decidedly worried look.

"No. Got it under control. What did you mean when you said everything was sort of okay?"

He took his time and looked around the kitchen, his gaze settling on my back door. He looked at the glass panels right above the handle. I thought I knew where this was headed.

"There wasn't anything broken or vandalized inside the shop

that I could see. It appeared like any place that's getting last minute touches." Unease tensed his shoulders. "There are a lot of vulnerable access points, though. Have you considered a security system?"

The coffee started to perk, and the room filled with the aroma. I've always thought psychiatrists needed a pot of coffee brewing all day in their offices, for the smell if nothing else.

"Sort of." I repeated his reply from a few seconds ago. "Mama and I knew we'd have a problem with people trying to pick up things inside the shop, but it never occurred to me someone might try to break in. Of course, I made it really easy for them tonight by not locking the doors earlier. Then again, maybe Marma Lee didn't hear anything. She does have a dramatic streak in her."

"I don't think it was her imagination." He hesitated. "Have you had a problem with people bothering you?"

Was he kidding? Didn't he know about my PCH winnings? I cleared my throat. "Let me fill you in on the last six months, Mick." I told him every detail about that glorious morning. The Mylar balloons, the camera crew that raced at me from the Publisher's Clearing House Prize Patrol Van was etched in my memory. I even described the moment when the sweetest-looking guardian angel I'd ever seen handed me a new life. To Mick's credit, his mouth only fell open once, when I told him the amount. "Within days the nuts arrived. In droves. People, most of whom I'd never heard of, began calling, knocking, begging, and sometimes insisting I give them money."

"They wanted you to simply give them money? Why?"

I nodded. "They wanted an easy buck. Call me stubborn, but I think able-bodied people should earn a living. Uncle Ardmore is a disabled veteran, and you won't find him asking for anything free. He works at Pansy's nursery and works rings around her son, Junior, who's a third Ardmore's age."

He smiled, and the whole kitchen took on a homey glow.

"Okay. So, maybe it was one of your nuts. But when was the last person you know about downstairs?"

I thought about Uncle Ardmore but dismissed him immediately. He would never come by without saying hello and goodbye, and he for sure wouldn't leave a door open. Security and detail were big deals to him. I shrugged. "There wasn't anyone down there after four o'clock this afternoon. Mama's writing group came and toured the shop. Why?"

"Mud is all over the carpet leading to the basement. It didn't start raining until a little while ago. The yard around the shop isn't landscaped yet, so there's a lot of mud outside. On top of that, the basement door was open." He shrugged and looked apologetic all at the same time. There went my last shred of hope. Someone had been in the shop and had probably fled from the basement entrance when Marma Lee arrived. Whether it was a local snoop, another loony asking for money, or Smitty's killer, I didn't know. I decided it was time to find a good surveillance company to install motion lights and a security system. That task would go at the top of my to-do list. I told him as much.

"That's good." He looked around. "What about out here?"

"Out where?" I asked, refusing to look him in the eyes. Whatever he had to say was not going to make my ears happy.

"Miss Casteel, isn't it?" he asked.

"Mary Clare, but my friends call me Mac." I realized I'd never properly introduced myself. Mentally, I slapped my forehead.

"Mac." He said it slowly, like he wanted to see how it tasted on his tongue. I'd never heard my name pronounced in such a delicious way before. "I like that." He stood straighter and perused the windows and doors. "You need security out here as well. I don't mean to be forward, but I couldn't help but notice your status." He raised his hand in the air and wriggled his ring finger. "If you're living alone, you need protection." As if on cue, Flash and Blur came in and sat beside me. I had to smile.

Here stood a perfect stranger in my house, and they hadn't even snarled. When I looked up, he grinned from ear to ear.

"Not another word. I'll call about a full security system. After all, I'll have guests staying here at times. It's important they feel safe."

"Mac," Marma Lee bellowed. "I'm going home."

"You sure you feel like driving?" I asked. "You could stay here."

"I'm fine. I'll talk to you tomorrow." She strode into the kitchen and handed Mick his jacket, thanked him, and waved goodbye. She didn't even attempt to flirt. The girl was either worn to a frazzle or sensed my own interest in Mick. Hmm. Maybe my pinch cinched it.

Mama curled up on the couch with an egg roll in one hand and the remote control in the other.

"She's still pale." I nodded at Marma Lee's retreating back.

Mick pulled out his phone. "I'll call a cab for her."

"You're still in a Memphis mindset. This is Pocket. The closest thing we have to a cab is Mutt's Grocery Truck." Marma Lee wobbled toward the door and started hunting her shoes.

"I'll follow her home if you'd like." Mick laid his phone on the counter. He turned. Maybe he wanted to check on Marma Lee's progress or maybe to see if we had an audience.

"You would?" This guy was too perfect to be real. "She's not a great driver. When she gets rattled, she's really bad."

He dug keys from his pocket. "I'll be glad to." Grabbing a notepad, I jotted down Marma Lee's address in case she got ahead of him. He could always use his GPS. He shrugged into his jacket and pointed to the kitchen door. "Lock it. I double checked the doors in the shop and secured everything. My plan is to stay at my shop tonight."

"Not on our account. It's completely not necessary."

He waved it off. "If you knew my uncle, you know there's a comfy bed in there. I'll grab some clean linens and clothes on my way back from seeing your cousin home and settle in next door."

I'd always been pretty good at math. Right now I estimated inches. My guess was fifteen and a half between us. The attraction couldn't have been more palpable had we been wearing heavy-duty magnets. "I'm sure everything will be fine," I managed to whisper.

"If you need me, call." His voice dropped to a dangerously low decibel. In some cultures, it might be considered a moan. He pulled a piece of paper and a carpenter's pencil from his pocket. "Here's my cell number."

It was inevitable our fingers would touch when he handed me the folded paper. I warned my fingers to behave themselves. They did. His fingers, however, misbehaved. After they handed me his phone number, they brushed my cheek.

I have no idea how Webster's defines caress, but I wager it isn't as accurate as the way Mick's fingers skimmed my cheek. My eyes closed, and I'm pretty sure I sighed. When I opened them, he smiled. Oh, my. It was up to me to put more inches between us.

I turned and slid the paper on the counter under a Pocket Change paperweight. Time to transition my mind to less dangerous destinations. My gaze locked on the top of the fridge where promotional items were in bags. We intended to hand them out during our grand opening. Bracelets, phone covers, pens, bumper stickers, bookmarks, and paperweights were sacked in plastic. I'd have to remember to put them by the cash register before we opened. Taking a deep breath, I turned back to Mick. Oh, good grief. Did he have to have such a broad chest?

Totally flustered, I nearly tripped over my own feet when I whipped around. Mick seemed a bit discombobulated himself. More distance. We needed more inches. Composing myself, I gestured toward the door. Without saying a word, he followed me. Just when I thought I was safe he leaned in and whispered.

"… for she was lovely to look at."

"Shakespeare?" I asked.

"Nope. Book of Esther. Chapter one; verse eleven." Smiling wider, he opened the door and strode to his truck. Within minutes I heard him pulling out of his driveway. As my Aunt Dovie would have said, I didn't know whether to faint or fan myself. Instead, I hiccupped. I used to hiccup after getting off the Scrambled Octopus ride at the county fair. Mick Walker had the same effect on me. Maybe this delayed reaction thing really did run in the family. Marma Lee went fuzzy. I hiccupped. I went to the kitchen, ran myself a glass of water, and stuck my chicken and egg roll in the microwave. There was still a big ol' smile plastered on my face as I meandered back to the living room. All the frustration of not being able to locate Mick online vanished. Who needed a status update when the real thing resided two minutes from my back door?

Mama stared into space. "I'll bet it was Verna May Peabody." Her definitive nod brooked no argument.

"You bet what was Verna May Peabody?" I nibbled on a thumb nail and thought about Mick's whisper. "Oh. That reminds me. She called and wanted to come over. Told her it wasn't a good time."

Mama snapped her fingers. "Yep. She's our cat burglar. The old busybody. She's been hinting for a month now that she'd like to see the shop. I told her to come on over anytime. Of course, only a nitwit would pick today, so she sneaked in tonight. She's like that. Did I tell you she asked me to ask you for a hundred grand?"

"For what?" My jaw dropped. Why did people still astound me? Since winning the sweeps, I'd seen some top-notch shenanigans. One in particular involved a tricycle and an almost clothed octogenarian. Come to find out, she needed money so she could enroll in an online dating service specializing in unique individuals. Yeah, buddy.

"Said she needed a full-body lift." Mama nodded at the idea.

The sound of a hammer rang out beside me. "What in the world is that?" Mama stuck her head around the corner and eyed the cell phone on the counter. "Did you change your ring tone?"

Uh, oh. Mick's phone was hammering up a storm. He'd laid it on the counter and forgotten to pick it up. I glanced at the screen and read the number and the initial below it.

"A. No name. Just A. Should I answer it?" I looked at Mama, but the phone quit ringing. I placed it back on the counter and watched it like it might jump up and bite me.

"Best to let sleeping dogs lie." She pointed to the cell, turned, and went into the living room.

"Hmm." Since it was passcode protected, I had no choice but to leave the phone alone. Within seconds, it locked. I retrieved my dinner but had trouble working up any enthusiasm over it. Maybe it was the idea of the process one would have to endure to give Verna May a body lift or maybe it was the nagging question of who A. was.

My thoughts turned to Mick, his phone contacts, and the fact I'd completely forgotten to ask him about the size of the footprints he'd detected on the basement carpet. The thought of a curious Verna May hadn't occurred to me. Somehow, in my heart, I didn't think we'd find little ladies' (or big ladies') footprints, but that would be easy to check out myself. The intruder would be long gone now. The rain sounded like big, fat pelts of pterodactyl poop hitting the side of the house. Maybe I should wait until morning. Telling Boomer could definitely wait until morning. But Mick might need his phone tonight. I yawned and listened to the rain pound the roof. Maybe he'd stop back by. If not, I'd run it to him first thing in the morning before breakfast. That reminded me.

"I'm going to ask Lurlene Huff if she'll consider cleaning the shop. Everybody in town says Maybelline's sister is the best."

"That's a good idea. You know…" Mama lowered her voice

as if we had an audience of a dozen around us. "Some folks poke fun at her, and it's mean."

"Why do they make fun of her?" I frowned. This was news to me.

"Well, cleaning is her life. She's a bit obsessed with it. That's why so many people hire her. She's good. She wears those yellow rubber gloves everywhere she goes. Sally out at Wal-Mart says she goes through three pairs a week. Course, she didn't used to be that way, but ever since the dumpster incident, she hasn't been the same."

I stared at Mama. How does she know all this stuff about people? "She was dumped in a dumpster?"

"Not exactly. It happened about fifteen years ago. She and Maybelline used to be just crazy about yard sales. They'd get all the nearby papers and chart out their routes just like a military operation. Come the weekend, they'd be up by four in the morning. By five, they'd be on their way to whatever residences they had rated with triple stars. They would only allow themselves fifteen minutes per stop, and then they'd move on to the next location."

I was amazed. I'd known the spinster sisters all my life. Or maybe not.

"One day, Maybelline was paying out and Lurlene spotted a sale across the street that hadn't been announced. It was one of those moving sales where they don't drag the stuff out to the yard, you traipse through the house and pay when you leave. Anyway, she went to check it out and about the time she walked in the front door, she saw somebody throw a perfectly nice wicker basket out the back door into a dumpster. Lurlene was beside herself. She couldn't imagine anybody throwing away a good basket, so she waited until the man went around to the front of the house then proceeded to climb into the dumpster and retrieve it. That's when the Doberman showed up." Mama tried her best to keep her lips from grinning, but it wasn't working.

Evidently, she had the same mental picture in her brain that was etched into mine.

"The dog's name was Chewy, and she was normally a calm, friendly dog." Mama giggled. "But when she saw Lurlene trying to steal the basket she had just birthed her babies in, she got a little riled."

I puckered up my face. "Ew. No wonder they were throwing the basket away."

Mama nodded. "Chewy bounded toward Lurlene with a vengeance. When Lurlene saw that canine cannon coming at her, she dived into the dumpster headfirst. It was right after that when Maybelline opened up the diner, and Lurlene started cleaning businesses. They both gave up yard sales for good. Said it was too dangerous."

I wiped the tears off my face with my shirt. "That explains a lot. Maybelline's always said she caters to yard sale shoppers."

Mama nodded. "She told me once it's sort of like when parents live their lives through their children. She enjoys yard sales via her customers. I've heard Lurlene dabbles in QVC, but she manages to keep it under control."

"You reckon she'll have time to clean Pocket Change?"

"Maybe. You won't be able to get her on Mondays. That's the day she drags all the tables and chairs out of her sister's diner and scrubs them. She scrubs the whole place down. It really is the cleanest diner in the tri-county area. Probably the cleanest anywhere. You never have to wipe off the booths in Maybelline's Diner."

The clock on the bookcase chimed on the quarter hour. I couldn't believe it was only six forty-five. This day had been three days long. I said as much to Mama.

"Yes, and your mama is tuckered out." She closed her take-out box. "You sure you don't mind me staying here tonight? I thought I'd get to move a few more things into the garage today, but..."

"Of course, you'll stay here. You may have a dog or two curled up with you in the morning." I grinned at her and pointed to the dogs at her feet.

"That's okay." They followed her into the bathroom as she brushed her teeth and washed her face. Flash sat beside her. Blur lounged in the tub with her head resting on the rim.

"You got a spare nightie?" she called.

"How about a Cat in the Hat sleep shirt?"

"The dogs won't mind?"

"Wear it wrong side out." I chuckled and rummaged in a box for the sleep shirt then, decided to double check the doors after making the pooches go to the bathroom. Phoning a security company would top my to-do list. I rubbed my hand, which still ached from Ruby's sturdy handshake during the writers' tour. I struck out with the Aspercream but located aspirin. Surely the medicine would kick in soon. "What time do you want to get up?"

"Early." Her yawn gave a view of the back of her throat and her two fillings. "I want to get gone for two reasons. One, to beat the curious passersby who are going to be ringing our doorbell and two, to nab one of Maybelline's pancake rolls before they're all gone. When she runs out of batter, that's it. Tomorrow is Saturday, you know. She puts bacon in them on Saturday."

My stomach rumbled. I would have to wait until morning, though. I wasn't going to have a bedtime snack. I still felt guilty over the Snickers. "How about seven o'clock? Don't forget I have Mr. Money Grubber Barlow coming over at nine in the morning. Boomer said he would witness the final payment." Both dogs followed Mama into the spare bedroom. The sound of her climbing in the bed and fluffing her pillow wafted across the hall. It wouldn't be long before she'd have bookends on either side of her. It was a good thing she was little, and the bed was big.

"Seven o'clock is fine." I heard her punch her pillow one more time, sigh, and the light went out.

"Honey girl?" Her voice echoed across the hall.

"Yes, Mama?"

"I hope tomorrow's calmer. Today's been a real killer."

The woman did have a way with words.

On my way to open the shop, I noticed Mick's truck missing from the lot next door. I tucked his phone into the pocket of my sweater and arrived at Pocket Change to find Boomer at the front door. It was eight-thirty. My, what an early bird. As I unlatched the oak entrance and stood aside, I tried to look perky but didn't pull it off. Without my first glass of sweet tea, I wasn't coherent. Mama thought that was crazy. She said normal people start their day with coffee. I told her I wasn't crazy or normal, I was somewhere in between, and needed cold caffeine to jolt my system into moving. I offered Boomer a glass.

"Don't you have any coffee?" he asked. These people and their ruts.

"No, but I'll make a pot." I headed into the kitchen to start the brew. Mama entered the back door with Flash and Blur at her heels. She spotted Boomer and nodded. For an instant I thought she intended to tell him about last night. Then she looked at me and apparently decided if it was to be done, it was my job.

"Mary Clare, these babies have to be fed. Where's their

food? I couldn't find anything in the cottage. They're starving." She bent down and patted each. Boy, did they have her trained.

"Their kibble is in the pantry, Mama. I saw you sneaking them bologna out of the refrigerator last night. That is not good for them."

She didn't even have the decency to look guilty. She hurried to the pantry, scooped out a generous helping for each, then filled their water bowls. The clink of ice cubes hit the rim of the bowls. Sheesh.

"Have you had breakfast, Boomer?" Mama asked.

Surely she wasn't going to offer him kibble.

"Yes, ma'am. I stopped by Maybelline's a while ago. Had two of her pancake rolls. Don't know where she got that recipe, but I've never tasted anything like it. You know today's Saturday. She puts bacon in them."

Was he licking his lips? I set his coffee mug in front of him and shoved the sugar and creamer toward him.

"That's a family recipe she modified," Mama informed him. "Maybelline's mama gave her the pancake recipe, and Maybelline tweaked it. Won't give the recipe to anybody. People have tried to buy it from her. She's become famous all through the Ozarks for her pancake rolls. The *Arkansas Times* even did a big write-up on her a few years back."

It was a quarter until nine. I wanted to get this over with and get a couple of pancake rolls myself. Maybelline had the best tea in town too. Sweetened just right.

"When is this Mr. Barlow supposed to arrive?" Boomer blew into his coffee. "That name doesn't ring a bell. Is he local?"

"He said he was from Westchester. If he's as rude to everyone as he was to me on the phone, he won't be making any close friends in Westchester or anywhere else."

"I apologize for that."

I whirled around and took in the strange man standing in my kitchen door. I hadn't heard anyone come in after Boomer. By the looks of the briefcase, business suit, and ramrod stance, this had to be Boyd Barlow. I'd never seen anyone quite like him. He pushed his glasses, which had a slight rose cast, up the bridge of his nose, and his shoulder twitched. He seemed a bit uneasy. Good.

"Mr. Barlow, I presume." I made no effort to apologize for my comment. I'd meant what I said. Rude people should expect to be justly appraised. I wasn't ashamed of my candor.

"I'm Mr. Barlow. Boyd Barlow. We spoke on the phone yesterday, and I want to apologize for my abruptness."

Maybe he wasn't such a twerp after all. Still, I didn't offer him any coffee or tea. I was glad Mama didn't offer him kibble.

He tugged at his too-short, red tie and adjusted his glasses again. His cell phone began chirping. "Excuse me." He unclipped the phone from its holster and stepped back into the main room. The quick exchange took less than a minute. Maybe Mrs. Barlow phoned to tell him to bring home a loaf of bread. His left hand revealed no wedding band. Nope, it hadn't been Mrs. Barlow.

He stepped forward and extended his hand. Regarding it with the same amount of eagerness reserved for boiled liver, I took it. A wimpy handshake. Not much surprise there. As he stepped back, I noticed his Reebok running shoes. They didn't quite go with his three-piece suit. Red, thinning socks were visible from beneath pants, which were about two inches too short. They matched his red tie perfectly.

"I do apologize for my bluntness on the phone, Miss Casteel. You must understand, however, I deal with all types. It's been my experience people like to pretend their responsibilities end if someone they're dealing with dies. It makes settling the estates difficult."

"What made you change your mind about me?" My curiosity got the better of me. The man was a changed creature. Yesterday he'd been insulting and arrogant. Today he was manners magnified.

"I had a client in my outer office who overheard my conversation. When they heard me call your name, they couldn't believe I would accuse a Casteel of reneging on a debt. Got rather huffy, to tell you the truth. Said your family has one of the best reputations in Northeast Arkansas and I should be ashamed of myself. I am." He hung his head. His cell phone chirped, and again he excused himself and stepped out of the room.

I know it's wrong to gloat, and I could mentally hear Mama Z snapping her fingers at me, but I enjoyed Mr. Barlow's apology. Casteels are good people. We didn't rob, we paid our debts, and we didn't lie. Ooh, conscience tug. "Boomer, there's something I need to tell you."

"That was my office," Mr. Barlow said from the door. "It seems I have a meeting in thirty minutes with someone not as credible as yourself. I hate to rush things along, but if we might complete Mr. Small's transaction, I'll be on my way and out of your hair." He seemed to notice Boomer for the first time. "Good morning, Sheriff. I hope I'm not interrupting something."

"No." Boomer shifted his cup and was going in for the power sip. "I'm here to witness Mary Clare's final payment."

Instead of showing signs of resentment, Mr. Barlow's smile widened. "A wise business call, Miss Casteel."

I pulled the check from its resting place in the Bible and showed it to Boomer then handed it to Mr. Barlow. Maybe he wasn't so bad. I'd save my highlighted present for another time. I placed the Bible on the desk and patted the white cover. Meanwhile, Mr. Barlow wrote out a detailed receipt explaining the nature of the transaction and handed it to me. I took it, snapped a picture of it with my phone which garnered another appreciative nod from Mr. Barlow, and slid it into the desk drawer.

"It was a pleasure meeting you. If I can be of service in the future, don't hesitate to call me. I'm sorry we got off to such a rocky start. My fault completely." He bowed. I've never been bowed to before. Was a curtsy in order? Before I could decide which foot I was supposed to lead off on for a curtsy, he was gone.

Boomer stood. "Wish the rest of my day was gonna be this easy."

"Sit back down," Mama ordered. "We're going to brighten your day even more." I guess Mama had read my conscience.

Boomer rubbed his hands over his face. He didn't look excited. "Maybe I'd better have another cup of coffee."

I picked up his mug and refilled it. Handing it back to him, I tried to decide the best way to broach the subject of last night's fiasco.

"Boomer," I began.

"Does this have anything to do with the reason you called me last night?"

"Kind of. What I wanted to tell you yesterday had to do with whether or not Mr. Barlow knew Smitty was coming into some money. That could be a motive for murder, you know. However," I paused, "you insinuated anything I had to tell you was silly, female drivel. That kind of rudeness rankles. I wasn't even going to tell you, but something happened last night to change my mind."

Boomer sat as straight as a toothpick. Looking from Mama to me he seemed to sense something was wrong. "What happened?"

"Someone was in the shop last night. Mama's writing group came by yesterday afternoon to set a meeting date. Marma Lee came back to get her cell phone and heard someone in the basement. She thought it was me, but I was in the cottage with Mama and Rennie. Mick Walker came over to make sure everything was okay. That's when he found muddy footprints on the steps going to the Children's Chamber. He also found the outside door to the basement open."

"The same door that guy used to deliver the books?" Boomer clamped his lips together.

I nodded. Mama had her chin cupped in her hands.

"I think it was Verna May Peabody," she declared. She went on to give Boomer her reasons. "If the delivery man didn't shut the door completely when he left, she could have sneaked in to pilfer."

"I'd better go." Boomer looked at his coffee with longing but left it on the table. Being the dedicated proprietor, I decided to go with him. Mama stayed in the kitchen talking to Flash and Blur. She told them she would bring them something pretty from Dollie's Money Mart.

"Who did you say came down here last night?" Boomer withdrew his pad and pencil.

"You mean to check out the trouble? That was Mick Walker. Nice man." Fortunately, Boomer busied himself examining the muddy tracks on my beautiful red carpet and didn't notice my flushed face was only a few hues short of matching the carpet.

He scratched his head. "Unless this Verna May Peabody has extremely large feet for a woman, these don't belong to her. I'd say a man made these. Take a look. And they're going down the stairs, not up. If Miss Peabody came in the basement door, she'd work her way up and out the front door, which you said was open when Marma Lee arrived. Whoever made these came in on the main level and went down to the basement. The size suggests a male."

Marma Lee said people with large feet usually have large hands. Large hands could choke a person. I mentioned that to Boomer.

"Our victim was strangled with something sturdy. Whoever did it probably brought it with them because they planned to kill Smitty. If we can prove that, then we'll prove premeditation. We just don't know why. You know, this means getting the Jonesboro men back over here. We need pictures, and they'll need to do a complete sweep for anything foreign. I wish you hadn't let that group in here. That will really complicate matters." Boomer's scowl spoke volumes.

He was right. Until yesterday, there hadn't been anyone down here except Mama, the UPS man, Smitty's work crew, and me. "I'm sorry, but you did clear the building. What do you want me to do? Ruby Holly is supposed to call to set up a time for her group to meet here. I'm already obligated."

"We can't take a chance on any more contamination."

"Could we meet in the cottage?"

Boomer chewed the inside of his mouth, frowned, and then nodded his head slowly. "If you make them park by the cottage and enter through the fence gate, I'll permit it. No one is to walk anywhere close to the building or the shed. I mean it, Mary Clare. This is serious."

"I'm really sorry." He was trying to keep us safe. Besides, the sooner he could get his job done, the sooner we could open for business.

"Do you need us here when the men come to take pictures?" I fiddled with the buttons on my sweater.

"No. I'll lock up when we're finished. Why, you going somewhere?"

"Yes. We're going to get out of Dodge, Sheriff. People are already flocking into town for the ten-mile yard sale. I do not want to have to field questions from all those people. We're going by Maybelline's for breakfast, and then we're off to Jonesboro."

"I have one of the deputies assigned to keep watch today. Rubberneckers will be by to check things out. Clarence Leonard's new. This will be a good detail for him. I may assign him here for a while."

If the intruder was Smitty's killer, why in the world would that person have come back last night? None of this made sense.

"Did you get scared last night?" Boomer's eyebrow quirked with concern. "You really should have called, you know."

"I was still peeved at you, but you're right. We should have called." I tap-danced around his question. The truth was it had shaken me up.

"Well, we'll get on it now. You and Lilly go to Jonesboro and have a good time."

We headed back to the kitchen when we heard the front door open. Boomer hurried to the main room. Ruby Holly closed the front door and wiped her feet on the welcome mat.

"Good morning." She glanced in my direction. For an older woman, Ruby had a youthful smile. You couldn't help but reciprocate.

"Hi, Ruby. What can I do for you?" I cast a nervous glance at Boomer.

"I'm sorry, Ms. Holly. I'll have to ask you to step outside." He motioned her to step back the way she'd come.

"What did I do?" I sensed Ruby's alarm.

"We're sealing off Pocket Change, Ms. Holly. We should have done it sooner." Boomer gave me a pointed look.

"I see. Mac. I tried to phone. No one answered. I came by to leave a note about the meetings. I guess we'll have to change our plans."

"Only a little." I explained the need to meet in the cottage as well as the parking setup. Ruby nodded. She would contact the group members and tell them of the changes. They would meet Tuesday night in the cottage.

"It's all set then. We'll expect everyone around seven o'clock." I smiled.

"This is a trying time for you." Ruby said. "Any word yet?"

Boomer shook his head and gave me a warning look. My goodness, the man must think I go around blabbing my head off.

"I'll tell Mama about the meeting," I called to Ruby as she

disappeared. "She'll be excited." Boomer secured the front door and followed me to the back exit.

"Okay, I'm out of here." I clicked the lock and looked up to see that Mama was way ahead of me. She brought my purse and keys from the cottage.

"You think their igloos will keep them warm enough?" She fretted over the greyhounds. "Maybe we need to think about getting a doggy door in the cottage."

"I don't think they make doggy doors their size, Lilly, and if they did, the doors would be large enough for a man to crawl through."

She paused to stare at Boomer. "Maybe that's not such a great idea."

"Mary Clare, was that your old blue Chevy in front of the store last night?" Boomer asked.

"Yes. It still runs fine. I'll let the clerks use it if they need to make deliveries. It'll save them from having to use their own wheels. Plus, Molly doesn't have a car. I thought she might need it to go back and forth from work."

"Very generous of you." Boomer waved and walked back to the shop. "We'll talk later, Mary Clare."

"Time to hit the road," Mama called. "I'm starving. I hope Maybelline hasn't sold out of those pancake rolls. I may have to get extra maple butter. Today feels like an extra maple butter kind of day."

"How does she make that stuff?" I asked, backing out of the parking lot.

"Don't know. She won't give anyone that recipe either. I've tried making it like honey butter, but it never turns out like hers. Wouldn't do any good to ask her for the recipe."

"Surely Lurlene knows."

She shrugged. "She says she doesn't. Did you ever call her about cleaning?"

"I forgot with all the commotion this morning. Maybe we can catch her at Maybelline's."

"Maybe." Mama settled in and buckled up. "Sometimes, if she doesn't have a cleaning job, she helps with the morning crowd."

We were in luck. When we walked into Maybelline's Diner, Lurlene swabbed the kitchen floor. Maybelline fussed at her for being in the way. "It was just a little dab of syrup, Lurlene. It doesn't take three buckets of mop water to get up a little dab of syrup."

We didn't hear Lurlene's reply, but Maybelline flew back into the kitchen, shaking her head and tugging at her big hair. Mama found a booth in the corner close to the window and plopped down. I smiled at Maybelline as she came back carrying three orders of eggs and bacon. On the way back, she gave me thumbs up, acknowledging my order. She knew me well.

"Make it two orders, Maybelline, with extra maple butter." I yelled across the room, any decorum thrown to the wind. She nodded, made the okay sign, and pranced back in five minutes with two huge pancake rolls. Maple butter oozed from the top and middle. The woman was a kitchen goddess. She plunked down hot coffee for Mama and iced tea for me.

"Heard about Smitty." Maybelline scanned the room, made sure her customers were okay, and pulled up a chair. "You two okay? That would have scared my gray roots right out of my head." She patted her hair nest. That's what Mama called big hairdos.

She examined the top of my head. "Not one gray hair in those red locks. I guess you weathered the surprise."

"She's as sholid ash a wock, Maybelline," Mama said around a mouthful of pancake roll.

"We may have to delay our grand opening," I grumbled and took a sip of the tea. Heaven. "Boomer is over there now, sealing the place up. But when he does give us the all clear, do you think Lurlene would consider signing us on as regular customers?"

"Prob'ly. I'll ask her." Maybelline flew off toward the kitchen.

I started to take another bite of my roll and noticed Mama wiping her mouth. "You're finished?" The woman was a machine.

"Nope, just getting started. When Maybelline comes back, I'm going to order some orange juice and an order of smacked-around hash browns."

"Mama, those things are loaded with grease."

"Yes, they are. That's what makes them so good, that and the chopped onion and garlic." She waved her hand in Maybelline's direction like a know-it-all student. Half the customers in the diner waved back. Only in the South. I loved it. I was about to dig into my own pancake roll when I looked across the room and locked looks with Mick Walker.

Not much can stop me from launching into Maybelinne's pancake roll, but one glance at those gorgeous green eyes, and I forgot about the delicious delight on my plate. Smiling, he raised his cup of coffee in a sultry salute. I saluted with my fork. It was like a scene from an old movie. Or at least it would have been if my fork hadn't been dripping with syrup. Embarrassed, I raced to the lady's room and spent five minutes trying to get maple sludge out of my hair.

Mustering as much dignity as possible, I sauntered back to our table. As I sat down, I glanced at his table. He was gone. Great. He was probably rolling around in the parking lot laughing his rear off. What if he posted that on the Internet? Would he do that? No, wait. He couldn't. I had his phone. I dug around in my sweater pocket and felt the rubber from his protective case. There was no sign of him anywhere. That was okay. I'd just play it cool and wait for him to return to his seat. Then

I'd pay Lurlene a hundred dollars to give it to him while I slunk out the back door.

Lurlene came trotting across the diner, wearing her signature yellow rubber gloves. Her cheeks rivaled the color of a fresh garden tomato. She shoved a replacement fork in my face. "Hey, y'all. Maybelline said you might have a job for me." She plopped down in the seat Maybelline had vacated.

"Do you think you could fit in cleaning both the shop and cottage, Lurlene? I know you're busy, but we wouldn't trust anybody but you."

"Be happy to. I have a hole in my schedule. I could fit you in on Tuesdays and Wednesdays. Would that be okay?"

"If I wasn't too stuffed to get out of this booth, I'd hug your neck. Tuesday and Wednesday would be great. Could you do the cottage on Tuesday and the shop on Wednesday? Mama's writing group will be in the shop Tuesday nights. You won't be able to start for a while, though. Boomer has locked the place up until all this mess with Smitty is cleared up. It won't bother you to work there, will it? I mean, with what happened to Smitty and all. It seemed to really upset Ruby."

"I'll bet this has been hard on her." Lurlene straightened her gloves.

"What's been hard on her?" I asked.

"Smitty's death." Lurlene straightened one finger on her yellow glove. "You know, he was the same age as her Cora Ann."

"Oh, my goodness." Mama put her fork on her plate with a loud whang. "I'd forgotten about that."

"What are you two talking about?" It was so frustrating to be clueless. To offset my irritation, I took another bite of pancake roll.

"Y'all talking about Cora Ann Holly?" Maybelline asked as she stuffed her order pad in her apron pocket. She'd appeared over Lurlene's shoulder like a hovering angel. It would be hard to find a halo to fit that hair. Mama gave Maybelline her order, and she whisked back to the kitchen.

I looked at Lurlene. "What are you talking about? Who is Cora Ann Holly?"

"Honey, Ruby had a daughter that was killed. She was Smitty's age, wasn't she, Lurlene?" Mama asked.

"Sure was. They were real good friends. The police just ran out of clues. That was a bad time for Ruby. Cora Ann had just told her mama she was pregnant."

Lurlene leaned over our table. Her gaze flitted around the room, then she leaned in to make sure nobody could hear her. "Ruby always thought Smitty was the daddy, but he denied it. He was real upset when Cora Ann disappeared, though. He helped that rescue team, but her body never did turn up. It nearly killed Ruby. What made it doubly bad was the fight she and Cora Ann had the day before, and they didn't even talk the next day. Then she was gone."

"That is so sad." My appetite was gone. Smitty's death meant Ruby lost another link to her daughter's disappearance. No wonder she looked sad. None of this affected Mama's appetite in the least. When Maybelline placed her plate of hash browns in front of her, she dug right in. The orange juice was gone in no time.

"It's not fair, Mama. You can eat whatever you want, and you don't gain an ounce. I have to watch every calorie, and I swear sometimes I gain weight in my sleep."

"You inherited your daddy's metabolism."

I shook my head and gave Lurlene a glum stare. If possible, she was thinner than her sister. "You too?"

"Yep. Sister and I drank milk shakes to gain weight when we were kids. Hate milk shakes to this day." She stood and pushed her chair back in place, squirted it with Mr. Clean, and wiped it down. "Give me a call when you get the all clear from Boomer. I won't take on another job."

"You sure it won't bother you, Lurlene? You won't be afraid?"

"Honey, nothing's as scary as having your rear chewed by a maniac mama Doberman. Trust me, a little crime tape won't faze me."

The woman was amazing, and so was what happened next. After we paid our bill, we headed to the car. There, under the windshield wiper, a napkin fluttered in the wind. On it was a message written in blue ink. *Marma Lee Mission Memorable. Arrived safely. Not sure how. I'll pick up my phone later today.*

P.S. On anyone else, Aunt Jemima wouldn't work. On you, it looked downright delectable.

Hmm. My day was looking up.

CHAPTER SEVEN

I t was almost ten-thirty by the time we slid into a prime parking spot in front of Dollie's Money Mart. With the motor still technically engaged, Mama leapt from the car and dashed for the door. She was small, quick, and a cheater. The rule had always been that we entered together, but her rebel side had kicked in. She darted inside the store and had the cart yanked out in the aisle before I'd gotten both feet over the threshold. Her tapping toes told me I tried her patience. Sailing past her, I headed for the customer service counter.

"Do y'all have any blue light specials going right now?" I asked. One glance at Mama told me she wanted to kick herself for not asking the girl the same question.

"There's one in the petite slim department, ma'am, but that's probably not going to help you any." After announcing this, she offered me an apologetic smile. I wanted to slug her, but my upbringing prohibited that. Instead, I silently prayed my O.S.P. then commented on the beautiful blouse she wore. Mama hurdled toward the short people department. The race was on.

Ten minutes into it, Mama yanked on my sleeve. "Mary Clare, that's you!" She pointed toward the electronics department, and I realized the ratty pink chenille-robed woman dancing around was me. I was displayed on every monitor in the place. Apparently, since I'd declined any and all requests for an interview after Smitty's body was found, the local media decided to run old footage of me from the morning of my Prize Patrol visit. Lord help. I looked like a high definition lunatic badly in need of makeup and a hairbrush.

"C'mon, Mama. That is just plain embarrassing."

"Don't you want to hear what they have to say? Maybe they've found out something about Smitty."

"Anything they have to say we'll either hear around town or Boomer will tell us. Besides, sometimes they just make things up. Reporters report what shocks people the most. The truth just gets in their way."

Two hours later we left the store with fourteen bags. Fourteen. One bag held my purchases. The rest belonged to Mama. She reasoned since most of her wardrobe was stuffed in packing boxes, she'd 'get a few things' for the change in the weather.

We parked our purchases and snapped our seatbelts. "Look at these cute little skunks, Mary Clare." She held two flat, black and white, synthetic critters in the air for inspection. "You think Flash and Blur will like these?"

Mama is not a spendthrift. In fact, most of the time she had to be threatened with bodily harm to buy anything for herself. But she loved buying for others, especially the dogs.

"Mama, you spoil them." I smiled at her and not for the first time thanked God for giving me the mother sitting beside me. The woman was an energy ninja.

"Buying toys for those dogs gives me a happy heart. It delights me to have the money to buy for them." Mama stroked one of the skunks and slid both back into the bag.

"Besides, dear, they're the only grandchildren I have. It makes no never mind to me that they have fur and four legs. I love them." I knew we were skating on thin ice. Any minute she was going to tell me again how she, too, had been afraid to obligate…until she'd met Daddy.

"Mama, what do you remember about Cora Ann Holly's death?"

"Oh, honey, that was thirty years ago. That girl's disappearance happened right after your daddy died. Naturally, I heard about it, but, to tell you the truth, nothing much registered. I do recall hearing Cora Ann's purse was in a ditch in front of some preacher's house. He turned it in. Ruby must have been beside herself. Her only daughter and no way to know what had happened to her, but knowing she might not ever get to hug her baby again." Mama reached over and patted my hand.

"Didn't they have any clues?"

"They may have, but I didn't follow the case. I'm sure there are still records in the papers. If you're really interested, you should do an Internet search on it. If that doesn't do any good, hunt around in the courthouse records or dig up the newspaper archives."

That wasn't a bad idea. It would be something to occupy my time until we could get back to work in the shop. "How did they know for certain Cora Ann died?"

"They didn't." Mama adjusted her heat vent. "I guess they assumed she did when she didn't come home."

"Lurlene said she and her mother had a fight, didn't she?"

"Uh huh. About the pregnancy most likely. It's been too long ago. It seems to me that if she planned to run away, she would take her purse with her or at least take some money."

"Yeah, you're right."

"I'm cold. Let's go to that coffee place on Windover and get a mug of something hot." She leaned forward and squinted. "Those clouds sure look like snow clouds to me, but we haven't had snow in October since you were a little girl."

At that precise moment, my phone dinged with a weather

alert. "Let's get a quick cup and check on the dogs and the answering machine."

We bustled into The Chug and Churn and ordered steaming mugs of white chocolate mocha topped with rich whipped cream. It would be a good idea to start watching my calories, or a return trip to Miss Polly's Nutrition Paradise would be a definite possibility. I could probably get a two-for-one deal and take the 911 gal with me. Which reminded me.

"Mama, did you tell everyone I went to a fat farm?"

"Of course not. I told them you went to a weight spa. Fat farm sounds so vulgar."

"You know, you didn't really have to tell where I went."

"I couldn't lie to them, dear. People were curious. Besides, you promised Miss Polly you'd tweet about her business the whole month of October. What's the difference in me telling them where you went and you tweeting about it? Advertising is advertising. I'm proud of you. You lost nearly a whole person. You haven't been in a size ten since you were ten."

I was sure a compliment lurked in there, but I didn't want to dig for it. I checked my cell phone, two o'clock. The clouds were more ominous. We left with Mama swiping whipped cream off the tip of her nose.

Forty minutes later, we hauled packages into the cottage. The second Mama let the dogs in, they headed for the fireplace and sat in front of it until she lit the gas logs.

"Mary Clare, these dogs are cold. We've got to come up with a warmer place for them to stay."

"Mama, they have the igloos. It was a total waste of money to buy two. They both curl up in one and don't come out until they hear us pull up."

"You think they recognize the sound of our vehicles?"

"I watched them one day. The minute they heard your car pull away, they climbed into one igloo. They snoozed until they heard you come back, and yes, they are smart dogs."

"Do you think Richard likes dogs?" Mama asked. This one took me by surprise. Mama had been thinking about what Richard liked. Hmm.

"I don't know. Maybe you should find out. What will you do if he doesn't?"

"Oh, I'm just thinking out loud. Don't mind me." Mama hadn't sported a blush on her cheeks since I was eleven and asked where babies came from, so it took me a moment to recognize it for what it was. Mama was venturing. It was about time.

"You know, Richard is downright smitten, Mama. You don't mind his hair?"

"He doesn't have hair, dear."

"He has a toupee, and it's really bad."

"No argument there. He's a nice man, though. Very thoughtful. He's from the old school and still opens doors and pulls out chairs for ladies. I like that. Your daddy always treated me like a lady."

Mama glowed the same glow she did every time she talked about Daddy. Even after thirty years, she still loved and respected the man he'd been. That kind of devotion was what I wanted, and I wanted her to know it again.

After checking Caller ID, I felt better. Only fourteen calls today. No calls on my cell phone other than Marma Lee, and it was from her landline number. She answered on the second ring.

"Hello." Her voice sounded stiff, like the surfboard she'd dragged in from one of her buying excursions.

"Hey. I missed your call. What's up?"

"Ruby said we were meeting in your cottage next Tuesday." Marma Lee's voice was as cold as a fish.

"That's what we decided this morning. Boomer's closed the shop for now. Nobody can go in until all this mess with Smitty is finished."

"This is upsetting my plans. I had my strategy all made for Saige. It involved perfume and the loveseat in the shop. I need to get all of Saige's contact information so we can spend some quality face time. You don't even have a loveseat in that dinky cottage. All you have is a couch and those two rocker things."

"They are rocker recliners, and I like them. They're comfortable. Why, and I'm probably going to be sorry I asked, is a loveseat so important? You can sit on the couch with Saige, and that kind of face time is a whole lot better, you dingbat." I rolled my eyes. Mama was nowhere around. I glanced at the clock on the mantle. I'd promised Basil, my book vendor, that I'd touch base with him about a shipment of books. If Marma Lee didn't shut up soon, Basil would lock up and head home.

"You're such a novice, Mac. The loveseat is important because the woman I bought the perfume from says it's alluring but subtle. If I'm too far away, he won't smell it, and I'll have blown one hundred and fifty bucks for nothing."

I tapped my foot, noting the time. "You spent a hundred and fifty dollars on a bottle of perfume. Are you nuts? Your mama snagged your daddy with a dab of vanilla behind her ears. That's a whole lot cheaper. What were you thinking?" I knew the answer. She was in the midst of Operation Saige, and no amount of lecturing on my part would do any good. "You'll have to take your chances. I'll roll in the chairs from the kitchen, and you can put one close to where he's sitting."

"This whole thing is inconvenient, Mary Clare."

"I agree. I'm sure Smitty would, too, if he could voice his opinion."

"Well, I plan on making an entrance, so I'll be running a little late. Arrange it so that Aunt Lilly is sitting in the middle spot on the couch, and of course, see that Saige is on one end. Then, when I get there, she can suddenly remember she has to check on something in the kitchen."

"I'll do what I can. You know you're obsessing again. You need to let things happen."

"Things don't just happen, Mac. God gave me gifts. I'm

organized and creative. He'd be disappointed if I didn't put those talents to good use. You have to make things happen. That's the difference between us. I am in charge of my destiny. You're just out there flopping in the wind."

I bristled. I took charge with the best of them, and I wasn't too shabby in the creativity department, either. "I'll see you Tuesday night."

"Have the fire lit too. And maybe some soft music playing. The lights need to be dimmed."

"How many candles would you like burning?"

"You have candles?"

Sarcasm is lost on some people. "I have to go now. I need to rest up to help you move the heavens and earth next Tuesday."

"Don't get snippy with me. I'm just trying to impress Saige."

"No, you're not. You're trying to hog-tie Saige. There's a big difference. He doesn't strike me as the hog-tied type."

She giggled. "He'll never know what hit him." The dial tone sang to me. I stood with the receiver in my hand and stared at it. Poor Saige was only days away from a full-blown maneuver, and Marma Lee was right. He'd never know what hit him.

I dialed Basil's Books, hoping to increase my order of young adult titles before he shipped them out. As I suspected, his phone went straight to voicemail. Pish. I hadn't really thought about what to say to his machine. Talking out the order with Basil would be so much easier.

Marma Lee's comment about 'flopping in the wind' floated to the top of my thoughts. There was nothing wrong with my ability to handle situations. Not with Mick. Not with the shop. And certainly not with a stupid answering machine. I'd simply tell Basil I needed to touch base with him and to call me.

No. Maybe I'd tell Basil I needed to talk to him and would call back. Phooey. The machine beeped its permission for me to leave a message. Problem was my brain hadn't processed what I wanted to say. With a deep breath, I tried to formulate my message.

"Basil, I need you and can't wait to touch you. Call me."

I hung up the phone, sat on the floor and thunked my head against the wall three times. Marma Lee was right. I was out there flopping in the wind. And now, a sixty-five-year-old man I hardly knew was likely either having a heart attack or racing to call all his friends at the Senior Center.

Sometime during the night, it snowed five inches. For Northeast Arkansas in October, that's almost unheard of. Traffic crawled, and there were only three stores open Sunday afternoon. Mutt's Grocery Store opened long enough for folks to get the essentials. Everybody loved Mutt. He stocked the staples. He let poor people charge until the first of the month, and he always gave well-mannered kids a free sucker. Mama said he'd been running his business like that for forty-two years.

Monteen's Virtual Mountain Climbing Store had its doors open, and they flapped to beat the band. Her store sat directly across the street from Pocket Change and beside Perty's Realty. People poured into the store in droves. They needed entertainment, and evidently conversing required too much work. Pity.

The third place was Mick's Bait Shop. I couldn't figure that one out since ice fishing wasn't big in Arkansas. This needed investigating. Leaving Mama a note, I slipped on my boots and made my way across the adjoining field. When I opened the door to his business, I smelled the reason for the full parking lot.

A little bell jangled when I walked through the door. Expecting to smell minnows, worms, or fishy odors, instead my nose was met by a pleasant surprise. The aroma of smoked pork filled the room. Mick stood behind the counter, handing someone a bottle of sauce. He saw me and winked.

I winked back. I WINKED BACK! I had never winked at a man in my life. When he started chuckling, I joined in. I might as well get used to the idea. When it concerned Mick Walker, I surprised myself. I'd have to tread carefully. Mick motioned for me to take the only empty seat at the end of the bar. A strip of duct tape ran down the middle of the faded red vinyl, and the back of it wobbled. The bar showed signs of wear. I loved it.

"Now I know why there's no room in the parking lot." My gaze took in the crowded room. "It smells wonderful in here, but I didn't know you had a diner. I thought you specialized in worms and all things wiggly."

"That was the plan." Mick wiped his hands on a washrag. "Then we dug out Dad's Bar-B-Que recipe and made a couple for some fishing buddies." Shrugging, he pointed to the newly painted sign behind the counter. Mick's Bait and Barbecue Shop.

"And the rest is history." I gestured around the room.

"Something like that. You might not care for the barbecues. They're pretty hot." He closed one eye and cocked his head. "You want to try one? Everything's on the house today. Some folks don't have electricity, so I thought I'd open up and cook for a couple of hours. Besides, yours would be a professional courtesy. Neighboring businesses and all."

His grin was contagious. "Sure. Could I have a Coke too?"

"Coming right up."

"Oh, and here's your phone." I'd lay odds my face was the color of his ketchup bottle in front of me. I handed him his cell and was rewarded with another wink. I probably should tell him about the call from A., but he'd see it when he checked his calls. Given the syrup mishap, the last thing I wanted to do was make him think I was meddling with his phone.

As he walked away, I swiveled my wobbly chair around to people watch. Everyone chatted, ate, and laughed. I liked this place. Mick certainly had brought it back to life. His uncle's idea of a busy day had been raising the shades. I spotted bags of birdseed by the door and decided I'd buy some for the feeders I'd set up outside the bay windows of the cottage.

I sat swinging my legs like a five-year-old and planning where I could build another feeding area for the birds when Mick came back carrying a barbecue sandwich the size of a salad plate.

My jaw dropped. "Your buns are huge." Okay. Maybe that hadn't come out exactly right. I ducked my head. If he ordered me out of my seat, I'd understand. Instead, he covered for me. The man was a saint.

"I special order them from a lady in Walnut Ridge. She makes them." He set the plate in front of me and went to get my Coke.

I picked up the knife he'd plopped down and cut the sandwich in four pieces. He'd brought a bag of plain chips and set them beside the plate. Acting as if I hadn't eaten in three days, I yanked open the chips with one quick tug. Picking up a quarter of the sandwich, I bit into it. The sweet, tangy taste of coleslaw on top of the barbecued pork was pure bliss.

"This is amazing." Okay, it wasn't lady-like to talk with my mouth full, so I tried to hide my happy, full mouth behind my hand. "What's in this?"

He plunked my Coke on the counter. "Sorry. Old family recipe." He leaned forward. "The only part of the secret I can tell you is that I put syrup in the sauce." His lopsided grin was adorable. My face flamed, and he went to check on another customer. The place held three small booths and six stools at the bar. Every seat was taken. Two more people walked in. Not having a place to park didn't seem to deter them. They went around the room talking to people they knew. Before long, two places opened up, and they slid in.

I dabbed at my mouth. Not a single crumb remained. Mick wore a pleased expression.

"You mind if I blog about your place? Not to brag, but I have a pretty good following and it looks to me like you are a hit."

"I hope so, and no, I don't mind. Blog away. When I decided to move back and reopen the shop, I wasn't sure how well the whole Barbecue thing would go over." We both looked around at the happy faces. "My uncle always talked about this kind of place, but his idea of a hard day was working past noon." He leaned close. "He wasn't real work-brickle."

"My Aunt Dovie used to say that about Marma Lee's daddy. Aunt Dovie said Uncle Marvin's goal in life was to master the art of immobility. The only time he moved fast was when he was behind the wheel. He taught Marma Lee to drive." I raised an eyebrow.

He threw back his head and laughed. "That explains a lot."

"I'm surprised you could keep up with her last night."

"If I had lingered much longer at your place, I couldn't have." His gaze roamed over my face. He certainly knew how to get a girl's heart racing. He nodded his head in the direction of the shop. "Being lazy must not run in the family. You seem to be a workaholic. I've seen you and your mama work way into the night."

"It doesn't really seem like work yet. We've had a ball. We can't do anything inside the shop right now, though."

"So, you can't do anything, and now you're battling boredom."

"I like to keep busy. Speaking of which, I'd like to buy a bag of your birdseed." I slid off the seat. "I'd better get going. I've hogged this chair long enough. Lunch was great. Thank you."

"Anytime. I'll have Doc carry your birdseed over for you. I'll put it on your tab."

"I have a tab?"

"You do now." He motioned to a teenager in the back. "His name's really Duane Odel Crawford," Mick whispered conspiratorially. "He hates it."

"Got it." I gave him an okay sign and headed for the door.

Maybelline hurried over to get my spot. "Hey, girl. Had to come over and check out these barbecues. They're the talk of the town. Any good?"

"You're in for a treat," I replied. The young man from the back came around the counter and slung a bag of birdseed over his shoulder.

"Ready?" he asked.

"Don't you need a coat?"

"Naw. Won't be gone that long. Lead the way." I waved to Mick and Maybelline and headed out the door. The snow came down again causing the space between Mick's store and mine to look like a mini winter-wonderland. I glanced at Doc's thin sweatshirt and felt guilty. He must have read my mind.

"Don't worry about me. I never get cold. I don't even own a coat. My mama says I was born with thick skin."

I spotted Boomer's car parked in front of the cottage and hurried toward the car. Doc put the seed inside the front door as I reached in my purse to give him some money, but he shook his head.

"No, ma'am. I'm glad to help. Anytime you need anything, you just call. Remember me this summer. I mow yards for extra money." He ducked his head for a split second, looking like a kid caught cussing. "I heard what you said to Mick about blogging. You think you could mention me in your blog? It might help me get some customers. Maybe you could keep me in mind?"

"I will. What a great idea. Thank you, Doc." He trotted back to Mick's. Doc and Molly were about the same age. I tilted my head back and winked at God. Winking was quickly becoming a favorite pastime.

Boomer strode away from the shed.

I waved as he ducked under the police tape. "What's up?"

"Just looking around. The shed door isn't latching properly.

It wasn't locked." He rubbed his head. "I need an aspirin. You got any?"

"Yes, sir." I saluted. "In the cottage. Follow me." He turned and gave me one of his police officer looks. I let my hand drop to my side.

He nodded. "I'm finished in here." He dropped something into a plastic bag then stuck the bag in his pocket without offering any information.

The snow came faster now. I glanced next door. Mick's parking lot overflowed. It couldn't hold one more car, truck, scooter or skater. Many more days like this and he'd have to expand. I told Boomer about the barbecues.

"Yeah. I went by his place yesterday. A person certainly doesn't leave hungry. I couldn't finish all of mine."

I didn't mention I'd had no trouble. "He seems like a nice guy, don't you think?"

"Yep. Hard worker. His daddy is too. He used to own a carpentry shop on the edge of town. Moved to Memphis about thirty years ago when Mick was just a little feller. Mick's dad retired last year. I guess they both decided they'd had enough of Memphis. He told me they stayed in touch with Mick's uncle, but for the life of me, I don't remember either one of them visiting. Mick's move surprised me, but I'm glad he's opened up the old shop."

I held the cottage door and took Boomer's coat. He sank into a rocking chair. I went to fetch the water and aspirin. I found a scribbled note from Mama saying she and Rennie had gone snow exploring. No one in the world loved snow as much as Mama. If I ventured a guess, I'd say the two were out doing donuts in an abandoned parking lot in my old blue car.

"You making it okay out here?" Boomer asked.

I handed him his medicine and nodded. "Everything is fine. The calls were down to five this morning and no calls from nuts, beggars or money grubbers." I sat in the recliner next to

Boomer's chair. There was something tranquil about rocking chairs. Flash and Blur curled up on the couch to ogle Boomer. I wondered for the first time what kind of comfort Boomer went home to and why his wife left him. "Boomer." I leaned forward.

"Hmmm?"

"Why haven't you remarried?"

He shrugged and looked at the dogs. "The pickins are slim in Pocket. Most of the women I know are high maintenance and don't want anything to do with a guy who makes the salary I do. That was the problem with Thelma. She wanted more than my wallet could give her. I guess I haven't been too interested in looking for a lady since she left. She walked out on me and sent me divorce papers last month. I haven't signed them yet." Boomer seemed to age a year for each word he uttered.

"I'm sorry, Boomer. I guess I missed Thelma's leaving this time while I was, um, away at the spa. You're a good man. God has a woman out there just waiting for you to melt her heart."

"I'm a slow mover. Sure does get lonely, though. I've been thinking about getting another dog. I miss Luke almost as much as my wife."

I caught him grinning. He was going to be all right, but Mama and I may have to make another trip to Memphis to get Boomer an early Christmas present. Plus, I needed a project that wasn't Smitty or Mick related. If this thing dragged on much longer, I'd go stir crazy.

CHAPTER EIGHT

oomer called Tuesday afternoon. Smitty's killer was in
custody.

"What?" I yelled.

"We made an arrest today."

"Who in the world is it?"

"You sitting down?"

I dropped into the closest chair. "I am now. Who'd you arrest?"

"Ethel Glacier."

"You have to be kidding. There's no way that fragile lady could strangle Smitty. You've got the wrong person."

"She's Smitty's wife," Boomer said quietly.

"What?" Much more of this and Boomer would have to be fitted for hearing aids. I apologized.

"It's okay. You're the reason we found out. I became a little suspicious when Boyd Barlow came to pick up your final payment. I started wondering who had authorized him to do that."

My conscience was doing a tango. I never told Boomer about

Barlow telling me he had been asked to continue Smitty's business transactions. Guess he'd figured it out without my help.

"…that's when we found out," he finished.

"Found out what? I drifted."

"When I went to question Barlow, he told me he had been approached by Mr. Small's wife to collect Smitty's wages. When I asked who Smitty's wife was, he told me it was Ethel. She stopped using her married name when she and Smitty separated. She got tired of his shenanigans and left. Ethel moved back to this area because she had money problems. She admitted to that. Smitty had a sizeable check book, and with him gone, she would inherit. There were never any children."

"She wouldn't have the strength to strangle him. The woman is frail."

"She told me she took self-defense classes in Little Rock. The coroner didn't check for unusual bruises, but I'm sure they're present. Kinda surprised he didn't notice them, but then again, he may have and assumed they were due to Smitty's work. The way I see it, she incapacitated Smitty then strangled him. Case closed."

"Did she confess?"

"No, but she will. I found a button, which she's identified as hers. Somehow we overlooked it during the initial search. I found it yesterday under a bunch of boxes in the shed."

That tiny object he'd bagged and stuck in his pocket. So that's what it had been. How could her button have gotten in the shed? I felt miserable. I couldn't believe Ethel, who loved animals and seemed so fragile, could murder her husband. "Couldn't someone else have put her button there?"

"That's stretching it. Who else would go to all the trouble of getting one of her buttons? Besides, we asked if she'd had anyone in her apartment recently. She said no. She's digging her own hole. She didn't even want to call anybody. Said she didn't want to bother anyone, and she hated to talk on the phone."

I thought of what Rennie had said about Smitty. His carousing had been going on during his marriage to Ethel. That could drive some women to murder. Maybe Smitty refusing to help her financially had been the final straw. "Why that night? Why not some other place, some other time?"

"She probably saw his vehicle and stopped to confront him. Doubt it was premeditated, though. More like a spur of the moment action. The result is the same. Smitty's dead. Just can't get her to admit what she used to kill him."

"Who will get the estate if she's convicted?"

"I don't know. Mr. Barlow will probably have to secure it until after the trial."

"Don't you think that's a little convenient? He did just pick up a check for over ten thousand dollars. Maybe he framed her."

"Stop watching television, Mary Clare. Barlow didn't do it. Ethel did."

"But you said she hasn't confessed."

"She will. When I start telling her we know about how Smitty treated her, she'll crack."

"She'll crack? Now who's watching too much television?"

"Goodbye, Mary Clare."

"Wait. Does this mean the investigation is over?"

"Yes. Consider yourself back in business. You can open to the public as soon as you want. Just don't sell that old trunk in the Cozy Area. I might want to buy that."

"Deal." I hung up the phone, but something niggled in my head. Boomer believed Ethel killed Smitty, but I didn't. Something wasn't right. In the back of my mind skulked a sneaking suspicion about Boyd Barlow which I couldn't shake. He'd done a complete turnaround in the shop when he'd seen Boomer there to witness the final payment. Maybe he felt remorse over his rudeness, or maybe he was an excellent actor.

I'd forgotten to ask Boomer how quickly we could have our casket back. It didn't really matter. There were tons of things to be done before next Saturday. Well, I wouldn't have to worry too much about landscaping. A quick trip to our nursery would be in order though. A bunch of mums and some hay and the front porch would be presentable. Landscaping around the porch would have to wait until spring, but that was okay.

"Mary Clare, you home?" Mama charged through the back door of the cottage with her hands full of grocery bags.

"What have you bought?"

"Thanks to you, I'm making peanut butter cookies for tonight's meeting, remember. You always were good at volunteering me to bake things. I got stuck making cupcakes for every party you ever had at school."

"Yours were always the best."

"Mine were the only ones that were homemade. Every other mother bought a package of cookies from the store."

"Yeah, but there were always dozens of those left. Not your cupcakes. They disappeared in no time. You remember my junior high English teacher. She told me she didn't care about getting any old plaque when she retired. She just wanted a batch of your chocolate cream cupcakes."

"Bless her heart. She got them too. She was awfully good to you."

"They all were. I had a good education, thanks to some very patient people. You remember Mr. Neece."

"The principal?"

"Yep. He never put his cupcakes aside like some teachers did. He would gobble them up right then. That's when I realized that teachers are real people. There's something about watching your principal lick frosting off his cupcake that puts him on the same level as the rest of us."

"He's a good man." Mama chuckled. "He's a little thinner since you graduated, though."

"Boomer called a few minutes ago."

"What did he say?"

"We're back in business."

"We are? You mean we can open on time?"

I'm sure Mama hadn't meant to hug the bread. Looks like we'd be having a lot of French toast for dinner. Maybe she could serve that to the group along with her peanut butter cookies.

"Yep." I relayed everything Boomer had told me. "I forgot to ask Boomer about the casket, so we might have to come up with a different display. That's okay, though. Once we get it back, we'll decide if we want to store it or sell it. Which brings up another point. Did you leave the storage shed open for anything yesterday? The door was open this morning."

"Haven't been out there and don't really want to go any time soon, honey, but I hope nothing's hurt. Smitty intended to change the latch because it wasn't working properly." Mama fidgeted with her scarf. "It may not have latched well the last time the police were in there."

The doorbell rang. My lovely, if somewhat scattered, cousin came marching through the cottage with a sack in each hand. My scowl should have slowed her advance. It didn't.

"Why do you ring the doorbell and not wait for an answer? I could have a visitor."

Marma Lee and Mama both looked astonished. "Who?" they asked.

"It's not impossible," I said.

"Yeah, right." Marma Lee shrugged out of her coat, which nearly touched her ankles. She placed it gingerly across a kitchen chair.

"What's all this?" I pointed to the bags.

"As I told you, Cousin, I never leave anything to chance." She pulled out five white tapers and five gorgeous crystal holders and a cell phone.

"You found your phone?" I reached for it, but she yanked it out of the way.

"Keep your mitts off this, Mac. This is the latest version, and you know how klutzy you can be. I'll leave my new number on the counter, and you can add me later. I didn't get my old number. I went with something more…alluring. Right now, I need you to pay attention."

I really didn't think slapping one's cousin constituted a basis for a lawsuit. I'm pretty sure that was in the Geneva Convention somewhere.

Marma Lee stroked the tapers. "These need to be on the coffee table. They'll highlight my hair and complement my complexion. Plus, heat activates the chemicals in perfume."

"She spent one hundred and fifty dollars on a bottle of perfume," I explained to Mama.

"Saige?" Mama asked. I nodded.

"Why don't we all sit in a circle on the floor holding a candle and put you in the middle? That way everyone could smell you from every angle. You could rotate like a pig on a spit," Mama offered. I have enough sense to know sarcasm when I hear it, but I think Marma Lee considered the idea.

"No, I would get my new outfit dirty. Besides, Richard would have trouble getting up and down. So would Ethel."

"You make Richard sound like a doddering old man." Mama crossed her arms and lifted her chin. "He can get up and down with the best of them. For your information, you won't have to worry about Ethel. She's in jail."

I caught the crystal candleholder before it hit the floor. Fortunately, Marma Lee only held the one.

"Ethel's in jail? Did she overcharge somebody for a trip?" Marma Lee asked.

"No. She killed Smitty," Mama declared.

I shoved a chair in Marma Lee's direction. She plopped down. "You're kidding."

"It's true. Boomer called a little while ago. They're closing the investigation, and he said I can open the shop."

"You mean we could meet out there tonight?" Amazing how she bounced back from shock.

"We could, but we aren't." Mama stood her ground. "We've already made arrangements to hold it here, and here is where it will be." She turned and marched upstairs. As usual, the dogs were right behind her. Flash looked as miffed as his mistress.

Marma Lee watched her aunt stomp from the room. "What's with her?"

"You insulted Richard. She likes Richard."

"I like Richard, too, but he would have a horrible time getting up off the floor."

"Never mind. Why are you here so early? It's only four o'clock."

"I can't stay. I just wanted to drop off this stuff." She proceeded to pull a variety of accessories from the bag. "Here's a bag of potpourri. I bought it at Dillard's last week. The saleslady said its special blends enhance romantic evenings."

"We're having a writers' meeting, not a Spin-the-Bottle Night. Don't you think you're carrying this thing a bit far?"

"No, I do not. I told you. I plan for detail. Now, don't put this too close to where I'll be sitting. I don't want it to overpower my perfume. It would work by the door. That will put him in the mood before he ever sits down."

"What else is in the bag?" I leaned over just as she pulled out the ugliest statue I've ever seen in my life. I could do nothing but stare. "What is that?" I finally asked after examining it from several angles.

"It's a Skarie Sculpture."

"Excuse me? Scary as in…boo?"

"No, you ninny. The spelling is totally different. You are so uncouth. I bought it in Branson at an estate sale. The auctioneer explained its origins. Each Skarie is unique, highly collectible and sculpted by Ernesto Skarie, a famous artist from Springfield, Missouri. I can't believe we've never heard of him before.

Everyone who is anyone owns one. I think it will set the mood for romance and ungirdled passion."

"Don't you mean unbridled passion, Marma Lee?"

"Oh, yeah. Maybe. Mary Clare." She moved closer, "I haven't told anyone this…but I think a wedding is in my immediate future."

"Another one?" Marma Lee excelled in withering looks.

"I heard wedding bells when I went back to The Landing." She put her index finger to her chin. "It could have been from the Dancing Waters display, but I don't think so because the most amazing thing happened after I got back to the room. I was unloading my packages from all the shops and the auction when I heard the glorious sound of wedding music."

Mama would forgive me this once for rolling my eyes. "Are you dehydrated, Marma Lee? You know what that does to your thinking processes. How much did you pay for this, and you better not have used my business allotment for it. It's the most hideous thing I've ever laid eyes on."

"It was a steal at seventy-five dollars, and of course I didn't buy it with your money. You always get a receipt for all your stuff. You know that. I bought it for myself, and I'm going to display it tonight for everyone to enjoy. It's a Skarie, Mac. Put it by the candles so Saige can appreciate its charm and culture. Good grief! Don't you even want to know what the amazing thing was that happened at The Landing?"

I started to shake my head but knew she'd suckered me in. "Okay. So, what happened?"

"I stepped out on the balcony of my hotel room and saw a man down below walking on that cobblestone walkway they have. You know, the one that runs the length of their outdoor mall? Mac, it was Saige. I didn't realize it at the time, but it was him. I'm sure of it. Now, he's right here in Pocket. It's a sign, Cousin."

One look at the candles and this stupid sculpture and the

entire group would label me as some cult person. I said as much to Marma Lee.

"No, they won't. They'll think you're 'cult'ured." Slapping her leg and snorting did not look good on her. "Now tell me about Ethel."

After her laughing fit, she pulled her chair up to the table. Everything Boomer told me tumbled out my mouth.

"Is Ethel really in custody now?"

"According to Boomer, she'll be in custody for a while. I don't buy it. Ethel murdering for money doesn't sound right." I told her my suspicion about Boyd Barlow.

"I met him at an auction not long ago. Extremely cheap. He won't even buy the food they fix at the auction barn. He brings his own in a brown paper sack, which he reuses. Not that there's anything wrong with that, but I overheard him bragging to someone he had recycled it twelve times. There's a cleanliness issue there. What's up with the hair parted down the middle? He looks like that kid from the Little Rascals. What was his name?"

"Alfalfa, but Barlow's hair doesn't stick up in the back, does it?"

"Not sure. I didn't pay that much attention to him."

"I'll ask around and see what I can find out. If he knew Ethel was Smitty's only heir, he could have killed Smitty and framed Ethel. He was on the premises to pick up my check Saturday morning. He could have planted that button in the shed. Ethel visited his office when she told him to handle Smitty's business. What's to say she didn't lose it then, and he picked it up?"

"Not a bad theory. Be careful. If he is the killer, he won't think twice about killing you."

She shrugged. "I have to go. It's past time for Toodle's dinner. This is her spaghetti night."

"That poodle is spoiled." I hefted the bag to the other hand.

"Like you have room to talk." She snorted and shrugged into her coat.

"You really need to have that hemmed." I pointed to her coat tail dragging the floor.

She wiggled her fingers and floated out the door. With the right equipment, say a scythe, she'd look a lot like the Grim Reaper.

"Is she gone?" Mama peered at me from the loft, hands on hips.

"The coast is clear. Come on down." I sounded like *The Price is Right* dude. "You've got to see this statue."

"You don't think Richard is an old coot, do you?"

"Every man's an old coot unless Marma Lee is interested in him. You know that. And no, Richard's not an old coot. As a matter of fact, I think he's kind of gorgeous."

"You do?"

"Yep. Plus, he has the soul of a poet. The man definitely has potential, Mama." I pointed to the Skarie Sculpture and studied Mama's face.

"Honey, that looks like something Blur does when she's had too much to eat," Mama said.

"This is maybe a little taller," I said.

"What are you supposed to do with it?"

"We are to put it on the coffee table to add culture to the joint and surround it with candles. Saige will be bowled over with how cultured we are. Oh, and you're supposed to make sure Saige sits on the couch and then sit beside him in the middle. Marma Lee is going to make a late entrance wearing her one-hundred-and-fifty-dollar perfume and a new outfit, then you are to give her your seat. She said she could take it from there."

"If that girl put half as much energy into keeping them as she does catching them, she'd still have Larry. There was nothing wrong with him, Mary Clare."

"I liked him too, but according to Marma Lee, so did several other women. Who knows?"

"Well, that couldn't have been the problem with Lum. He was ugly as homemade soap. But, he had a good heart."

"According to Marma Lee he gambled and had an affair."

"Oh, pshaw. He couldn't have gambled that much, and what woman with good eyesight would…"

I shrugged and dismissed Marma Lee's romances. "Poor Ethel. I can't believe someone who enjoyed such peaceful surroundings could be a murderess. There had to be a mistake."

I didn't tell Mama about my suspicions. I'd wait and think about this for a while. Her status as a compulsive worrywart was growing, and if she thought I was nosing around about Boyd Barlow, she'd have a fit. I decided to take Flash and Blur for a walk.

The crisp air made all three of us prance a little. The snow may have stopped, but the clean feeling lingered. As the sun set in one final golden burst, the town slowed down. That was one of the nice things about Pocket. When it got tired, it rested. Most little towns operated the same way. No all-night grocery stores, laundromats, or restaurants. By ten o'clock, most folks were parked in front of their televisions listening to how the rest of the world dealt with disaster. It was a good place to live. I was glad Mick Walker decided to return.

Void of all common sense, I allowed the dogs to lead me in the direction of Mick's shop. No sign of his truck. His neon blue welcome sign reflected on the snow. The dogs and I peeked through the oversized front window that went almost to the ground. The lingering smell of tangy sauce and pork wafted around us. Maybe that's what drew the dogs. That's not what attracted me.

"Out for a walk?"

I nearly wet my pants. Two startled dogs and a nosy neighbor spun around. There stood the man himself. *Oh, Dear God help me out of this one.* "Yes," I all but screeched. I cleared my throat. "I guess the dogs wanted to investigate the smell. Not that it's a bad smell. It's a wonderful smell. They aren't used to it, so I brought them over to…" My voice trailed off like a dying buzzard. I was so busted.

"I have leftovers. I ran to Mutt's to get some foil." He waved the box in the air. "Wait here, and I'll get the pooches some chow."

Gladly. I'll just root to this spot and shovel up some witty explanation for why I'm snooping around your shop. Unfortunately, he returned before I could even scrape up the beginnings of a likely excuse. I threw up my hands. "I was on a snooping expedition. Where's your truck?"

He placed a couple of paper plates on the ground for Flash and Blur and patted them on the head. "I don't think I've ever had a woman spy on me before." He cocked his head. "I like it. I left my truck at Mutt's. When I saw y'all, I worried the truck might scare them. It's kind of loud."

I smiled despite my tattered ego. "You're not mad?"

"Mad?" He stood and moved closer. A lot closer. "What man in his right mind would be mad about having an attractive neighbor checking him out?"

I started to shrug. Then I stopped. "Attractive? You think I'm attractive?"

He raised his eyebrows. Then, right there in front of God and Flash and Blur, he planted the most precious kiss on my lips. It made me grateful to be a nosy neighbor. I felt so grateful, I kissed him back. With vigor.

"Yes." His breath puffed a little cloud. "I think you are… quite attractive."

I blinked several times. At some point my arms had wrapped around his middle, and the leashes went willy-nilly, but I needn't have worried about the dogs running off. The two of them sat on their rumps downright mesmerized. When Mick laced his fingers through my hair, they appeared positively pleased. I had news for them. I was pretty pleased myself.

He pulled me closer, if that were possible. "So, are you going to tell me why you and the kids were spying on me?" I loved the smile in his voice.

"Just curious." His chest muffled my voice. "I thought I might catch one of your admirers hanging around." I'm pretty good at reading body language, and for a moment his arms stiffened. Whether from the cold or from my comment, I wasn't sure. When I pulled my head back to look at his face, his mouth smiled…but not his eyes.

Five minutes later, after gathering up their leashes, we were being escorted home. Just before he opened the cottage door he brushed his lips against my forehead and whispered, "Don't forget to lock this as soon as you get inside." I nodded and stepped over the threshold. "Would you like to come in?" I asked.

"It's getting late." He looked at my face intently, as though trying to memorize every freckle. I thought longingly of my makeup bag upstairs. The dogs ran into the house. I could hear them shoving their food bowls around. He laughed. "Besides, they're ready for their next course."

I focused on Flash and Blur. "I'm afraid they're a bit spoiled."

"You have a kind heart, Mary Clare Casteel." For the second time that night, I reveled in how right it felt to be kissed by this man. And how tangy a Bar-B-Que-cooking neighbor tasted. Without another peep, he turned on his heel and crunched back across the field.

The little cottage smelled of peanut butter and oats. The candles were in place as well as Marma Lee's Skarie Sculpture. The packaged potpourri came open with a healthy pull. I went in search of a bowl to put it in. Then a dash upstairs would be in order if I had a hope of getting cleaned up and changed before the meeting.

I dumped the fragrant mixture into a cut glass bowl and

placed it by the front door. Not bad. It had a fruity smell. I wondered what effect it would have on Saige.

"Well, what do you think?" Mama twirled around.

"Whoa. Where did you get that?"

"I ordered it online. They called it 'the sophisticated woman's lounging ensemble.' Do you think it's too casual?" She backed toward the stairs, ready to scramble up and barricade herself in the bathroom.

"You're stunning. It's the perfect outfit for hosting a casual business meeting. Sophisticated, yet feminine. It's got that flirty little flip at the hem plus you can see the fuchsia sparkles through the jacket. You've got bling, Mama. Don't change a thing."

She exhaled for at least three minutes. "I've never had anything like this. I'm used to wearing the same old clothes, and I've never paid ninety-nine dollars for an outfit before in my life, but I just love it."

I hugged the woman in the sophisticated woman's lounging ensemble and said another thankful prayer for the money God sent our way.

"If you're going to look that snazzy, I'd better find something a little dressier than these old jeans. You need me to do anything before I grab a shower?"

"No, dear. I have Marma Lee's props in place, and the goodies are all baked. You run along and take a hot bath. I'll feed the babies their supper."

I skedaddled out of the room without confessing the babies had already had their dinner and I my dessert. Instead, I nodded and went off in search of a suitable outfit. The cupboard was bare, so to speak. I hadn't unpacked most of my winter clothes but found a nice tunic and a pair of tights that would serve the purpose. I placed them on the bed and went to another box to find my turtlenecks. After scrounging for fifteen minutes, I dug out a brown, wrinkled mess and tucked it under my arm. I'd let the steam from the shower loosen the wrinkles. The iron could be in a hundred places, and there was no time to go hunting for it. Besides, between Marma Lee's plot to snag Saige and Mama's lounging ensemble, I seriously doubted anyone would notice even if I showed up in my bunny slippers and flannie pajamas.

CHAPTER NINE

At six-fifty p.m. the area writers began to arrive. Ruby came in with a flurry of leftover snowflakes. I offered to take her coat. She opted to keep her briefcase. "It contains the evening's program, Mac. I'll just put it here by my side. My, it smells wonderful in here." She took a big whiff and sighed.

I noticed Mama casting some anxious glances toward the entrance and shooed her back in the kitchen. "Don't worry about a thing, Mama. I'll man the door." She patted my face. I had a feeling Marma Lee wasn't the only one wanting to make an entrance.

The next knock announced Ralph. He came in stamping snow. "It's cold as an iron wedge out there." He stepped inside, handed me his coat and gloves, and tugged his overshoes off. Ralph had no sooner cozied up to the fire to warm his hands when the next knock sounded.

Saige and Rennie entered laughing. "You just wait. I'll get you when we leave." Saige closed the door behind them.

"Not if I can help it, you won't. I'm sneaking out the back.

I'm not afraid to admit I'm a coward." Rennie shrugged out of her coat.

"What in the world are you two talking about?" I asked.

"Saige threw a snowball at me and missed. Mine hit home." Rennie pointed to the top of Saige's head.

"You didn't." I covered my grin with my hand.

Rennie threw back her head and laughed. "He started it. I can't help it if I'm a better aim than he is."

Saige laughed and went to sit on the couch. Very good. I told Rennie to sit on the other end.

"Why?" she asked.

"I'll tell you later."

She waltzed over to the fire, rubbed her hands together, and settled on the other end of the couch. With a smile of contentment, she kicked off her shoes and pulled her legs up under her, yoga style. This was going well. Marma Lee would be pleased.

Another knock announced Richard, who came in carrying a folder and a bouquet of daisies. He had to duck his head a fraction to clear the top of the door. He thrust the flowers in my direction. "I thought I'd bring some flowers to the lovely hostesses."

Thanking him, I took his coat and was about to tell him to make himself comfortable when I saw Rennie heading for the kitchen. By the time I'd hung up Richard's coat, he'd settled into Rennie's spot on the couch. Oh well. This way, Mama would get to sit by Richard until Marma Lee arrived. Pivoting, I rummaged around under the kitchen sink in search of a vase for the daisies. They looked lovely on Mama's heirloom drum table she'd given me.

Ruby glanced at her watch again. "Where is Marma Lee?" Ruby asked. "For that matter where is Ethel? It isn't at all like her to be late. Maybe I should phone."

"Ethel won't be able to join us tonight, Ruby. I'll explain later." I'd explain near the end of the meeting. The last thing I wanted was to put a damper on the evening before it began. "Marma Lee will be along in a minute. She mentioned she might be running late."

"Oh my." Richard gazed over my shoulder. "Don't you look lovely?" For a moment I thought he was talking to me. Mama, standing just behind me, had brushed her brown curls again. They shone in the soft light of the candles. I was sure no one else noticed that pretty little blush that spread across her cheeks.

"Please, come sit." Richard patted the seat beside him.

I gave Mama a tiny shove. If this thing worked out, we might need to have the doorframes adjusted to accommodate Richard's height. We couldn't have him bumping his head. It would knock his toupee off. I hurried to the kitchen to check the back door. I thought I'd heard a noise. Maybe Marma Lee planned on coming in the back way. No sign of her. Mick's idea of a security device flitted through my head.

When I returned, I sensed Ruby's agitation. "Why don't you begin?" I said. "Marma Lee can slip in, and you won't have to lose any time."

"We'd better. We're five minutes behind schedule. Since we have a new member with us, Mr. Saige Nichols, we'll begin by informally introducing ourselves and sharing with the group what type of writing we do. I'll begin. My name is Ruby Holly. I'm a longtime resident of Pocket and a retired schoolteacher. I founded this group about five years ago and enjoy historical research and genealogical searches. Most of my writing is nonfiction."

Short and sweet. She pointed to Rennie.

Returning from the kitchen, Rennie sat on the floor cross-legged and hugging a pillow. She finished her cookie and launched into her introduction. "My name is horrible, so I don't use it anymore, but because I like you, I'll tell you what it is." Everyone laughed. Saige seemed particularly amused. "My given name is Renesta Dymes. I've never been married so my name has always been Renesta Dymes. I taught dancing at a fine dance school in Memphis, and then I decided to try my hand at writing. Now I write children's books and my pen name is Little Miss Bellybutton. My weakness is critiquing my own work, which is why I am grateful to have a group to help me. My friends all call me Rennie, and if you want to stay my friend, you'll never tell anyone else my real name." She playfully shook her finger at Saige. Leave it to Rennie. She had a way of putting everyone at ease. Ralph volunteered next.

"My name is Ralph Perty." He stood and nodded to those assembled. "I run the Perty Real Estate Agency across the street. My family has been in the real estate business for generations. But," he shrugged, "I'm also interested in fiction. I compose short stories. I've even had one published. A copy of the ten-dollar check is hanging in my den." Everyone laughed. "That's 'Perty' much it." Despite his flat pun, he turned on his cheesiest grin and bowed. Richard was next.

"My name is Richard J. Lorch. The J stands for Jesse, who was my father. I'm a retired restaurant owner, and I've been writing poetry for greeting cards for the last four years. It's surprisingly lucrative, which is fortunate, since being a retired restaurant owner isn't. My writing started out with mysteries, but I decided on the greeting card business, and I've allowed my mystery imagination to go stale."

Mama's eyes lit up. Her wheels were turning. She was writing a mystery, and now she and Richard had one more thing in common. She volunteered to go next.

"Since we're confessing full names," Mama said, winking at Rennie, "mine is Edie Lilly Casteel. I'm new to the group, too, and my work in progress is a romantic suspense." She slipped a side peek in Richard's direction. "I hope to share it with you in the near future. I haven't written enough to read tonight." Drats. There went my hope of getting a peek.

As if on cue, the doorbell rang. I glanced at Mama. "Places, everyone" was plastered all over her face. She rose from her coveted spot on the sofa to see about the snacks. With flair to spare, I opened the door to admit Marma Lee. She took in the potpourri and gave me a discreet thumbs up. Like a good servant, I relieved her of her satchel and coat. When she turned around, my jaw dropped. She wore the same ensemble as Mama. The two outfits were identical, right down to their peek-a-boo jacket and fuchsia sparkles.

Richard noticed first. "Why, you look lovely tonight. Did you and your Aunt Lilly go shopping together?"

Marma Lee looked confused until Mama pranced into the room carrying a tray of cookies. Mama beamed at Marma Lee. Marma Lee blinked. After a split second, Marma Lee recovered.

"Aunt Lilly liked my outfit so much, she decided to buy one just like it, didn't you, Aunt Lilly?" She walked over to Mama and plucked a cookie from the tray. "I just didn't realize we would both be wearing them tonight." Her growl was barely audible.

Mama pointed to Marma Lee's sacred seat. Evidently Mama was forgiven because Marma Lee hugged her and swayed her way to the couch. The candles cast a beautiful glow that bounced off the crystal, resulting in dancing prisms of light. Marma Lee slid into her seat and turned to smile at Saige.

"What's that smell?" Richard asked. "Lilly, have y'all had the exterminator in today?"

"Uh, Marma Lee, maybe you'd better go next," I said. She shot daggers at Richard. His blissful ignorance of her glare was a blessing.

"What?" Marma Lee asked, tearing her eyes from Richard.

"We're introducing ourselves. It's your turn." The best way to calm my cousin was by putting her in the spotlight. Worked every time.

"Oh." Smoothing her hair and rising, she offered the group her best Nichole Kidman smile. She cleared her throat. "Many years ago," she began, "I decided to follow my dream of writing. Although most of my creations are romance, occasionally, I write poetry. When I first started, I wrote rhymed poetry and have advanced to unrhymed poetry." None of us bothered to tell her that one wasn't a graduation from the other. She continued. "I've come to learn how to express myself in this manner, and while most of my writing is romantic fiction, I hope you will allow me to read my poetry piece aloud. I know we don't usually do this, but I feel compelled."

Compelled, my foot.

"This piece is entitled 'Love's Savage Passion.' I hope you enjoy it.

> *"Why, oh why, does the wind blow so?*
> *Why, oh why, does my heart break?*
> *Why, oh why, do the birds sing a song?*
> *When they know I walk alone."*

Everyone sat still as a rock. No one wanted to tell her it was lousy, but the sudden desire from all present for a cookie should have tipped her off. Mama's tray emptied in record time.

"My, oh my." Mama grinned. "I'll get more."

"That was, intriguing. Your writing is coming right along." Ruby nodded her head and turned on her heel to face Saige. "Now, Saige. You know about our little group. We'd love to hear about you." The rest of the group focused on Saige like he was a life saver.

"I'm Saige Nichols. I travel quite a bit from place to place hunting for different stories. My Grandmamma Gladi lives here, and I came back to visit her. I've decided to stay for a while."

Marma Lee was probably finding it hard not to do handsprings around the room.

"I don't write much fiction, and I don't know anything about poetry." Saige managed an apologetic shrug.

Slick move. He neatly sidestepped having to critique Marma Lee's poem.

"I write nonfiction. My specialty is unsolved mysteries. I research real crimes." The matter-of-fact way he stated it elicited goose bumps on my arms.

Everyone in the room unconsciously eyeballed Ruby. No one breathed. Not even Marma Lee. Ralph saved what could have been an awkward moment.

"That's fascinating, Saige. We've never had a true crime writer in our midst. It must lead you to interesting places."

Saige seemed oblivious to Ruby's past. He described his work on a case in Mountain View and his most recent in St. Louis. Before that, he worked in Chicago, Denver, and even Canada. The man did get around. It was no wonder he never married. Or maybe he had, and she didn't like the traveling or his work. It happens. I'm sure Marma Lee would find out and fill us in. She hung on his every word.

"Since I didn't have a current project, I planned to ask around about Smitty Small's murder. It seems to be a bit of a mystery."

"Not anymore," Marma Lee blurted.

"What?" Saige hunched forward on the edge of the couch.

"Mac, you didn't tell them?"

I glared at my cousin. "No. I wanted to wait until the end of the meeting."

"Well, there's no mystery anymore. You might as well go ahead and tell everyone." Marma Lee shrugged.

"Tell us what?" asked Ruby.

"The police believe Ethel killed Smitty. It seems she's Smitty's wife, and he refused to help her with money when she needed it. Ethel is in custody. Boomer called me this afternoon." I finished and searched each face in the room.

Ralph spoke up. "I knew there was something fishy about her. She was all gung-ho about finding a house when she moved here. Then, all of a sudden, she decided to stay in a motel. I guess she knew she'd be inheriting Smitty's house."

The room hushed, and heads shook while each tried to figure out how a nice woman like Ethel could be moved to murder. From the looks on the faces, they were having as much trouble believing it as I did.

Saige moved all the way to the edge of the sofa. Whether his intention was to get more comfortable or move as far away as possible from Marma Lee's perfume was iffy. Richard excused himself on the pretext of finding the restroom. When he returned, however, he drew up a chair from the kitchen and sat next to Mama. Marma Lee had not moved over. She remained next to Saige. I felt sorry for the guy. If I'd had a gas mask, I would have offered it to him. Everyone else had moved discreetly. Ralph reclined his rocker as far as it would go. Rennie, who had taken a seat in the other rocker, swiveled toward the door and inhaled deeply every few minutes. I was tempted to open the door. I don't think one person would have objected.

"How old are the cases you investigate?" Richard asked. Were his eyes watering? He placed his arm on the back of Mama's chair. Mama glowed. Whether from Marma Lee's fumes or Richard's charm, I couldn't tell.

"They vary," Saige replied. "Some are recent. Some date back a decade."

"What will you do since Smitty's case has been solved?" Ralph asked. "There's not much in Pocket in the way of crime. We're a boring little community. I guess this will change your plans about staying." He turned to Ruby. "You know, we'll have to find replacements, Ruby. With Ethel and Saige gone, we'll be left with only six members. We need at least eight."

Mr. Skarie's sculpture was in jeopardy of being thrown. It would leave quite a whelp on the realtor's head. While the thought of his coiffed hair being messed up by a big, white bandage enticed me, I hated for Boomer to be dispatched to our residence again. We could get a reputation. I caught Marma Lee's eye and sent a silent warning. She wouldn't want Saige to see her lose her temper. I'd seen it at work when I was six. I still have the scar on my ankle where she bit me.

"Would you consider investigating an older case, Saige?" Ruby's voice was firm enough to get everyone's attention.

"Maybe. What do you have in mind?"

"My only child, Cora Ann, disappeared thirty years ago. I never heard from her after the day she walked out. Actually, it was evening when she left. We had a horrible dispute. The last time I saw her, she grabbed her purse and told me she hated me. She was twenty-one." Ruby trailed off then sat straighter in her chair and continued.

"Much of the story was publicized in the local paper as well as some of the major Arkansas newspapers. I know she isn't coming home. I knew the next day. I think a mother senses things. I'm an old woman, Saige. I'd like to know what happened to her. May I ask what your success rate is?"

Saige cleared his throat. "Of the five cases I've researched, four involved murders. Three of the murderers were found because of my involvement."

"The other murder case, what happened regarding that one?" Ruby cleared her throat and paused.

"The mystery wasn't who committed the murders. The man confessed to several killings, but he would never tell exactly how many or where he placed the bodies."

"Did you find them?" Ruby inquired.

"Yes, ma'am, I did, but one family told me they wished I hadn't. As long as their son was lost, they said they could hope. The mother told me without hope, she had no reason to live. They found her two days later in her bedroom, holding a picture of her son. She died from a heart attack. I think she died from a broken heart.

"That happened two years ago. I haven't researched another

case since. Maybe that's why I came here. My grandfather was a minister. He's passed on now." He sighed. "As long as I felt I helped people, I enjoyed my work, but when I found out about that mother's death, I felt responsible." He looked away for a moment, and we all knew he was remembering. It's hard to evict a ghost once it sets up house in your heart.

"You did what you thought was right." Ruby searched his face. "That mother was angry and confused. Her guilt and remorse shouldn't be yours to shoulder."

Saige studied Ruby for several moments. Their eyes locked, and neither blinked.

"I've kept my daughter's room exactly as she left it. Foolish, I know, but it brings me peace. Did you come here to research Cora Ann's disappearance?"

He sat straighter as though pinched. I looked for signs of Marma Lee's straying hands, but they were clasped demurely in her lap. "No, Ruby. I had no idea about your daughter. I hope you don't think I planned this."

Ruby examined him for a long time. Saige never wavered. He looked at her earnestly. This was not part of the agenda. The rest of the group watched the proceedings like a tennis match.

Finally, Ruby spoke. "No, I don't believe you did, but I don't believe in coincidence either." She shrugged. "Perhaps you ended up in Pocket for a reason. I've waited a long time to find out what happened to my Cora Ann. I'd like you to investigate her disappearance. Would you do that?"

Saige hesitated then nodded once. Ruby smiled. It wasn't the smile of contentment. Ironically, Ruby's writing program was about tying up loose ends. Interesting coincidence.

CHAPTER TEN

"I can't believe you showed up wearing my outfit, Aunt Lilly."

"I'm sorry, dear, but I had no way of knowing we had the same ensemble. You did look lovely, though."

"I spent a fortune setting the right ambience for the evening. I had no idea you would wear anything like that." Marma Lee managed to look huffy and chastened at the same time. No telling how long she'd worked on that look.

"Normally, you won't see me in such an outfit. It was a pure splurge, and I'm not sorry. I do regret we chose to wear them the same evening. With the exception of that little mishap, the meeting went rather well." She plopped a box of books on the floor. We were unpacking boxes delivered last week. These were going in the middle grade section.

"It wasn't boring," I chimed in.

"Richard almost ruined my whole plan when he started complaining about the place being fumigated. He was talking about my perfume. He's incapable of appreciating a refined aroma."

Marma Lee was skating. Mama gets quiet when she gets

mad. I always knew as a child when I'd gone too far. I would experience the same eerie quiet witnesses of tornadoes talked about just before the big funnel comes down and swoops up everything in its path. Without looking at any gauges, I knew the barometric pressure in the basement had just taken a dangerous dip.

"Your perfume had quite an effect on everyone. Richard and Saige seemed overcome by your vapors. Rennie finally asked if it would appear rude to open a window."

"Why, Aunt Lilly!"

"It's true." Mama stood straight as an arrow. "I thought we were going to have to dig out the smelling salts. They were positively woozy."

"It wasn't from my perfume. It was Ruby Holly's bombshell."

"I'm with Mama on this one, Marma Lee. That perfume is ruined. I'd ask for a refund. Evidently it stays on for a while. I can still smell it this morning." The stuff was starting to sting my nose.

"There's nothing wrong with my perfume, and I can't get a refund. I bought it from a lady I know. You two are used to wearing those cheap knockoffs. We'll get another opinion."

"From whom?" I asked. "Saige? If you come at him with that stuff again, you'll run him out of town. I'm not sure he won't leave anyway. He was flustered by the end of the evening."

"It wasn't his fault. He didn't know about Ruby's daughter. That was thirty years ago." Marma Lee tried her best to defend her prospective man.

"How do you know? Don't you think it's odd he researches unsolved mysteries for a living and has a grandmother who lived here during the time of Cora Ann's disappearance, and now he just happens to join the group which her mother founded? Come on, Marma Lee. Did those vapors get to you too? Wake up. Saige knew there was a story here way before Smitty's death. I don't believe for a minute he came to visit his granny and liked it so much he decided to stay awhile. It doesn't make sense."

"Not everything makes sense, Mac. Love is often irrational."

"You're not being poetically compelled again, are you?" I frowned.

"No, I'm not, but we might as well settle this issue about my perfume. I have it in my bag." Mama and I backed away.

"Don't you dare spray that down here where children will be. It's toxic," Mama screeched. Her words came out a bit muffled since her hands were clamped over her nose and mouth.

"I wasn't going to spray my one-hundred-and-fifty-dollar perfume like an air freshener, Aunt Lilly. Where are my car keys? I'm hungry. Let's go to Maybelline's. I'll buy all of us a late breakfast. We'll ask her about my perfume."

"What does Maybelline know about perfume?" I demanded.

"I've seen her and Lurlene shopping in Dillard's at the perfume counter. They have an appreciation for finer scents."

Marma Lee thought everyone who shopped at Dillard's was a cut above the rest of us. Some day she would realize the Dollar Store had a charisma all its own. They had great prices, plus the employees always said hello when you walked in the door.

But I was hungry, and she was buying. "Let's go, Mama." I grabbed a wet wipe, one of the best inventions of the twentieth century, and gave my hands a good scrubbing.

"Oh, all right, but we can't lollygag. We've work to do. What does Maybelline put in her pancake rolls on Wednesday?"

"Sausage." Marma Lee and I answered together.

"I'll get my coat." Mama ran for the closet.

We piled into Marma Lee's Chrysler and took off. My mind was already on the side order of fried bread I intended to order.

"You know, I'm going to enjoy being a member of the writing group. It was an exciting night." Mama's seat belt clicked into place.

"Have you started on your story?" I waited for her to answer and could have smacked Marma Lee for jumping in before Mama had a chance to respond.

"If you ask me, you went a little overboard with the Ethel thing."

"What are you talking about? It was your fault I had to make the announcement. If you had arrived on time, you would have known I wasn't going to explain about Ethel's arrest until the end. What good did it do you? Saige isn't any more enamored with you than before."

"I wasn't talking about your explanation of Ethel's arrest. It was your dramatic declaration of her innocence. She did it. She had the perfect motive. You're crazy if you think otherwise. The police are convinced. Get over it."

"I'm not so sure." I could be stubborn when necessary. "She likes animals."

Marma Lee hooted. "What does that have to do with anything? Don't you remember that guy in Rockford who was a vet? He was a serial killer. Loving animals does not mean you are a stable person, Mac."

"Neither does shopping at Dillard's," I retorted. We pulled into Maybelline's Diner before Marma Lee had a chance to reply. We hurried inside and found an empty table. The place smelled just like it had the last time. Wonderful. I couldn't wait to take a picture of my order and post it on my new blog, *Pocket Change, Anyone*?

Maybelline deposited glasses of water in front of us. "I'm so mad I could spit nails." She hissed as she slammed down the glasses along with three orders of pancake rolls. It was nice to come to a place where they know you like the back of their skillet. She also knew I didn't need fried bread.

"What's Lurlene done, honey?" Mama asked, hanging her purse on the back of her chair and digging into her food.

"It's not Lurlene this time. It's that man over there in booth number three." Maybelline jerked her hair nest to the right. "He had the gall to tell me my sausage was undercooked, and he isn't paying for his breakfast. It didn't keep him from eating it, though. He even drank all his coffee and asked for a refill. I told him that was fine but not to darken my doorway anymore, or I'd show him what really undercooked sausage looked like. Then he asked if I was threatening him. The man is mean."

I stopped chewing long enough to turn to look at the person who needed his taste buds examined. "That's Boyd Barlow."

"You know him?"

I nodded and proceeded to share our few conversations with Maybelline. She calmed to a simmer. "So, it's not just me he's picking on. Sounds to me like it's his nature to look for things to complain about." Whirling around, she flounced off to the kitchen. She returned, carrying a large, white bucket.

"What are you going to do with that?" Mama asked. "Honey, if you stick that over his head, he really could sue you. Let's find a more subtle way of dealing with him, okay?"

"It's not for him, although that's not a bad idea." She stroked the bucket and glanced in Mr. Barlow's direction. "I have a leak by the door. This old roof is in bad shape, and this wind isn't helping. Every time I look out the window, I see another shingle fly by. We need to fix it, but it's going to cost a lot more than what's in my savings. I'm trying to make it through until next fall." She shrugged and made her way toward the leak.

Marma Lee scoped out Boyd Barlow as she popped a bite of sausage into her mouth. She swished her napkin at my arm. "Watch," she whispered. "He's going to walk out with Maybelline's paper."

Sure enough, Barlow rose nonchalantly from his table, tucking under his arm the copy of *The Jonesboro Sun*, which Maybelline subscribed to for her customers. The regulars knew to put it back for the next person to enjoy.

"Yoo-hoo, Mr. Barlow," I called. "Since you're leaving,

would you mind letting me have Maybelline's paper? I haven't read it."

"Nice move, Cousin." I think she actually meant it. Mr. Barlow turned three different shades of red. He heel-toed it to our table and handed me the paper.

When the door closed, I waved Maybelline over. "Tell Lurlene that Boomer gave me the all clear, and she can start at Pocket Change any time she wants."

"Will do." She disappeared into the back.

Lurlene came out. "So, you're open for business?"

"No, but we will be Saturday." I took a sip of my sweet tea and dabbed at my mouth.

"Do you need me to come in tomorrow and help with anything? I could use the money. We've got a drippy roof. I'm trying to work some overtime at some of my regular jobs to get it repaired. Maybelline thinks it will hold until next fall, but I don't believe it. We haven't started winter yet, and if we have a wet spring, we're done for."

We all looked at the drippy ceiling. A water spot had already started forming.

"We could use the help, and I'll pay extra since it's short notice. Would seven-thirty in the morning be too early?" My mind made mental notes for later.

"Mercy no, girl. I get up around four. God gave me the gift of get-up-and-go. I never sleep more than five hours. I'll be there in the morning with bells on."

"Y'all about finished? We need to get to work." Mama tapped her nails on the orange Formica.

"Oh no, you don't. The deal was I'd buy breakfast so I could prove there's nothing wrong with my perfume. I'm going to show you two olfactory-challenged women this perfume is refined, subtle, and alluring." She motioned for Maybelline to come over to the table.

"Maybelline." Marma Lee whipped out the offensive bottle.

"I'd like you to smell a fresh, delightful fragrance. I know you appreciate fine perfumes." Marma Lee plopped the atomizer on the table.

Maybelline's eyes grew big. "Don't spray that in here. The health inspector could come in. There's been a recall put out on that stuff." Maybelline sniffed. "You didn't put any of that on your skin, did you?"

I managed to keep my composure for five seconds. To Marma Lee's credit, she neither argued nor pouted. She returned the bottle back to her purse and thanked a confused Maybelline for her time. She paid the bill, added a twenty-dollar tip to the table, and walked silently to the door. I suspected she thought twice about unlocking the passenger side doors, although she finally did. We rode in silence for two blocks. Mama kept glancing at me from the front seat.

"Reckon I could sell it to the termite people?" That was our Marma Lee. You might have to hit her upside the head with a board before she finally got the point, but she came around eventually, laughing at her mistake.

Mama chuckled. "That stuff is too potent to spray under a house. You need to contact the toxic waste people or maybe the government. Chemical warfare is lucrative. That stuff is pretty potent. Have you showered today?"

"Twice," Marma Lee admitted.

We were all laughing when we arrived at the shop. It died when we saw the massive front door standing wide. Snow had blown in on the hardwood floor, and the winds from outside had scattered papers all over the room. At least that was the impression. As I got closer, I suspected something a little stronger than wind had caused the mess. Muddy footprints were everywhere. They looked like the ones leading downstairs a few days ago.

The land phone rang. Mama, her mouth gaping, plucked the receiver from its base. She listened for a minute then came over to stand beside me. "That was Boomer. He's coming over."

"How did he know anything was wrong?" Marma Lee asked. All I could do was stand and stare.

"I called him." Boyd Barlow stood under the arch leading to the basement. He held his cell phone.

The man must have been part panther. He was just there, ready to pounce. "What are you doing here?" Okay, some might call my question blunt. They'd be right. "And why is my shop in such a mess?"

"I passed by and noticed your door open. I knew you were at the diner and thought it a bit unusual you would leave your premises vulnerable. When I stepped onto the porch, I heard someone inside. I came to investigate. After your recent difficulties, I felt it well-advised to phone Sheriff Boomer."

"Why did you go to the basement?" Mama demanded. She wasn't buying his story either. One look at his face said it all. He had been caught.

He hesitated a split second. "To make sure no one was hurt. I came back up and called the police."

"Boomer said the call just came through," Mama confirmed. "He didn't take the call, though. He said the dispatcher sent word to him." We all turned at the sound of the cruiser's tires crunching on the snow. The front door stood open. No one had bothered to close it. Boomer was out of the car and up the steps in record time. Big men could be surprisingly lithe.

The look on his face could have set a thunderstorm into action. He took in the scene. His trained eyes stopped roving when they reached Barlow. "Why are you here?" Boomer asked the same question I had. Barlow gave the same response. The little man glanced around at the wreckage then to his briefcase by the door.

I followed his gaze. "Why did you bring your briefcase in with you? If you were checking on intruders, you wouldn't need to bring your briefcase."

"Mary Clare, if you don't mind, I'll ask the questions, and I'll ask them at the station." He frowned at me. I frowned back.

"Mr. Barlow, if you would follow me." Boomer gestured toward the door.

"Am I being arrested for calling the police?" His shoulders rolled back, and his eyes widened.

"No. You are not being arrested. I have some questions, and it might be more conducive to the situation if you followed me to the police station. You are welcome to ride with me. I'll bring you back when we're finished."

Barlow looked like a guppy sloshed out of its bowl. His mouth opened and shut, but I guess he realized arguing would only make matters worse. He trailed Boomer down the steps and slid into the cruiser's front seat.

I pulled out my cell. "That guy gives me the creeps. There's something wrong."

"Who are you calling?" Mama demanded.

"I'm calling Lurlene. Maybe she can come in this afternoon."

"You can't have Lurlene come in and clean until we hear from Boomer," Mama said.

Marma Lee nodded in slow motion. She didn't say anything, but her hips looked like she was trying to hula. Here we go again. She bobbed her head a couple of times. Mama led her to the sofa. Marma Lee gave her a look of surprise.

"Give me a minute." She took a couple of deep breaths which seemed to steady her. "Now, we all agree looks can be deceiving. Barlow may look like a crook, but he may be a normal guy who puts his foot in his mouth a lot."

"Why would he come in here to investigate? He impresses me as the type who would be afraid of his own shadow." I tugged my ponytail and glared at my cousin.

Marma Lee huffed. "I just told you, you cannot judge people by their looks or by your first impression. You don't really know anything about Mr. Barlow."

"Why did he go down to the basement?" Mama asked. "I'm not buying that story of his for a minute. A normal person would have waited for the police to arrive. He knew we weren't in danger. We were at Maybelline's."

"Why would he call Boomer at all, unless it was to cover his tracks when he heard us pull in?" I had to admit Marma Lee had a point. Even though the tracks did resemble those in the basement, Barlow's story could happen. I would have to wait and find out what Boomer said.

Mama had a point too. I couldn't call Lurlene until Boomer called me. Frustrated, I stomped into the kitchen. Open house was in less than three days, and now I had a huge mess to clean up in the front room along with all my books to unpack and a new neighbor to snag—get acquainted with. I really wanted to kick something. Instead, I grabbed my coat, stepped out the back door, and marched directly into aforementioned new neighbor. I blinked twice. He had on a billed cap and a heavier jacket than the last time I'd seen him. His smile, however, was the same.

He leaned down to look in my eyes. "You okay? I saw Boomer leave with some guy in a suit. Neither looked happy."

"A rough morning. Someone came into the shop and left a bunch of muddy footprints again, and I now have a ton of paperwork scattered all over the front room."

Mick frowned. "Was it caused by the guy Boomer hauled off?"

"I think so, but I'm not sure. He gave us some stupid story about seeing the front door open and coming in to investigate, but I don't believe him." I told Mick about being at Maybelline's earlier and seeing Barlow. "Maybe he thought we'd be gone longer, and he'd have time to come in and rummage around."

"What would he be looking for?"

"I don't know."

"What does your gut tell you?"

"My gut tells me not to trust him, but I'm not a trusting

person, I guess." I looked down. Now was probably not the best time to tell him about Roger, aka the reason I had trouble trusting people.

He seemed to sense a change of subject was in order and turned me toward the cottage. It took a few moments of confused gazing to spot what he pointed toward. In front of the bay window stood a new bird feeder at least three feet tall. It sat atop a three-foot pole and nestled with the ones Mama and I erected. It looked for all the world like a tiny replica of my cottage. The only difference was the wide wrap-around porch.

"This is beautiful." I hurried over to the feeder. He'd already filled it with a mixture of seeds. Several apples had been sliced in two and slathered with peanut butter and sprinkled with seed. The birds scattered when we approached. They sat twittering on a nearby cedar branch.

"Where did this come from? It's exquisite." I stroked the structure, awed by the craftsmanship.

"I took some liberties with the porch, but the little fellas have to have somewhere to perch. As to where it came from, I had Dad build it. Consider it a 'bird' house-warming gift. Do you like it?"

"I love it. It's perfect. How did you put this up without me knowing about it?"

"I saw y'all leave a while ago. Dad finished it yesterday, and I've been waiting for an opportunity to sneak it over. Scared the living daylights out of me when Boomer pulled up. I thought a neighbor called him because of me. I walked around the side of the shop about the time he escorted that gentleman to the car."

"Your dad built this?" I was amazed. Little wooden tiles made up the roof.

"Yeah. He's had this pattern for years. He used to build birdhouses for Mom before she passed away. She loved to watch the birds feed. He only had to make a few minor adjustments to the plan to make it resemble your place. Seemed like the perfect gift."

"It's ideal."

He shrugged and looked shy. "I should get going." He picked up his hammer and pick. With the ground being so hard, it would have been hard to set the feeder pole in the ground. He'd gone to a lot of trouble.

"Would you like to come to dinner tomorrow night?" I blurted.

"That sounds great."

"I'm afraid I'm not a fancy cook, but if you'll tell me what you don't like, I'll steer clear of it."

He hoisted his toolbox. "I've never been fond of cauliflower, beets, or cottage cheese. Other than that, I'm a human disposal."

"I promise none of those will be on the table. Would you like to come in for some coffee?"

"Thanks, but I need to get back. Dad's running the store for me, but it looks like he and Doc may be getting busy."

Apparently, a visit from Mick could erase my frustration. I felt like doing a little tap dance. "How's seven o'clock for dinner?"

"That's great. I close up about six."

"I'll see you tomorrow, and thanks for the birdfeeder. Tell your dad he's an artist."

He hesitated and then jerked his head toward the feeder. When he spoke, his words came out low and husky. "Be sure to read the inscription." He turned and walked back toward his shop. Shivering, I dashed back, bent down, and hunted for a message. I found it etched along the porch railing. Matthew: 6:26. "Look at the birds of the air; they do not sow or reap or store away in barns, and yet your heavenly Father feeds them. Are you not much more valuable then they?" I stroked the bird-house and reread the scripture. My new neighbor had given me more than a bird feeder. Come to think of it, God had given me more than a new neighbor.

I hurried into the shop. Sometimes my daddy's voice still whispered in my ear. This was one of those times. Rubbing my hands together, I scampered to find the phone book. It was time to make good on those mental notes I'd taken in Maybelline's. According to Daddy, good deeds are meant to be passed along. It was time to call a roofer. Maybelline and Lurlene would have to find other uses for their buckets.

CHAPTER ELEVEN

Mama and Marma Lee were cradling cups of cocoa when I got back to the shop.

"Mick's cute," Marma Lee observed.

"And thoughtful." Mama played with the marshmallows, dunking them into the cocoa.

"How do you know he's thoughtful?" I asked.

"We were listening at the window, dummy." Marma Lee smirked.

"Mama." I turned and gawked at her.

"Honey, I tried to drag your cousin away, but we couldn't help but overhear part of the conversation. What are we fixing for dinner tomorrow night?"

"I could fix my famous spaghetti sauce." Marma Lee clapped her hands once and stood.

"Don't you mean Ragu's famous spaghetti sauce?" I narrowed my eyes. "All you do is add extra mushrooms. Besides, when did you get invited?"

Marma Lee huffed. "You're lucky to have someone like me to advise you, Cousin. Your problem is you don't have any real art appreciation. I will allow you to keep the Skarie Sculpture for now. That will give the joint some class, and you still have the candles."

"This calls for a new outfit, dear." Mama turned and nearly knocked me over with her dazzling smile. Had my sunglasses been handy, I'd have slung them on my face. Her toothy grin was blinding. "We should leave immediately and find you something. Would you like slinky or flowing?"

"Mama, this is just dinner."

"It's never just dinner, Cousin."

"It's never just dinner with you, Marma Lee. I do not try to rope every man who sprints by."

"You haven't tried to rope anybody since Roger. Maybe it's time to get back in the saddle."

My withering look would surely have crippled an ordinary person, but my cousin came from hardier stock. I turned and headed for the basement.

"Now you've done it, Marma Lee," Mama fretted. "She isn't ready to talk about that yet. She didn't try to rope him. Don't you have a thread of tact?"

"It's time, Aunt Lilly. It's been two months. Roger is a dud and a leach. The jerk took advantage of Mac's goodness, and I'm not the least bit sorry I ran over his foot. He had it coming. Not that it did much good. He's still hovering around like a vulture. Men like him aren't worth…"

I didn't hear the rest of the conversation. I was too busy stomping down the stairs. Who did she think she was, anyway? She zipped through men like most women go through their email. What did she know about real relationships?

I'd located the perfect box to kick when footsteps sounded on the staircase. The phone booth was handy, so I kicked it instead. Something inside rattled and tinkled, but holding my throbbing toe took a lot of energy. I was too busy thinking of ways to throttle Marma Lee to pay much attention to it. I hoped with all my heart I had not dislodged one of Superman's more important body parts.

"Now, honey." Mama reached out and patted my head. Marma Lee stood with her hands on her hips.

"Look, Cousin. I'm sorry I brought up Roger, but it's time to move on. Think of him as an Etch-A-Sketch goof. Time to shake things up and start over. Why are you hopping around? You look ridiculous."

Maybe I growled. Mama made a cooing noise and came to help me over to the reading bar. I plopped down on one of the stools and removed my tennis shoe.

"Thanks to you, I don't have to worry about Roger. After you ran over his foot with your car then sent him that note, he was glad to leave. You really are going to have to learn to mind your own business, Marma Lee. You know, you never did explain how you got stationery from Bagram's Psychiatric Institution. You're lucky he didn't have you arrested for terroristic threatening. I can take care of myself. Maybe Roger isn't so bad. It's possible he just had a few issues."

"Yeah, and a few warrants for his arrest." Marma Lee snorted. "Look, I know you thought you liked the guy, but you really only felt sorry for him. You did the right thing by dumping him. You can't turn a lump of mud into a diamond. Trust me. He is a lump. He didn't even have the decency to pay you back the money he owed you, and I know you loaned him two hundred and fifty dollars."

I glowered at Mama. "How did she know that?"

Mama had the decency to squirm. "I might have let it slip. It broke my heart to see him using you. Marma Lee's right, you know. The only time he was nice was when he wanted something."

"We were together almost a year, Mama. I know him a little better than the two of you. He had potential. Maybe I made the wrong decision. It's possible all he needs is someone to steer him in the right direction. But Rooster Cogburn here," I said, jerking my head toward Marma Lee, "threatened to have his anatomy rearranged. How was that supposed to help?"

Marma Lee sniffed. "I did what I had to do, and I'm not sorry."

Had Mama not been patting my right hand, I might have walloped Marma Lee. Instead, I wiggled my toes gingerly and began putting my shoe back on. I wanted to spit nails but knew everything my dingbat cousin said was true. Roger deserved a flat toe or two. He left me with a broken heart and some serious trust issues. Why on Earth do women think we can fix the broken men in the world?

"Hello. Anybody home?"

"Boomer, is that you?" Mama called. With one last fretful look in my direction, she hurried to the staircase.

"I thought you ladies might like to know the latest on our Mr. Barlow." Boomer's head came into view as he descended the stairs. "You'll probably see him around town, so I want to tell you why."

"What do you mean, 'You'll probably see him around town?' How can he be around town if he's sitting in your jail?"

"I've released him."

"You did what?" Who knew my jaw could drop so fast? "Tell me you're joking. The man's story was full of holes. Surely you can hold him for something. Can't you?"

"Nope. There's no evidence to prove Barlow did anything. Plus, Monteen from across the street said she saw a kid running out of your shop just before Barlow arrived. According to her, Barlow couldn't have been in the store long enough to have caused any real damage. I've finished questioning him, and I believe his story. He's not the type to leave a big mess like the one upstairs. He's too neat. He straightened that red tie a dozen times during the questioning, and those creases in his pants don't come from a dry cleaner. He creases them himself with a special iron he owns. He told me so. Did you lock up when you left to go to Maybelline's?"

"No, Mama did. She was the last one out the door."

"I may have forgotten to turn the lock, dear."

I turned to stare at my mother. Was this the same woman who insisted on locking her Avon jewelry in the safe?

"Barlow admitted he was here to leave you a note." Boomer strolled to the nearest beanbag, gave it a questioning glance, and headed for the stool I had vacated. I followed behind like a limping puppy. "According to him, he was up the front steps before he noticed the open door. He saw no reason to take his briefcase back to his car, so he entered the building to investigate. I think he hoped he could catch someone trespassing and get on your good side."

"Why on earth would he want on my good side?"

Boomer's cocked head gave him a comical look. "He thought you might be interested in letting him handle your money affairs."

I had to get off my feet. It was affecting my hearing. "Would you repeat that? I could have sworn you said that little skunk wanted to handle my money."

"That's what he said. He's quite earnest."

"He tried to steal Maybelline's paper this morning. I wouldn't let that weasel touch our money with a ten-foot pole, much less manage it."

Boomer shrugged. "I'm on my way to question Monteen. I wouldn't have known about the kid if she hadn't called the station. That's why I got here so fast. I was already on my way when the dispatcher called. You've got a good business neighbor."

"Did she give you a description of the kid?" My temples were beginning to ache like my stubbed toes.

"There wasn't enough time when she called, and I didn't want to call her back and question her in front of Barlow. I'll let you know as soon as I find out. Sounds like it might have been vandalizing that got nipped in the bud. You should probably thank Barlow."

I sniffed. "I think I'll wait."

"Suit yourself." Boomer headed for the staircase then seemed to notice Marma Lee for the first time. "I've never known you to be so quiet. You okay?"

"Maybe we haven't really scrutinized the ingredients in this murder."

"Meaning what?" demanded Boomer.

I stepped closer. "She's suffering from a brain bubble. Pay her no mind."

"No. I'm serious, people." Marma Lee took hold of Boomer's elbow. "First, we had a murder, and now we have vandalism. Maybe Smitty was targeted because of something he knew. Maybe because somebody didn't want him around anymore. Or maybe," she said, gaining momentum, "Smitty just got in the way. He could have been killed while trying to stop a break-in."

"Assuming you're right," Boomer said, "why didn't the same person, maybe this kid, try to hurt Barlow?"

"Because the kid panicked and ran before Barlow arrived." Mama looked at Marma Lee. "You know, she could have a point."

Boomer shook his head. "That won't wash, Lilly. Ethel had means, motive, and opportunity. What motive would anyone have to vandalize Pocket Change? You haven't even opened yet."

"I can't believe Ethel murdered Smitty." I shook my head. "As much as I hate to entertain the thought of Marma Lee being right, maybe she is. You have to remember Smitty thought he was coming into some money. It is an aspect we haven't focused on."

"We aren't going to focus on it, either. You can't let your

personal feelings about Ethel blind you to the fact she had a strong motive for killing Smitty. Now, I'm going to talk to Monteen, and I'll get back with you, but I don't expect this to be tied in with the murder. Look on the bright side. If it were related, I'd have to close down your shop again."

With a moan, I held up my hand. "Go talk to Monteen. In the meantime, I'll call Lurlene and see if she can come in and start on the mess upstairs."

"I'll allow that unless you want me to try and get prints so you can press charges against whoever made that mess."

"I guess it's possible the door could have blown open since someone failed to secure it." I glared at Mama.

"The wind could have played havoc with the papers. Lurlene said the gusts were blowing shingles off her roof left and right. If that's true, it could have blown the papers around," Marma Lee pointed out.

"I couldn't find anything missing or destroyed, so there's really no reason to pursue the matter. It's time to get back on track and open on time."

Boomer nodded. "Then call Lurlene or Mr. Clean or whoever, and I'll leave you to it. Good afternoon, ladies."

"Thanks for keeping us posted," Mama called as the door shut.

"Were you really serious, Marma Lee? Are you beginning to question Ethel's guilt?"

"No. I still think she did it. I just don't think any rock should go unturned. This is a murder investigation. Besides, it's fun to watch Boomer's jowls turn down when he's aggravated. It's kind of sweet, don't you think?"

"I try not to think about Boomer's jowls." I turned to Mama. "I can't believe that little pip-squeak thought we would allow him to handle our money, Mama. What on earth was he thinking?"

Marma Lee shrugged. "Let's get back to the business of your love life, Cousin."

I picked up the nearest thing I could grab, which happened to be an empty box, and hurled it at Marma Lee.

"You never could throw worth a dime." She watched the cardboard whiz past her. "You're a tad testy, but that's understandable since you haven't had a date in…a while. What are we going to do about your dinner plans? Aunt Lilly, why don't you take her shopping this afternoon? I'll work on the menu."

Mama beamed. "That's a wonderful idea."

"Now hold on a minute. You two are taking over, and this is not going to work. I'll tell you what we're going to do."

Both women looked at me expectantly.

"Don't rush me."

"Clock's ticking." Marma Lee pointed to the clock. "A date has to be well-executed. You haven't bought any new clothes since you lost weight. All your stuff is saggy. Why don't you go to Annabelle's Shop and see what she has? I can handle the rest of these books. I'll call Lurlene and line up a time for her to come and start cleaning upstairs."

My gaze lingered on the five remaining boxes. "You remember where I want them?"

Marma Lee nodded, pointing to the young adult section.

"You really think I need a new outfit, Mama? I don't want to appear over-anxious and make things uncomfortable with Mick and me."

"Leave it to me, darling. I'll make sure Marma Lee doesn't go overboard, but yes, it's time for new clothes. Going to Annabelle's is the best idea your cousin has had in a while. I'll grab our coats and pull the car around so you won't have to walk as far. Be back in a wink." She positively raced out the back door after depositing me in the chair.

I rubbed my foot and evaluated the mess across the room. Had wind really blown the stuff around? Probably. Gusts of wind were blasting the door now, but who was the kid Monteen saw running from the shop, and why had that person been here?

Mama bustled back with our coats and had me hustled out of the shop in under five minutes. The only thing she loved more than finding bargains at Dollie's Money Mart was shopping for me. I hated it. Our tastes rarely ran in the same direction. Which was why at age ten, I had been one of the last kids parading around in polyester. I'd finally talked her into letting me wear jeans my junior year in high school.

Halfway to the car, I spotted Boomer and Monteen talking animatedly outside the video store. Shushing Mama, I nodded my head in Monteen's direction. Mama waved, but Monteen's hands were busy rubbing her arms then pointing. She shook her head then pointed like a hunting dog in the direction of Mick's shop. Boomer turned and looked then gestured from Pocket Change to Mick's. Monteen nodded once, crossed her arms, and started to do a little dance. She wore short sleeves and no coat. The woman had to be cold. Why weren't they inside talking? When I caught sight of him heading in our direction. I punched Mama softly in the arm and cleared my throat. We turned to face Boomer.

"Why didn't you interview Monteen inside?" I asked. "It's freezing out here."

"Staying outside was her idea," replied Boomer. "She didn't want the kids who work for her to hear what she had to say."

"She knows who it was?" I asked.

"Sure does. She saw him go into your place, stay about five minutes and run out."

"Where did he run?"

"He fled right into Mick's Bait Shop. According to Monteen, the kid's name is Duane Odel Crawford. She said he goes by Doc."

CHAPTER TWELVE

I blamed Boomer's bombshell about Doc for the outfit I hauled home from Annabelle's. Mama seized the opportunity and took advantage of my fragile frame of mind.

Two hours later, when I finally dragged Mama out of the shop, I made a beeline to Boomer's office. As my luck would have it, he wasn't in. Why was I not surprised?

"I'm sorry, Miss Casteel. He said you'd probably come by, but he had to go out. I'm Deputy Clarence Leonard." The man sat as straight as a rod.

"Deputy," I began, "I would appreciate it if you would have Boomer call me when he comes in."

"I'll give Sheriff Boomer the message the minute he returns, ma'am."

I looked at Deputy Leonard's desk with a raised brow. It was questionable whether he'd seen the top of it in several days. I doubted he'd ever locate a pad of paper on which to write a note. Most people forgot to deliver oral messages. A freaky fact that had been proven true too many times.

Sending Boomer a text would be the fastest way to reach him. I remembered I didn't have his personal number. "I have a piece of paper in my purse, Deputy. If you don't mind, I'll jot a note and put it in Boomer's chair."

"That would be fine, Miss Casteel, but I'll be happy to do it for you."

"Oh, no problem." I fished for a pen when Mama came up behind me.

"I don't believe we've met, young man," Mama cooed and extended her hand.

"Deputy Leonard, ma'am." He all but saluted. Mama's face lit up like the neon sign at Maybelline's.

"Are you married, Deputy Leonard?" Mama asked innocently.

Where was that pen?

"Why no, ma'am. Are you?"

Mama blinked a couple of times and changed strategies. "Do you like children? You look athletic. You must work out. Are you dating anyone?"

"Aha!" I yelled, holding up the pen. "Mama, we've taken up enough of this nice man's time." I jotted a quick CALL ME note and signed my name. I dropped it onto Boomer's seat. He'd spot it the minute he pulled out his chair. I practically dragged Mama from the station.

"If you'd given me a few more minutes, I could have invited him to dinner. He's kind of cute, Mary Clare. If things don't work out with this Mick fellow, you have a backup plan."

"Mama, he has pimples all over his face. He's probably not even twenty-five yet."

"Age isn't important. Older women marry younger men all the time. Anyway, it wouldn't hurt to consider young Deputy Leonard."

"Young being the operative word."

"Won't hurt to have one on the back burner, dear."

"Mama, I don't have one on the front burner."

"Exactly. You know, Roger is ten years your senior, and look what a chump he is."

I didn't screech to a halt when we pulled in front of our store, but Mama did say later she might have a slight case of whiplash. Served her right.

While Mama retrieved our purchases from the trunk, I hurried up the steps. My foot was back to its usual size eight, and the throbbing had stopped. I could hear the landline ringing as I opened the front door. Lurlene, clad in her usual yellow gloves, lifted it off the charger.

"Pocket Change," she sang.

"Wow." The front entry was spotless. I'd been gone only two hours, but the place positively glistened. This woman was a miracle worker. Marma Lee sat by the fire, munching a leftover cookie.

"Wait a minute. She just walked in." Lurlene shoved the phone at me and motioned she would go help Mama with the packages. Mama seemed to be stuck in the front door. She and the boxes were larger than the opening.

"Boomer?" I practically yelled. Maybe I should cut down on caffeine. "I came by while ago, but you were out. I met your new deputy. I guess you found my note."

"Couldn't miss it. I guess you want to know about my chat with Duane Crawford."

"No. I thought we might discuss global warming. Of course, I want to know about Duane, I mean Doc. He hates being called Duane."

"How do you know that?" asked Boomer.

"Mick told me."

"You and Mick getting to know one another?"

"We're having dinner tomorrow night. He's new to the area, and it's only polite to make him feel welcome in the community." Why did I feel obligated to confess my every action to people?

Marma Lee snorted. Lurlene hooted. Mama chose to smile.

I ignored them. "You didn't call to ask about my social obligations, did you?"

"No. I promised I'd call when I found out something. Monteen proved helpful, and so was the interview with the kid. He swears he only went to the shop to give Mick a message. Duane, or Doc, knew his boss was there to put up a bird feeder, but he didn't realize it was in back of the cottage. He thought he put it in front of the shop. According to Du…Doc, he went to Pocket Change, didn't see anybody outside the front of the building so he knocked on the door then went in. When he saw the mess, he got scared and left."

"What do you mean, he knocked on the door? The door was already open. That's how the mess was made."

"Not according to Doc. I tend to believe him. Mick said the minute he arrived back to his shop, Doc came over to tell him somebody named Angelica had called, and he was to call her back. Mick said Doc was nervous. When he asked him why, he told him about the mess which he already knew about because you'd told him. He quieted Doc down and tried to send him home. The kid was pretty upset. Said he hadn't finished his work yet so he wouldn't leave. How many of 'em would worry about not having their work done?"

I grunted my agreement. "It wasn't the wind that blew all this stuff around?"

"Nope. The door was closed, and the mess was already here."

"Did Doc shut the door when he left?"

"He said he couldn't remember. It's going to be hard to say if Mr. Barlow told the truth or not. My guess is Doc forgot to shut it. Which means from the time you left for breakfast until Doc arrived, somebody rummaged through your place looking for something. It also means somebody knew you were gone. Did you mention your plans to anyone?"

"No. It was just Mama, Marma Lee, and me. No one came by."

Boomer grunted. "I guess I should come back and see if I can lift any prints. Maybe we'll get lucky."

I stared at the gleaming room. "Save your time. Marma Lee called Lurlene, and she's just finishing up. Any prints are gone."

"I'm sorry, Mary Clare. This entire case has me flummoxed, but I won't give up until I've figured it out. Is there anybody that has it in for you? Maybe someone's mad about you winning all that money. Stranger things have happened. Maybe it's one of those people who asked you for money."

"No, Boomer. That doesn't make sense. What would any of those people gain by any of this? Nothing. It wouldn't get them any closer to me handing them over money. And you know this means Ethel couldn't have murdered Smitty. She's been in custody, and don't even try to tell me these two situations aren't connected."

"I'll agree you have a point. However, she could have an accomplice. I'll question her and see what I can come up with. In the meantime, I'll have Clarence drive by every hour. It'll give him some surveillance experience and maybe give you a little peace of mind. You need to remember that the only reason I'm keeping you in the loop is for your and Lilly's safety."

"Okay."

"Mary Clare, there's just one other thing."

"What is it?" I wasn't sure I could handle any more surprises today.

His voice dropped to a whisper. "This is a little embarrassing."

"Boomer, speak up. I can barely hear you. Hold on." I punched the speaker button, and Boomer's nasal breathing could be heard across the room.

"There. That's better. What is it you want to tell me? Do I need to sit down for this? Are you shutting me down again?"

Taking a deep breath, I tried to calm my tongue. "Boomer, are you shutting me down again?"

"No. It's..." His voice fizzled out.

"I still can't hear you."

"Mary Clare, if I'm going to have Clarence check on you and Lilly, you'll have to have Lilly promise not to hit on him anymore. Clarence said something about your mama coming on to him. Is that true? He's pretty young for her, you know."

The barometric pressure in the room hit bottom.

"Why, that little ingrate!" Mama exploded. I punched the speaker button off.

"Uh oh. She heard that, huh?" Boomer went silent.

"Oh, she heard it all right. You might want to tell Deputy Leonard to stay a safe distance away tonight. Mama's a little upset."

This, of course, was an understatement. Never in a million years would Mama have stepped on Blur's tail. When Blur yelped, Mama immediately reached down and patted Flash's confused face. Blur ran to the kitchen and licked her wound, putting one paw over her eyes when she finished. Mama sputtered like a cappuccino machine.

"What's all that commotion?" Boomer asked.

"I'd better go now, but for the record, Mama tried to fix me up with your deputy, not herself. I'd appreciate it if you could explain that to your deputy while letting him know I'm not interested."

"I should have known it was something like that. It's just that Clarence was so surprised. So much for his power of observation, I guess."

"I wouldn't put him in charge of doing criminal profiles just yet. I really do have to go. This is Mama's third lap around the room. I've got to get to the Snickers stash before she does."

"I sure am sorry about this. I'll speak to Clarence."

"Goodbye, Boomer." I replaced the receiver and vowed to

never use the speaker on the phone again. Alexander Graham Bell had the right idea. One receiver on each end.

"Now, Mama."

"Mary Clare, how can you be so calm? That silly deputy practically accused me of being a floozy. Imagine someone his age thinking a refined woman like myself would throw myself at him. I've half a mind to go over there and give him a tongue lashing. I've never been so humiliated in all my life."

"Mama, you're starting to screech."

Lurlene cleared her throat. "Lilly, I've met Boomer's new deputy, honey. I'm sure he didn't mean anything. He's not what you'd call the sharpest knife in the drawer, if you know what I mean. He probably got all flustered, and his ego took a little trip. I wouldn't worry about it. Everyone in town knows you are the salt of the earth."

Mama smoothed her dress pleats and sniffed. She sat on the edge of the loveseat and immediately had a dog chin posted on each knee. "I guess you're right. I suppose my questions could have been confusing to someone who is obviously dim. Thank you, Lurlene."

The storm had passed. Mama busied herself showing Lurlene and Marma Lee my new duds. I cringed as she lifted the dress from its tissue-resting place. Why hadn't I put my foot down when Mama yanked it off the rack? Its lime-green velvet shouted *please buy me. I need a home.* But it was the front bodice, which, according to Mama, was "adorned" with imported lace and freshwater pearls that had sealed my fate. There was a bow on each shoulder. It looked like a Loretta Lynn castoff. Lurlene was agog. Marma Lee was speechless, and Mama beamed. It wasn't too late. I could still call Mick and postpone the dinner. Or maybe we could arrange to meet in the next state.

"Good gracious." Rennie gasped. I nearly jumped out of my skin. I'd no idea she had come in the back door. Her frown spoke volumes. "Lilly, you aren't going to actually wear that thing, are you?" she demanded.

Mama stood her full five feet. "No. I am not going to wear this gorgeous creation. Mary Clare is. She has an important dinner date with Mr. Mick Walker tomorrow night."

Rennie shook her head. "Unless you're planning to take him to a costume party, I'd change my mind about that outfit, Mary Clare. That thing's been hanging in Annabelle's store for the last four years. Bet you got it for a steal."

"The tag says it's been marked down from eighty-nine dollars and ninety-five cents to ten bucks." Lurlene held the white tag in her hand. "Hey, that is a bargain. If you decide you don't want it, I'd like to buy it off you. 'Course, I'd need to take it up a little, but I could wear it to the ladies auxiliary dance next week. It's dark in there. Nobody will see it."

I grinned like an idiot as I waltzed over to Lurlene and placed the dress back in its box. I shoved it in her arms. "It's a gift. Enjoy."

Rennie gave me a thumbs up and plopped down on the couch. "Lilly, why is your face red? I'm sorry, honey, but that dress isn't Mary Clare. I didn't mean to make you mad, though. Why are you breathing so hard?" Which, of course led to an explanation of Deputy Leonard's faux pas.

"Oh, Lilly. I run into that sort of thing all the time. You just have to blow it off and go on."

"What do you mean you run into this all the time?" demanded Mama.

"Some men are peculiar. They don't think before they act. Of course, a lot of women are the same way, but I think women generally tend to shy away from younger men. I do. I prefer someone who remembers Colonel Sanders and Ronald Reagan when they were alive. Not to say being the same age is the most important component to companion-ship, but I do think it helps." She took a deep breath. What a speech. Why did I get the feeling she was trying to convince herself?

"Sounds like you've given this some thought." Mama reached for some packing tissue gone astray.

"Actually, I've been thinking about it all day. Saige asked me out." Rennie raised both shoulders and shrugged.

"He what?" Marma Lee couldn't have stood faster had she been shot from a cannon.

"Saige called this morning and asked me to dinner. I told him no. He's a nice guy and all, but he's also forty-six. That's ten years difference. He said he wanted to talk about Cora Ann's murder, but I don't think that was it. I mean, I wasn't even here when that happened. I was already in Memphis by then."

"Of course, that must be it." Marma Lee chewed her lip. "He knows you're acquainted with a lot of people around here and could give him the lowdown on everyone. Since he hasn't been here long and doesn't know many older people, you would be a likely candidate. I mean, he couldn't very well ask Ruby, and he knows Aunt Lilly has her hands full right now."

"If it's just information he wanted, he could ask his grandmother." If Lurlene's eyes twinkled any brighter, we'd all need sunglasses.

Marma Lee scowled. "I'll make some iced tea."

"What's up with her?" Rennie's hand flopped in Marma Lee's direction.

"She's after Saige. Didn't you tell her the night of the meeting?" Mama asked me.

"I forgot. Sorry,"

"Open mouth. Insert foot. I better do something." Rennie leaned forward.

I waved her back down. "She'll get over it."

Lurlene announced she was going to the cottage to run a dust rag over everything that didn't move. She sailed out. Marma Lee sailed in. Contentment shone on her face. The tip of one finger poked her lemon wedge into her tea. "You know, I've been helping unpack those books all day. I'll bet Saige tried to call, and I was unavailable."

"Oh, honey. I'm positive that's it," Rennie assured her.

"I'll probably hear from him tonight. Now, Mac, this means I'll have to cut our planning session short." She faced Mama. "Aunt Lilly, can you handle the arrangements without me? I don't dare trust her," she jerked her head in my direction, "to prepare for tomorrow night's event."

"You make it sound like a sports match, Marma Lee," I complained. "I'm not competing for the world's heavyweight belt, you know."

"You could have a couple of months ago, Cousin." She drained her tea glass and handed it to me. "You look good since you've lost weight, though. You may actually have a shot at this guy." Fancy footwork on her part is the only thing that kept her from a total KO.

Lurlene came trotting into the shop a bit later. "I freshened up the beds and cleaned the top of the fridge. How come you've got bracelets and doodads up there? I was afraid to move 'em. I sort of scooted them around to dust."

"Those are for the grand opening," I explained.

"I wanted to order little whistles to hand out to the kids, but Mary Clare said we'd have tooting all over the shop," Mama said.

Lurlene clamped her mouth shut and headed to the door. "Y'all come on over to the diner Saturday. Maybelline's fixin' breakfast on the house. We won a free roof job, and we want to pay it forward. I think that's what Maybelline called it. Ain't that a kick? We need a roof, and God hands us one on a silver platter. That just beats all." With a shrug and a grin, she made her exit. A flash of yellow rubber gloves, and she and her new lime-green duds danced out the door.

"Mama, I'm going to the basement and check on Marma

Lee's alphabetizing." I hurried down the basement steps. I stopped long enough to straighten the cap on an antique doll displayed on the wall. One eye closed in a permanent wink. I winked back.

Running my fingers down the shelves, I processed my cousin's efficiency. She'd done a superb job. I was stupefied and said as much out loud.

"Yeah, I'd be surprised too. She's pretty stupid."

I whirled around. Not eight feet stood between me and the man I almost married. "What in the world are you doing here, Roger? And how did you get in?" I started to put my hands on my hips then thought better of it. Throwing something seemed like a better idea. Like a cast iron toy car.

He nodded toward the basement door. "I've come to talk sense into you, Mary Clare. I'll still have you if you want to get married. You ain't never had a lot of prospects, and I'm willin', so let's just do it, sweetheart. I know you didn't mean it when you said we was done. And I didn't mean it when I called you a cow. I like a woman with a little meat on her bones. But the skinny look is okay too. You look real good. You and me gonna have a good time. Now, I don't have all day, Mary Clare. Let's run to the courthouse, and I'll marry you."

The man's dishwater-blond hair didn't shine nearly as bright as I remembered it. Maybe it was the hair product he had slathered all over it. I knew for a fact he went through six tubes a month and bought them at a tent along the ten-mile-long yard sale route.

I took a closer look. Had he shrunk? What I'd once described as a taut physique just looked wiry and wormy. How could I ever have fallen for him? And to top it all off, the weasel was rude.

I had no prospects. He'd marry me? Who was he kidding? Okay, he'd been right about the cow part, but I'd remedied that problem.

"Listen closely, Roger." I stepped toward him and held tight to the toy in my hand. For a split second, he smiled. He'd always been a bit slow on the uptake. When he finally figured out my intention, he backed up.

"Now, Mary Clare. This makes sense. You know it does. I'm the one for you. You and me—why, with all that money, there ain't nothin' we can't accomplish. What're you planning to do with that iron car in your hand?"

"She's going to clobber you senseless, you scrawny little puff of a man." Usually Mama made more noise coming down the stairs. "Mary Clare?" Mama stood her ground, gripped the handrail, and glared a hole through Roger.

"I've got this, Mama."

"Don't listen to that old hag, Mary Clare. She's nothin' but a nuisance."

That did it. In two strides, I deposited the cast iron car on Roger's foot. It would be incorrect to say I simply dropped it. What I lacked in prospects, I made up for in agility and strength.

It was unfortunate the car fell on the same toes Marma Lee had flattened when she ran over them with her car. It was, however, effective. Scrawny men with injured feet can exit at amazing speeds when motivated. He did, however, manage to topple over three cartons of books, probably to keep me from running after him. Watching him hop around on the same spot I'd hopped around earlier was icing on the cake.

"I'll have you arrested if you ever set foot on this property again, Roger. We. Are. Over. If I so much as see your face near here, I'll tell people the real reason you had to go to the emergency room that last time." My shouting was met with a loud gasp and a slamming door.

"I wanted a go at him, Mary Clare, but he moved too fast." Mama clomped down the stairs and hugged me close.

"What in the world did I ever see in him, Mama?"

"I never knew, honey. Maybe you needed to see the really

bad so you will appreciate the really good when it comes along. You okay? Should we wait about working down here?"

"No. I'm fine." It was time to shake off the bizarre buzzard and get back to business. "Before I was rudely interrupted," I bent to pick up the car, "I was bragging on Marma Lee and what a good job she did with the pricing." I placed the car back on the shelf and patted it for a job well done.

Mama nodded. "Marma Lee has her moments. I've been giving some thought to her idea about vandalism. You know, she may have something. Maybe Smitty was in the wrong place at the wrong time. It's something to think about."

"Who would go to all the trouble of killing him and then stuff him in our casket? I don't know about you, but there's a lot that doesn't add up. I feel like there's some part of the puzzle missing."

"I know what you mean." She cocked her head and listened. "Did you hear that?"

We both froze as footsteps sounded above our heads. Good grief. Was Roger back? Roger had always been a wienie, but one never knew what a moody, mad wienie of a man might do. Roger might be more rogue than I gave him credit for.

I switched off the basement lights and herded Mama toward the door, but it was blocked with toppled books. Instead, we ducked down behind the reading bar. I scrolled down to find the sheriff's number on my phone. The light from the screen shone like a beacon. Between its glow, the glimmer from the twinkle lights, and Superman's phone booth, we might as well have been a main attraction at a carnival. The Man of Steel hid our heads, which were barely above the countertop. We could hear the padding of feet as they descended the stairs. I shoved Mama's head below the bar and tried not to scream when she pulled my hair. She motioned for me to lower my own head and cover my phone.

Having my head exposed was not wise, but I had to know

where our intruder was and what, if any, kind of weapon he had. I looked around for one of my own. Throwing a copy of Moby Dick wouldn't incapacitate anybody for long. I picked up a miniature baseball bat instead. We'd planned to hang it on the wall but had used it instead to prop open a stubborn cabinet door. Mama picked up Moby Dick. Just as well. She was a much better pitcher than me.

The sound of a hard thump was followed by a loud crash.

"Oh, Hallmark!"

"Richard? Is that you?" Mama dropped Moby and raced to the man lying prone at the bottom of the steps. First, she slapped him, then she began what appeared to be mouth-to-mouth resuscitation.

"Mama, are you sure that's Richard? You may be kissing a murderer or worse, Roger."

"Of course, it's Richard. I'd know his voice anywhere. Turn on the light."

By then, the figure sprawled on our floor was coming around and asking for more. Mama might have obliged had it not been for the sight of blood oozing from his head. "What on earth happened to your head?"

Gingerly, he touched his temple and winced. "I hit it on the overhang on the way down. I didn't hear anyone upstairs, so I thought I'd come looking down here. I forgot to duck my head."

Mama patted his hand. "Are you all right?"

"I'm fine, Lilly. Just a bit clumsy. I'm sorry I made such a mess." He eyed the red drops on the carpet. "Let me clean this up."

"Nonsense. Mary Clare can do that. Let me help you up the stairs, and I'll get you a nice cup of tea."

It was entertaining to watch the twosome make their way up the stairs. Resting his hand on Mama's head, Richard steadied himself. It played havoc with Mama's perky new hairdo, but it served her right for pulling my hair. I made for the restroom and turned on the cold water. I drenched a paper towel and scrubbed up Richard's blood. As I finished, I spotted something shiny under the stairwell. Probably something Richard dropped on his skid down the stairs. I reached for the glittering object and froze.

The missing skeleton key.

CHAPTER THIRTEEN

I carried the key upstairs and slipped it into the side pocket of my purse, checking to make sure my key was still in its usual place. It was. Hurriedly, I reached for Mama's purse and found her turtle keeping watch over her copy. Boomer returned it the previous day. This one had to be Smitty's. Someone dropped it. I didn't believe for a minute the culprit was Richard.

Mentally, I tallied up people who had been to the Children's Chamber. The first person that came to mind was Roger. But all he was after was me and my money. Besides, he was too dull witted to plan a proposal, much less a murder.

Then there was Mick Walker. I immediately dismissed him. He'd have no reason to have the key. He'd offered to check the premises after he'd heard Marma Lee and me screaming. He hadn't even known Smitty. Had he? They both had ties to Memphis. Nope. Not Mick. My reverie was interrupted by Mama's excited voice.

"Mary Clare, do you think you'd be all right for a few hours alone?"

I'd forgotten she was on the planet, much less playing Florence

Nightingale. "I'll be fine, Mama. I have a zillion things to keep me busy." Let her assume those things had to do with the shop. In reality, I was overdue some quality online time. I could check statuses, post pics, and chat with a few friends. My tweets were woefully few. The list went on and on. "Are you going somewhere?"

She and Richard scurried into the main room. He rearranged his hair, which had gone askance in the fall, and helped Mama slip into her coat. "Richard is redecorating his kitchen and would like my opinion about a few things." Mama looked at him and beamed. "I'm going to help him with his drawers."

"Excuse me?" I cocked my head and leaned forward, trying to not laugh out loud.

Richard coughed and explained. "I'm thinking of having my cabinet doors and drawers refinished, and I'd like Lilly's ideas. Could you spare her for a while?"

"You two run along and have a wonderful time. I may take Flash and Blur for a little ride then come back and start dinner. Why don't you join us, Richard? I'm fixing Stromboli and salad. Mama could whip up some of her fried chocolate pies."

Richard caved. "Chocolate pie is my favorite. Are you sure it's not too much trouble?"

"No trouble at all." Mama squeezed his arm.

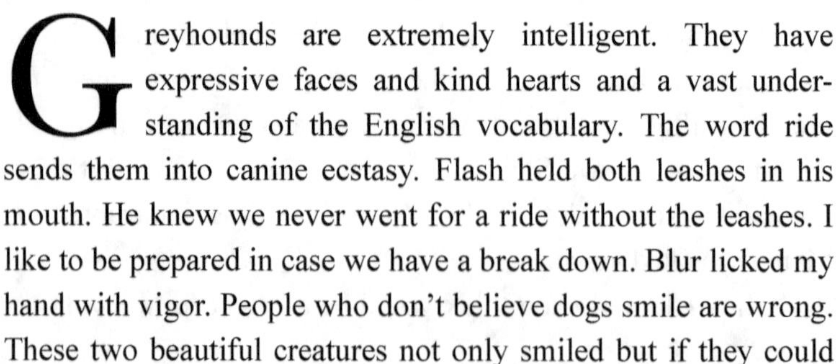

Greyhounds are extremely intelligent. They have expressive faces and kind hearts and a vast understanding of the English vocabulary. The word ride sends them into canine ecstasy. Flash held both leashes in his mouth. He knew we never went for a ride without the leashes. I like to be prepared in case we have a break down. Blur licked my hand with vigor. People who don't believe dogs smile are wrong. These two beautiful creatures not only smiled but if they could open the front door, they would have ushered me through in style.

"I have to grab my coat. You two don't have to worry about that." Still, I grabbed their favorite sheepskin rug and threw it in the back of the vehicle. Within three minutes, they were snuggled together, both chins propped on the back of the seat. "You know we're crazy, don't you? We should be sitting in front of the fire, snoring."

Their rears wagged faster, and their smiles widened. I turned the heat up, put the car in reverse, and switched on my playlist. Glancing at Mick's store, I noted the full parking lot. Then I stomped on the brakes.

Boomer said Doc had been on his way to Pocket Change to tell Mick Angelica called when he discovered the open door. Who was Angelica? No. I would not allow myself to be jealous. It was an overrated emotion. I turned to my two furry companions. "Neither of you knows how fortunate you are to live such uncomplicated lives."

I headed toward Annabelle's Dress Shop. I'd let Mama talk me out of what I wanted. She'd sworn it didn't have enough oomph. I'd had about all the oomph I could stand. Blur yipped in the back. I think she said, "You go, girl."

It took less than five minutes to drive the short tree-lined drive. A few brave leaves clung to the branches. The blustery wind would take care of those by the end of the day. The carriage lights on either side of the front door were lit, and Annabelle stood at her front window. She opened the door as I raced up the steps.

"Good grief, Mac. The weather bureau is calling for a regular blizzard tonight. A blizzard, girl. Can you imagine that in Pocket? This dinner tomorrow night must be pretty important for you to tromp around in this kind of weather." Her pink hair, which had once been strawberry blonde, swung back and forth as she shook her head and winked. "C'mon over here, sweetie. I've got it ready for you."

"You've got what ready for me?" I wondered how she knew I'd return for an outfit for tomorrow night's dinner.

"That darling little sweater you were eyeballing this afternoon. I know you. Your mama is the frilly one. You, on the other hand, have more practical tastes in clothes. I saw the way you lit up when you spotted that coral sweater. It's perfect with your auburn hair. Hope you don't mind, but I matched it with a pair of winter white pants and a scarf. Honey, knock him for a loop."

"Annabelle, it's only dinner. I don't want him getting the wrong idea. We're business neighbors, and he helped Marma Lee and Mama and me out the other night. I'm repaying a favor."

"Well, this outfit will be attractive and versatile. You can wear it to the church bazaar next week. That old basement is always drafty. This will keep you warm. The sweater is cashmere, you know."

As I ran my hand over the sweater, its softness sang. The price tag shrieked. My thrifty nature did a back flip. Annabelle noticed my astonished look.

"Cashmere isn't cheap. You've earned it. Actually, it's cheaper than what you'd pay in Jonesboro. There were only two in this shipment, and I nabbed the other one. Go on, try it on."

"I know it will fit, and I do love it. I'm not used to being extravagant." I sneaked a peek at the tag on the slacks and scarf. They, at least, were more reasonable. I knew Annabelle was honest. "I'll get my purse. I left it in the car."

"I'll send you a bill. You need to get on home. The snow's already accumulated since you came in. I'm glad my little apartment's in the back of the store. I don't like to drive in this weather."

I thanked Annabelle and headed for the door. Before I made it three steps, I spotted the most absurd bra and panty set ever designed. I wasn't sure whether to laugh or jerk it off the hanger and hide it. The thing came complete with feathers, a fishing net, and a pamphlet.

"I know what you're thinking, Mac. Not my usual stock. A customer ordered it for her anniversary and then chickened out. The company has gone bankrupt and won't accept it, so I'm stuck." She raised her hands in a helpless gesture.

"Mind if I take a picture of it and send to Marma Lee as a joke? She's already planning her next honeymoon."

"Be my guest. Send it to anyone else you think might snatch it up. I'll give them a great price on it."

Remembering how aggravated Marma Lee'd been over the duplication of outfits she and Mama had worn to the writers' meeting, I chuckled as I snapped the picture and added a message. "One of a kind. Would this fit into your plans?"

With a wave and a grin, I hurried out the door, trying to hide my excitement over the sweater I'd purchased, and buying it several sizes smaller than last season was almost as good as winning the Publisher's Clearing House. Almost.

I'd left the car running so the dogs wouldn't get cold. One of them accidentally bumped the horn, causing my head to jerk upward. Smoke came from the direction of the old dump. I shook my head in disbelief. Only a moron would try to burn trash in this weather.

A quick stop at Mutt's Grocery to pick up butter and the rest of the ingredients for my homemade Stromboli was a must. Mrs. Mutt swept the entry way and poured salt in front of the door to melt the icy patches. Both Mutts were thrilled beyond words.

"Mac, look at those clouds." Mrs. Mutt all but jumped up and down. "I'll bet it snows all night." Her rosy cheeks were snow flecked, and I caught her sticking her tongue out to catch flakes. The woman was a ringer for Mrs. Claus. I scrambled into the store.

"You need extra marshmallows?" Mr. Mutt asked from behind the old counter. "There's nothing like roasting marshmallows when it's snowing. The missus and I are taking three bags home. We could all be snowbound by morning." He rubbed his hands together.

I took in the overcast sky outside the old plate glass window. "You may be right. Better throw in a bag." I didn't mention I had gas logs and couldn't roast them. That was okay. We could always use them in hot chocolate. He helped me carry my bags and was greeted by wet nuzzles from Flash and Blur. As I pulled out of the parking lot, I noticed a snow angel on the ground. I caught Mrs. Mutt disappearing around the side of the building, brushing snow from the back of her coat. I loved my town.

Within minutes I pulled around to the cottage and parked next to Richard's gray Lexus. The dogs and I paraded in the front door. Richard jumped up to help me with my packages.

"I was a bit worried about you. The weatherman is calling for heavy snow tonight." He studied the clouds. "Perhaps I should start home."

"Nonsense. I've already started the pies." Mama stood in the kitchen, a stern expression on her face. "If you stay, you can take the rest home with you. It's a heavenly concoction." Her voice faded away as sirens approached. "Now what do you suppose that could be?"

We hurried to the window. The sirens faded, and we all heaved a sigh of relief when they didn't stop at our place.

"Mama, why don't you call Marma Lee and make sure she's home?" I took the opportunity to race up the stairs and stash my new outfit. The dogs kept Richard occupied.

Mama returned as I sauntered back down the stairs. "She's home, honey, but she's all sulky."

"Why? She loves snow. We've only had three flakes in the last five years. I thought she'd be ecstatic."

"She's happy about the snow." Mama heaved a sigh. "Saige didn't call her."

"Oh."

Richard wore a confused expression, and I began explaining. "I don't believe Saige is interested in your cousin. After the meeting last night, Saige said he was reassessing his decision and may stay only a short time."

"Did Marma Lee hear him?" Mama pulled on her oven mitts.

"I don't think so." Richard pitched the dogs' bouncing balls toward the kitchen. "No one else was around. He seemed uneasy. I suppose the turn of events surprised him."

Richard's tact impressed the phooey out of me. I wasn't sure if he referred to Ruby's request or Marma Lee's advances.

"A man like Saige is looking for adventure. For him, that means digging into unsolved crimes, which requires a great deal of traveling. That would never work for me. I enjoy my present surroundings." Richard glanced in Mama's direction.

Mama glowed. Which was a good thing, because the electricity chose that moment to go out. The only light in the room came from the flicker of the gas logs. Both dogs stopped in mid-romp, balls forgotten. They looked at me as if I were responsible. I shrugged.

The next half hour we hunted up leftover candles from Marma Lee's props. Positioning them around the room created a cozy atmosphere. The gas fireplace kept the room warm, and the glances between Mama and Richard kept things interesting.

I peeked outside to see if the rest of the neighborhood had electricity. Black as pitch. It was time to deliver the bad news.

"I'm sorry to bring this up, gang, but what should we do about tonight's dinner. The oven has an electric igniter, and since the electricity is kaput, it won't light. We have salad stuff."

"I know just the thing," Mama chirped. "Mary Clare, do you remember what you and I used to fix when you were little, and it snowed?"

"Yes, I do. What a great idea, Mama." I rushed to the kitchen to help her open cans of tomato soup and ready the skillet for grilled cheese sandwiches. We added cream to the soup, sprinkled grated parmesan on top and poured fresh milk into large glasses. Within fifteen minutes dinner sat in front of us. Thank goodness for gas stovetops.

We bellied up to the bar and marveled at the wonder of snow, the blessing of comfort food, and the snoring ability of dogs. Mama fixed each dog a miniature grilled sandwich and sprinkled it with their kibble.

Richard and I washed the dishes while Mama traipsed off in search of cards, a few board games, and a radio with batteries. "Your mother is a remarkable woman."

"She's amazing, Richard."

"Lilly Casteel is the kindest woman I've ever known. I never married, you know. Came awfully close to it once, but she died."

"I'm sorry. May I ask what happened?"

"I haven't talked about it in so long, but I suppose it's time." He settled in, collected his thoughts, and arranged his words. "I was twenty years old and fell in love with a girl I'd known all my life. We were best friends regardless of our different stations in life. You see, my family didn't have any money. Her parents came from a long line of comfort. When our relationship started changing, they let me know right away I wasn't acceptable husband material. She was everything to me."

I'd never seen this side of Richard. He'd always been so reserved. I tried to imagine a younger version of this gentle man. It wasn't hard. He must have been quite handsome, but something etched a permanent worry line on his forehead.

"I tried to explain to her parents how much I cared about her, but they wanted someone better for their only daughter. I'd started working two jobs to save enough money to buy her a ring. That's how I got into the restaurant business." He stopped and smiled at a long-ago memory. "I began as a dishwasher and worked my way up. I was proud of my accomplishments, but to them I was an embarrassment. They didn't want their daughter associating with someone like me, so they devised a plan. Being expert sailors, they decided an extended cruise would bring her to her senses, I guess. The day they left, she left a note for me at the restaurant where I worked. Their yacht capsized a week later during a storm. I didn't even get to tell her goodbye." He straightened a bit and clasped his hands between his knees. "I never married, and I've never really been attracted to anyone else…until now. God led me here. Does that sound crazy?"

I thought of Mick Walker and the bird feeder sitting out front. "Certainly not. You're a wise man for following where He leads you. I'm sorry you were treated badly. You didn't deserve that. Her parents were foolish."

"Foolish or not, I learned a lesson. She listened to her parents. She was of legal age and could have done as she pleased. She needed them more than she loved me." He shrugged. "It's true what they say about blood being thicker than water. I couldn't stand to go through that again."

It took me a few seconds to grasp what he said. "I'd never stand in your way. Mama is a wonderful woman who's experienced a lot of grief herself. The two of you might find you have a great deal in common. If you don't mind my asking, how did you end up in Pocket?"

Richard hesitated then continued to wipe the counter down with his damp cloth. "I loved everything about the restaurant business. The only thing that kept me sane after her death was work. Every waking hour was spent learning the business. When my boss decided to retire, I paid him what I could and financed the rest. I stayed until I decided I had enough of city life. I wanted something simpler."

"I admire you for that. Seems like a lot of people spend a lot of time doing things they don't really want to do and call it success." I sat back and crossed my arms.

"Exactly. I'm weary of that facet of life. Writing's always been a secret desire, and I began sending a few poems out to some of the greeting card companies. Pretty soon, I was successful enough to warrant an agent. One day, I received a personal note from him suggesting I spend a few days in the South. The card companies were thinking of launching an entire line geared for Southerners.

"I caught a flight to Memphis and began exploring. I found Jonesboro on the map, headed in that direction, and kept going. The sign for Pocket caught my eye. The minute I drove into town, I knew. I happened onto Mutt's Grocery. He was arguing politics with a bunch of men. I joined right in, and no one once asked who I was or what I was doing there.

"Before I left, I asked Mutt where I could find a realtor. The next day I put a down payment on the house I live in." He chuckled. "Ralph tried to unload that old Weatherly place on me. I'm not surprised it hasn't sold yet. He tried to spruce it up with paint and new shutters, but it's a wreck. Anyway, I've never regretted my move. Although, I do sometimes miss the restaurant business."

"I'm glad you're here, Richard. God's a good navigator."

He nodded. "That He is."

Mama clambored down the stairs with a mini flashlight in her mouth, the dogs on her heels, and a box full of entertainment in her hands. Flash kept nudging Blur, who was too excited to mind. How the three descended the stairs without breaking bones, I'll never know.

"Mary Clare, give me a hand, will you?" Mama peered over boxes. "You'll never guess what I found."

I hurried to help her. "Isn't this my old Monopoly game?"

"Yes. I also found a box of cards, your daddy's old checkers, and a diary. I didn't know you still had a crush on Dickie Richardson in the eighth grade. What did you ever do with all those marbles he won for you?"

"Now I know why it took you so long up there, Mama. You're not supposed to read other people's diaries, you know."

"I couldn't resist." She plopped the boxes on the kitchen

counter and pulled the radio out of the box. "We can take the batteries out of this flashlight and put them in the radio."

"Is that an old Rubik's Cube?" Richard asked. Mama and I glanced at each other. He took the cube to the couch and began working on it in earnest.

"Isn't he the most remarkable man?" she whispered.

"You've no idea," I whispered back.

"Huh?"

"Tell you later."

"Okay." She shrugged. Within minutes, the batteries were switched to the radio, and Mama tuned in the local station.

"Six-to-eight-inch accumulation expected tonight." The announcer sounded downright gleeful. "Travel advisory for all counties in our listening area."

Richard stopped fiddling with the cube. Mama gnawed on her thumbnail.

"I suppose I should go." With reluctance, Richard stood.

Mama's hands were closing in for a good wringing. "Richard, I don't think it's safe to be driving. You could land in a ditch."

"I'll be fine. The snow isn't packed yet. It's still powdery." The little pings on the windows at that moment told us it was no longer snowing powder but pelting ice.

"You are not driving on ice. You can take my room, and I'll sleep with Mary Clare. Besides, you haven't even tasted my chocolate pies yet."

Richard appeared to blush, but it was hard to tell in the darkened surroundings. He caved, admitting he had never had fried pies.

"It's settled then." Mama rubbed her hands together. An action she'd no doubt picked up from Marma Lee. "You two set up the Monopoly board, and I'll get dessert." She scurried to the kitchen, humming "Let It Snow."

Richard set up the board game as I cleared off the coffee

table. Mama brought in an entire plate and handed out plates and napkins and plopped a dab of whipped cream atop each and tucked paper napkins under our chins.

"Now!" She rubbed her hands together. "Let the games begin."

We settled cross-legged on the floor. Time zipped by with the candles flickering on the end table we'd pulled up. I was just getting my little car out of jail without collecting two hundred dollars when we noticed blue lights in front of the cottage.

"It's nearly midnight." Richard glanced at his watch and frowned.

I jumped up from my place on the floor with Mama and Richard close behind. Mama nodded her head with pride at Richard's agility. She probably couldn't wait to tell Marma Lee he had no problem hopping up from the floor.

I opened the door as Boomer heaved himself out of his car. At least five new inches of snow covered the ground. Sleet glazed the top. It glistened under his lights. He stood gaping at the three of us. Fatigue filled his eyes.

"Boomer, what in the world are you doing?" Mama scolded. "Get in here before you freeze to the ground."

Boomer trudged to the front door, stomped his feet on the rug, and dumped the ice from his hat.

"Mary Clare, why don't you fix some cocoa on the stove? Boomer looks like he could use something hot." Mama looked at Boomer like she might a wet kitten.

"That would be wonderful." Boomer shucked off his jacket.

"You're soaked!" Mama exclaimed. "We have to get you out of these wet clothes right now. You'll catch your death."

"I'm fine. I drove a refrigerated truck for fifteen years. I'm used to being cold."

"Being cold and being soaked and cold are two different things. Mary Clare go upstairs and get a quilt. I'll get the duct tape and start the cocoa." Mama herded the lawman inside.

Boomer didn't even raise an eyebrow. The guy had to be exhausted. Even Richard acted as though duct tape and cocoa naturally went together. If his Lilly suggested it, it must be a wonderful idea. I, on the other hand, knew what Mama had in mind.

"Are you sure about this?" I asked on my way upstairs.

"Of course, dear." She waved her hand. "I used to do it to your father all the time when he'd come in from shoveling the snow. He'd always get wet from head to toe. Of course, I won't be able to do it for Boomer. We'll let Richard help him."

"If you're sure."

"I'm sure. Get a clean sheet from wherever you have them packed, and get the Vicks salve from the medicine cabinet. You do have some, don't you?"

"Of course. You said it's a mortal sin to be without that stuff."

"I'll get the tape and send it up with Boomer and Richard." She whisked off to the kitchen, and I trotted up the stairs. I could hear Boomer questioning Mama about what she intended to do with the duct tape.

A few minutes later, our entire little group moved upstairs with Mama in charge. The two men stood gawking at one another doubtfully, neither wanting to insult Mama by questioning the suggestion Boomer rub Vicks salve all over his chest then allow Richard to tape a flannel sheet around him.

Boomer finally asserted himself. "Lilly, I am not driving home in a flannel sheet."

"You aren't driving anywhere. Thanks to Thelma, your house is all electric, which means you have no heat, and you can call your dispatcher from here and tell him your location. You can also inform him there's no need for that dippy deputy of yours to come patrolling the premises. Richard is staying also. The two of you can sleep together."

Four eyebrows rose simultaneously.

"I'll take the couch," Richard offered.

"Lilly, we have to talk. I…"

"We'll talk once Richard has wrapped you. Now go in the bedroom and rub your chest down. I'll know if you haven't. I have a sensitive nose." Mama tilted it upward for inspection.

"It's true," I agreed.

"Once Richard gets the flannel sheet taped on you, you can wrap up in this." She handed him one of my quilts. "Now Richard, don't tape him too tightly. Just make it snug enough that it stays in place."

Boomer resigned himself to the task of greasing his chest. Richard followed him into the bedroom, and one of them shut the door a bit harder than necessary. Flash barked.

We had just put the hot chocolate on the table with the rest of the pies when Boomer and Richard came into the room. There's nothing quite as astounding as seeing a six-foot-four man clad in a floral quilt. Mama's frown reminded me to close my mouth.

"That's rude, dear," she chided.

Boomer squared his shoulders and called his deputy. We could hear snatches of his conversation. Clarence. Surveillance. Casteel's. Morning.

"I told Clarence I'd take care of surveillance tonight, and I'd see him in the morning. The dispatcher will call my cell if he needs me."

I shoved Mutt's bag of marshmallows in his direction. He dropped a couple in the steaming mug, sighed, and finally relaxed. "No one makes hot chocolate like you, Lilly."

We sat in comfortable silence for a while, sipping and finishing off Mama's calorie-laden concoctions. Then Boomer livened things up. "Smitty Small's house was torched this evening."

Granted it was now past one o'clock and my hearing tends to get a little fuzzy after midnight, but there was no mistaking Boomer's words.

"Are you sure it was arson?" Richard's brows knit together.

"Yep. We found some gas-soaked rags somebody dropped on the ground. Some people on the way to the dump noticed the fire and called it in. The place was drenched. I called the fire chief. Didn't take him long to determine arson."

I remembered seeing the smoke as I left the dress shop. "Whoever did this must be trying to hide something. This will help Ethel. She's been in jail the whole time."

Boomer shook his head. "I told you, Ethel could have an accomplice, and besides, Ethel was released this afternoon. Her attorney said we didn't have enough to hold her. I've been all over this town looking for her. Even her lawyer doesn't know where she is. Ethel Glacier is nowhere to be found."

CHAPTER FOURTEEN

No one rose in a good mood the following morning. Richard had a crick in his neck from sleeping on the couch. His duct tape job proved to be inadequate when Boomer bellowed from the bathroom that half of his chest hair was now stuck to exposed tape. Mama hadn't sipped coffee. I hadn't chugged iced tea. We weren't properly prepared for cricks and bellowing.

"Mama, unless a miracle happens, there's no way we're going to open Saturday. I've already advertised all over the state. What if people drive from way off? They'll be furious and never come back."

"People aren't going to drive if the roads are bad. Be sensible."

"I want everything to be perfect. So far, nothing has gone right. On top of all that, I can't find my to-do list. Lurlene may have tossed it when she cleaned." I sighed. "At least the electricity is back."

"All things work out for the best. Trust in the Lord, and don't fret. Besides, if Boomer's chest hair really did get yanked out, the grand opening will be our least worry. He may arrest me for brutal assault. The duct tape was my idea, you know. I don't understand it. It always worked so well on your father. And with you and me."

"We don't have chest hair." I pulled on my warmest turtleneck and sweatshirt. "Is that makeup you're putting on?"

"I always wear makeup. You know that."

"Not at five thirty in the morning, you don't."

"We don't always have gentlemen in attendance at five thirty in the morning. Besides, it will save me time later."

"I'm going downstairs to take Richard something to rub on his neck." I plodded down the steps. The sight that met me nearly sent me scuttling back up the stairs. Poor Richard stood in the middle of the room with what appeared to be a small, dead ground hog clutched in his hand. Upon closer inspection, I decided it was his toupee. Beneath it, on the floor, lay chewed-up ringlets. I began to get the picture.

"Mary Clare, what in the world am I going to do?" Richard whispered anxiously. "I can't let your mother see me like this."

I stood back and gave Richard's nearly hairless head the once-over. "I like the look." And, I really did. I glanced at Flash who hid in the corner of the room, fake hair hanging out of his mouth. "To think I bragged on you for not being a chewer."

Boomer came bounding down the stairs in his wrinkled, but dry, uniform and stopped abruptly when he spotted Richard. "Well, I'm real glad to see I'm not the only one who lost hair during this little sleepover." He didn't smile, but his grunts were friendlier after that.

Mama came down next. The only thing missing was a tiara. Her attire made both men stop and whistle. Richard temporarily forgot about his handful of hair. Boomer stopped rubbing his chest.

Mama was a knockout, which shouldn't be allowed that early in the morning. She wore a new silky caftan sashed at the waist. Her tiny feet were slipped into gold house shoes, and her hair was perfect. I caught a whiff of Wind Song as she glided past me. Her signature scent.

"Why, Richard, you look dashing this morning," she cooed. "I'm so glad you've decided against that old toupee. You have a perfectly shaped head. It's a shame to hide it under that mop."

He grinned like a drunk.

She turned toward Boomer. "Are you all right? I'm sorry about your chest, but at least you aren't sick with a cold this morning, are you?"

"It'll grow back." He groused and rubbed his chest.

Mama beamed. "I'll get the coffee started. I'll make it strong. The kind that'll put hair on your chest, Boomer."

Mama managed to smooth the ruffled feathers and salvage the morning. Both men sat at the kitchen table and stared at her. If she wasn't careful, Richard might not be the only one seeking her attention.

Within a few minutes, smells of bacon filled the cozy kitchen. Flash and Blur pranced in from the living room and settled themselves beside Richard. Surely they weren't asking for seconds.

"Mary Clare, do you have any idea where Ethel would have gone?" Boomer asked.

"No. I'm sorry. Does she have any family in this area?"

"None she told us about. This looks really bad for her, you know. It makes me more certain she's guilty."

"Not me." Mama stood firm, but when she turned from the counter both men swooned. Evidently, the sight of a woman whipping up a batch of scrambled eggs was too much for them. It had to be the outfit. They didn't react that way to me shoving the biscuits in the oven.

"Marma Lee's theory has credence." Mama rinsed her hands and patted them dry. "I believe Smitty was in the wrong place at the wrong time. He found himself either outnumbered or outweighed and couldn't defend himself. I also believe those same people decided to break into his house, get anything valuable, then burn the house to get rid of any evidence." She poured her eggs into the skillet with a flourish. I could tell from the tilt of her head and the gleam in her eye something perked in Lilly Casteel's head and wondered if she was contemplating a plot line for this new book project. This little scenario would work nicely into a manuscript.

"They didn't take anything from the shop," Boomer insisted. "It's filled with valuables. I can't see Smitty owning anything with any resell value. Besides, if someone snuck into the shop the night Marma Lee came in…"

"There was someone. The basement loading dock door was left wide open. Whoever was in the Children's Chamber got scared and left from that door." Mama jabbed her whisk into the air.

"Same way they could have left when Barlow heard someone." Boomer nodded.

"Barlow didn't hear anyone but himself. He also dropped the other skeleton key while he was down there." I tidied my hands on the dish towel and tossed it on the counter.

Six eyes turned to stare at me, ten if you count Flash and Blur's. "It's true." Smugness isn't something I'm proud of. Sometimes it just jumps out. "I found the key yesterday after Richard fell down the stairs. While Mama took care of him upstairs, I cleaned up the mess."

Richard cringed.

"Oh, don't worry. It was no trouble at all." I patted his hand. "Anyway, that's when I found the key. It was under the stairwell, back by one of the beanbag chairs. I believe Barlow dropped it the day we caught him nosing around."

"I leave you people alone for a few hours, and this is what happens. When exactly were you planning to tell me about the key?"

"Well, things have been busy." He was right. I should have told him sooner.

"Where is it now, may I ask?" Boomer folded his arms, and the furrow in his brow could give me nightmares for weeks.

"It's in my purse." I scurried to locate the key and dropped it into Boomer's outstretched hand.

"I guess you know the prints have been compromised. Lilly, you got a plastic bag around?"

"Sorry," I muttered. "I didn't think about that."

Mama presented him with a bag and me with a withering look. "Why didn't I know about this?"

"We were all excited about the snow. I forgot to mention it. Boomer has the key now, and whoever used it to get in is now out of luck. I personally think it was Barlow."

"Well, I don't," Boomer stated. "I know the guy looks seedy, but he had no motive to kill Smitty. He's just an accountant." He stood. "You're right about one thing, without the key whoever's been gaining entry will have a harder time getting in. I need to call Clarence. I'll be right back."

"Speaking of Clarence," Mama said from the stove. "He has the intelligence of a carrot."

Richard looked confused but offered no comment other than, "Do you have any jelly, Mary Clare?"

Boomer turned back. "Don't worry. Clarence is still a newbie and a little anxious, but he has the making of a good lawman."

By seven o'clock both men took their leave. Boomer went home to change and report for duty. Richard left with the promise of returning to help in the shop. Mama was ecstatic.

"Mama, don't you think it's odd that Smitty's house burned? The timing's a bit suspicious."

"That house burned down for a reason."

I smoothed the damp towel on the counter. "It almost seems the killer wanted to get rid of something, doesn't it? What was out there? What did Smitty have that someone else would want to destroy?"

"From what Boomer said, the entire house and all the contents are gone. He'll figure it out. He's an intelligent man. He's nothing like his deputy." She sniffed and poofed her hair.

"I feel so restless. If the weather would break, we could get ready for the open house." I glanced out the front window. "Look!" My well-intended alert came out as a shrill shriek.

"What is it? Please tell me it's not another body. I can't do any more bodies." The greyhounds were immediately on either side of Lilly, waiting to soften the blow if she chose to faint.

"Look out the window, Mama. The sun is shining. Where's my phone? I'll check the weather forecast."

An impatient pair of dogs and an overactive mother danced around while I tapped the weather app. Today's forecast called for temperatures in the forties with sunshine. The big thaw was on. Already we could hear plinking sounds of melted snow pelting the ground. Soon the roof would be clear.

"Your daddy always said if you don't like the weather in Arkansas, stick around and it will change the next day. I guess he was right."

"You know this means the grand opening is back on, Mama. I'm going to straighten the upstairs and head over to the nursery to see if they have any pumpkins and mums that aren't frozen. Hopefully, Uncle Ardmore will be there, and I can check on him. You want to come along?"

"No, you go ahead, but give Ardmore a hug for me. I'll wait for Richard. Have you ever met anyone more sincere?"

"Richard is a special man." I proceeded to share his story.

"I had no idea he'd suffered such unhappiness. It must have been painful all these years. When your daddy died, I was devastated, but at least we had a chance to experience love and a family. I had you to think of, and that helped me get through his death, but poor Richard. And to think he cared about how you'd feel. He is a wonderful man, isn't he?"

"Yes, he is, Mama. He's also vulnerable. I'm not trying to tell you what to do, and I'm certainly no expert in matters of the heart." I cleared my throat, "But I think you should take this slowly. Richard's still new here. If you start a relationship and it ends, he'll have no one to turn to. He's made no close friends yet."

"You're perceptive, Mary Clare. I have to admit, I'm terribly attracted to Richard. He certainly does jiggle my Jello. I turn to mush every time I'm around the man. You know, I haven't felt attracted to anyone like this since your daddy, but I'm not sure I'm ready for anything as serious as what your daddy and I had. I may never experience that kind of love again. I'll need to be completely honest with Richard. I couldn't bear to hurt him."

"You'll do the right thing, Mama. You always do. Pray about it. You have my blessing, for what it's worth."

Within the hour, I had a load of clothes washing and had stashed the broom in the closet. I grabbed my coat and slipped my feet into the boots by the door. Marma Lee pulled up as I unlocked my car door. I threw a small sack in the back.

"Hey, where are you going?" she called. She slipped as she hurried to the car. "Did you know Smitty's house burned last night?"

"Yes. Boomer came by to tell us." I omitted the rest of the story. If Marma Lee got wind of Boomer's duct tape escapade, it would be all over town. "I'm going to get some pumpkins and hay. You can ride along if you'll behave."

Jumping in, she buckled her seat belt. "You know, Cousin, we have a nut running around town."

"Isn't that the pot calling the kettle black?"

"What do you mean?" Her voice held enough starch to stand a shirt on its end.

"Boomer thinks Ethel burned Smitty's house." I enjoyed Marma Lee's flabbergasted look.

"I thought Ethel was in jail."

"Not as of yesterday afternoon. Her lawyer said they didn't have enough to hold her, so they let her go. Then she disappeared. Boomer can't find her. Her lawyer doesn't even know where she is. It has Boomer quite baffled."

"A baffled Boomer. Now that's something you don't see every day. Of course, he doesn't have many murders to solve around here. His duties usually don't get more interesting than organizing funeral processions." She flipped the passenger side mirror down, fluffed her hair, pinched her cheeks, and flipped the mirror back in place. "It's not like Pocket is a hub of crime."

"It is right now, and we're included in it. At least the shop's not closed down. The grand opening is back on. That's why I'm headed to the nursery."

I pulled in. Snow covered many of the bedding plants displayed by the front gate. Hay sat forlornly by the entrance, waiting to be hauled home for someone's fall decoration. I hopped out and hurried inside with Marma Lee bringing up the rear.

"Do you need me to help Saturday?"

I knew she only offered out of duty, but I jumped on it. "I really would appreciate it if you're sure you don't mind. I'm not certain what to expect. I've advertised in every major newspaper in Arkansas, Tennessee, and Missouri, but with the weather being so unpredictable, I don't know if we'll have two or two hundred."

"I'll help you, Cousin. I refuse to wait by the phone for Saige to call. Besides, he has my cell." She polished her nails and stuck out her left hand. Was she getting it ready for a ring? The girl certainly possessed a healthy dose of confidence.

We ambled up the steppingstone path, or at least what we

could see of it through the slush. "When is that new guy getting into town?"

"What new guy?" I was already eyeing an eight-foot scarecrow.

"The one who's supposed to motivate the town."

"Sam Dawson? He won't get here for another month. Why?"

Marma Lee shrugged. Uh oh. Looked like my cousin was reassessing her possibilities. I did not have time to think about this right now.

"Mac." I glanced up in time to receive a bear hug from the owner. "I haven't seen you since you won all that money. You look good. Money agrees with you." She laughed and patted me on the shoulder.

I'd known Pansy since I was little. She still offered me licorice every time I visited the nursery.

She turned to Marma Lee. "How are you, dear?"

"I'm good, Pansy, but Mac is working me too hard. She said I had to haul hay today. How's your son?"

"Junior's fine. He's married, you know." She stared pointedly at Marma Lee who ignored the hint.

"Is his wife nice?" I asked.

"I guess so." Pansy shrugged. "She doesn't drink iced tea, and," she lowered her voice, "she doesn't have a clue how to make country gravy. My poor son has to sneak over here to get his gravy."

Marma Lee and I made appropriate sympathy noises. Truth be told, her poor little son could afford to lay off the gravy for a while. But that was neither here nor there.

I was on a pumpkin and mum mission. The selection was amazing. Pumpkins of all sizes were neatly grouped together.

"How did you know to bring them in?" I asked.

"When you've been in business as long as I have, you learn a few things. I knew it would come a humdinger of a snow last night. Ardmore and my boy stacked them yesterday morning.

We've sold hundreds, but we still have a good selection left. You need a couple?"

"I need a couple dozen. I also need some corn stalks and hay if you have any left. We're going ahead with our grand opening Saturday. I want to put the pumpkins all through the shop. As a matter of fact, I probably need three dozen pumpkins rather than two. Could Uncle Ardmore and your Junior deliver them this afternoon? If they could, it would be great. Do you have any mums left?" I eyed the gorgeous ficus tree to my left.

"Honey, I've got the prettiest mums you've ever seen. I even have purple ones. You want to see them? They're in house number seven. Marma Lee, what are you doing, honey?"

"Nothing." Marma Lee edged nearer to me. "I thought I saw something move over there in the corner. I was trying to see what it was."

"Probably a snake," Pansy answered calmly. "We get that all the time after it first turns cold. People don't think about it, but sometimes it turns cold so suddenly it catches the poor little snakes by surprise. They start looking for a warm place to hole up. I'll have my son take a look before he starts loading up your order to make sure there aren't any snuggled in your plants or hay. C'mon, girls. Let's pick out some pretty mums."

I stared in amazement as Pansy marched through the back door, leaving the snake to slither to its heart's content. She certainly was casual about her unorthodox critters. I was glad her son would be delivering the hay, cornstalks, mums, and pumpkins. After the week I'd had, I wasn't sure I could deal with a runaway snake in the back of my vehicle and whispered as much to Marma Lee.

"They won't stay in a place where there's a lot of activity," she said with confidence. "Their tongues are sensitive to vibrations. They prefer a quieter environment. There's a lot of vibration in this little hut." She nodded at the plump owner. "Besides, you've already dealt with one snake this week."

"You mean Barlow?"

"Yep. I don't think the guy killed Smitty, but I do think he has a little reptile in him."

I stopped dead at the entrance of number seven and stood staring at the sea of multi-colored plants."I've never seen anything so beautiful. These are magnificent."

"We take real good care of them. They're easy to plant when you're finished with them as decoration. They'll come back every year."

"I want five of each color," I exclaimed. "Would you mind picking them out for me? If you like, I'll advertise your business during open house so everyone will know they came from your nursery. Do you have any cards?"

"Sure do. I'll get them. I appreciate the plug. I can always use the business." She plodded back to the hut. She handed me two licorice sticks with my change then waved goodbye from the front door and told us to expect the delivery about two o'clock. According to my watch, I still had plenty of time for a slight detour.

"Are you in a hurry?" I asked Marma Lee, handing her a licorice stick.

"Not really, but won't Aunt Lilly need us?"

"Nope. She called in reinforcements. If I know her, she's already commandeered Richard to help with the cider and the sweets."

"So where are we going? You better make it snappy. I have to tinkle."

"We're going to the dump. I have something to throw away."

"Isn't Smitty's place out that way?" Marma Lee gazed at her reflection in the mirror again.

"Uh huh."

CHAPTER FIFTEEN

Chewing on my candy, I headed in the direction of the town dump. When we reached the site, I lifted the small bag from the back and tossed it into a dumpster. It held the remains of Richard's toupee. Marma Lee appeared puzzled but didn't ask. I didn't offer. I intended to sneak a peek at what remained of Smitty's house. Instead, I found myself waving to Boomer, who was headed back toward town. It didn't take a genius to put two and two together.

"What do you suppose Boomer is doing out here?" Marma Lee mused.

I rolled my eyes and thanked God I received the common sense that obviously had been denied my cousin. Turning the Enclave around, I headed back toward town.

"Would you look at that?" Marma Lee exclaimed as we passed a yard filled with a flock of plastic flamingos. "Did you know," she said, shaking her licorice, "there are more plastic flamingos in the United States than real ones?"

"No, Marma Lee. How could I have lived all these years without knowing that riveting piece of news?"

"You're being sarcastic. I hope that licorice goes straight to your hips."

I studied the last three inches longingly then tossed it out the window. Honestly, sometimes my cousin could be the biggest oaf.

The oaf spoke. "Why is Boomer turning in at your shop?"

I didn't answer but concentrated on parking between Boomer and a hearse. On any other day, this would have seemed odd. Now, it was just business as usual.

Marma Lee hopped out and ran inside. Pity the fool who stood between her and indoor plumbing.

I stared at Boomer sitting in his car. He gave the impression of being a rapper without rhythm. His neck jerked from one side of the car to the other, bobbing up and down. He appeared to be watching Mama and Richard through the bay window. They were supervising the arrival of the casket. The men who were moving it seemed anxious to get the job finished and skedaddle. I walked inside with Boomer right behind me.

"Put it here for now." Mama pointed to the display window.

Reverently, they parked it on its stand and turned to leave. "Hold it right there."

The four men stopped in mid-step. We all watched as she went to the casket and bravely raised the lid. Tucked inside was Bo. After a thorough examination of the skeleton and every inch of the casket, she dismissed the men. I'd never heard a hearse squeal tires before.

"Does everything seem to be in order, Mama?"

She nodded and began dusting it with the skirt of her apron. The one I'd made for her in home economics class. The lopsided bib held a multitude of stains and one of the strings that tied in the back was way longer than the other. After seventeen years of use, its rattiness bordered on tattered, but it was her favorite go-to apron.

Mama noticed Boomer. "Why, hello. Is there something you need?"

I'm pretty sure I was the only one who heard Richard mutter "duct tape." I could seriously get used to having this guy around.

"I'm just coming to check on the casket. It looks fine." Boomer never cast a glance in its direction. "Have you looked it over, Lilly? I want to make sure it isn't damaged. I know it's expensive."

"It seems to be in excellent condition," Mama assured him. "We're having it relined, you know."

"That's nice…" Boomer's voice trailed off.

"Are you all right?" Marma Lee asked, coming into the room. I gave her credit for being observant.

"I'm fine." He scratched his chest. "I have to go now." He looked at Mama, shrugged, looked at Richard, shrugged, and then looked at me. I shrugged. As he left the building, I followed him to his cruiser. Helping to find a murderer I was okay with, but there was no way in the world I would get tangled up in a love triangle. That was a battle he'd have to fight himself, and he really needed to come up with a better excuse to see Mama than to check out an old casket.

For now, I had questions.

"Boomer, did you find anything interesting at Smitty's?"

"Why is Richard in the shop? Don't you think he's spending an awful lot of time around here? I thought he had a job."

"He does. He writes greeting cards, so he can set his own hours. Mama asked him to come over today and help get the shop ready for the grand opening Saturday."

"Why aren't you helping?"

I gritted my teeth. If I wasn't careful, I'd soon have them ground to nubs. I composed my thoughts. After all, the man suffered from sudden hair removal.

"I was helping. Marma Lee and I went to the nursery, and then we went out to the dump."

"The dump," he repeated.

"Yes. We saw you driving from the direction of Smitty's house."

"Yeah, well?" He craned his neck toward the window Mama was silhouetted in.

"Are you paying attention?"

He nodded, his gaze never wavering from the window.

"Marma Lee and I hid behind Smitty's trees. We were dressed like gypsies. Marma Lee played the tambourine, and I yodeled. One old man asked to have his fortune told."

"What in blue blazes is Richard doing to her?" Boomer huffed and puffed, but he didn't budge from the car. From my vantage point, Richard appeared to be retying one of Mama's flapping apron strings.

"Would you like for me to tell your fortune?" I'll admit I raised my voice just a tad. If I weren't a nice person, I would have grabbed a fist-full of shirt, thus yanking out the few remaining chest hairs lurking under Boomer's badge.

"Huh?" Mama and Richard moved out of his line of vision. His eyes were beginning to focus. "What are you yammering about? I have to get to my office with evidence I found at Smitty's house. Get to the point."

"I've been trying to get to the point for the last five minutes, but you're acting like a lovesick goat. Pull yourself together." Okay. So maybe that was a snarky thing to say, and apparently Mama wasn't the only one who could bellow.

"Did you just call me a goat?" He straightened his cap.

"I'm sorry. That was harsh, but you need to gather your wits about you. Mama and Richard are thinking of having a relationship, and she's not the type to play one against the other. Your timing is way off. Besides, why are you making your move now? You've known her forever."

"I don't know." He frowned. "While Thelma was with me, I wasn't looking. When she left, I swore off women. I didn't notice anybody. I've seen Lilly all my life, but it wasn't until today that I really noticed her. How serious is this thing with Richard?"

"You better talk to Mama about this. I need to talk to you about what you found."

Boomer snapped out of his romantic reverie with effort. "Okay. I'll tell you, but this goes no further. I found a gas and paint can in Smitty's workshop."

"So? That's pretty common stuff for a workshop, isn't it?"

He shook his head. "Sorry, I've probably told you too much already. I trust your discretion, Mary Clare, and your ideas. However, don't you tell a soul what I just told you. It could ruin this case and delay your grand opening again."

Now he had my attention.

"I'll talk to you later." Boomer headed for his car.

I turned on my heel and hurried back up the steps to the shop. Smugness flowed through my being. I'd ordered the fall decorations and arranged for Marma Lee to help with last minute pricing and dusting. I reveled in the smoothness that was my life. I entered the front door with the confidence of a newly elected official.

"What are you serving Mick for dinner tonight?" Marma Lee inquired.

"Dinner? How could I have forgotten about dinner?" I looked at the clock. Eleven fifteen.

Mama spoke up. "Calm down. Mick's not due until seven o'clock. We'll all lend a hand. I've called Rennie, and she's coming to help Richard and me with the baking. I've decided to make a few other things besides the pumpkin cookies and pecan cups."

I glanced at Marma Lee, who smacked her lips. Pumpkin cookies were her favorite. "I haven't even thought out the menu."

"You didn't get to fix your Stromboli. Why don't you serve

that with a nice salad and some of your homemade bread? You have some in the freezer, and you have all the makings for the other. I'll fix a nice German chocolate cake, and you'll be in business. I'll stay out here working while you and Mick eat in the cottage."

"I've been thinking about that." I edged toward the kitchen. "I'd like other people around. I didn't specify dinner for two. He's probably expecting you to be there."

"Does that mean I can come?" Marma Lee's eyes sparkled. "I love your Stromboli. Will you put mushrooms in it? I'll serve. I do a much better job of serving than you do. My servings go on the plate, not the laps."

"All right. You can come, but NO interfering. This is a casual business dinner. As a matter of fact, Richard should be here too. He's done more than his fair share of helping. Richard." I turned to speak to him. "Would you be available for dinner at seven o'clock this evening?" I glanced at Mama. Her hands were tucked behind her back, which meant she had her fingers crossed.

"I'd love to." Richard accepted the invitation with a wink. "What may I bring?"

"Not a thing. I really appreciate you helping Mama and Rennie in the kitchen."

"I'm delighted." His brilliant smile rivaled the rays bouncing from his head.

"Mama, why don't we ask Rennie too? She's not going to feel like cooking dinner after helping us all day. How is her book coming along?"

"She finished it last night. When I called this morning, she was celebrating with a batch of frozen bananas dipped in chocolate. That's her little celebration ritual."

For two hours I tied tags to antiques and collectibles. By the time I got downstairs, Marma Lee was nowhere in sight, but everything shone. I could hear voices in the kitchen area and followed the pumpkin aroma. There, I found Marma Lee, a cookie in each hand.

"How many of those have you consumed?" I demanded.

"Six."

"Polish off those two, and let's go to the Children's Chamber. If I leave you up here, you'll eat all the food."

Mama flashed me a grateful smile. Rennie waved from her flour-covered workstation as Richard pulled a batch of something out of the oven. One thing was for sure, the customers would not leave hungry on Saturday.

Flash and Blur stood guard over Mama's workspace. Something told me they were her official taste testers. I grabbed a pecan cup on my way out as well as Marma Lee's arm. I pointed her in the direction of the picture books, and she went to work. By four o'clock, we were both pooped and more than a little dusty. I sent her home.

"Lotsa stuff down here." Uncle Ardmore clomped down the stairs with Junior at his heels.

With his signature flap cap pulled over his ears, he resembled a WWII fighter pilot. He picked a purple mum petal from his sleeve and tucked it behind my ear. "Pretty petal for a pretty young lady."

"Uncle Ardmore!" I dumped my duster and hugged the man who planted money and delivered sunshine wherever he went.

He hugged me back then searched my face. "Penny for your thoughts?"

The man was intuitive.

"Oh, just lots on my mind with the opening and all."

He squinted harder, and I swear he could read the worry in my head like yesterday's headlines.

He tilted his head back and closed his eyes. "'Do not be anxious about anything, but in everything, by prayer and petition, with thanksgiving, present your requests to God.'"

"Amen." I hugged him again.

"Can't stay. Work to do." He gave me a wink and motioned for Junior to get moving. "Always sittin', this one. Always sittin'. Got labor to do, Junior." Uncle Ardmore stopped in his tracks when he saw Christopher Reeves and the phone booth. "Nice. Shiny stuff in it."

He liked shiny stuff. It was right up there with Miracle Grow. He helped heft Junior off a step, told him to pull up his breeches, then trailed behind him up the stairs.

"You'll be here for open house, won't you?" All I got was thumbs up and a grin. I turned back to retrieve my duster. What was on the floor? I reached down and chuckled. A shiny new penny. Uncle Ardmore. He'd given me a penny for my thoughts. So far, my store had acquired $1.01, and it was all from my dollar-planting, penny-dropping, Fred Astaire-wannabe, quirky uncle.

At the top of the stairs, the amazing scent of cinnamon wafted throughout the shop. It almost kept my eyelids from drooping shut. I slid onto a barstool and studied the threesome in front of me. Not one of them looked wilted, yet each out-aged me by at least twenty years. I needed vitamins, or chocolate, or both. I looked around for the bananas.

"They're in the freezer." Rennie is quite adept at reading my mind. "Help yourself, sweetie. Are you tired?"

I nodded. It took less energy than speaking. I helped myself to the frozen treat. "Maybe I should call and postpone this whole thing."

"Absolutely not." Mama patted my hand. "We'll keep the conversation rolling, and if you nod off I'll nudge you. Besides, Richard already has your salad tossed, and we have your bread thawing on the counter. All you have to do is make your famous Stromboli, pop it in the oven, and get dressed." Mama's floured hands flew to her cheeks. "Honey, you don't have anything to wear."

"Mama. I have something new."

She winced. "It's not those brown overalls you bought at Wal-Mart, is it? Honey, those are fine for working outside but not for a dinner date."

"It's not a date, Mama. It's a casual dinner with a business neighbor." Maybe I should have that statement printed on a poster and wear it around my neck. How many times had I said that in the last few days?

"Show me the outfit," she demanded.

"Nope. You get to see it tonight."

Richard and Rennie stood with folded arms, smiling at the exchange. Richard looked pretty spiffed with a white apron tied waiter-style around his waist. The flour on the top of his head didn't even detract from the effect, and it matched Mama's cheeks exactly.

"Thanks for fixing the salad, Richard." I truly appreciated the thoughtfulness of this man.

"Think nothing of it. It was the least I could do." He eased the door closed on his way out.

"It might be hard to go at a leisurely pace with a man like that. He's the sort that sweeps you off your feet without even knowing he's doing anything special."

"I know." Mama grinned. "It's his nature. It's a shame there aren't more men like him." Flash and Blur curled up in a huddle by the pantry, no doubt guarding their kibble. Flash had his paw slung over a dreaming Blur. She yelped and twitched.

"Now that's companionship." Mama nodded at the two. Flash roused and nibbled Blur's ear. She jumped up and slapped him with her paw.

"Yep. That's companionship," I agreed.

By six p.m. everything was on schedule. The Stromboli bubbled in the oven, and thanks to Mama, the table resembled a slick magazine advertisement for hospitality. New candles glimmered on the counter, and the smell of freshly baked cookies still lingered in the air. I pranced in the back door of the shop wearing my new duds.

"Honey, you look lovely."

"Are you sure, Mama?" I asked with exaggerated sincerity. "If you think it's too much, I can always wear my overalls."

I wouldn't admit it for the world, but I'd taken a few pains with my makeup and even went to the trouble of trying a new hairdo. I'd found a nice little ivory barrette tucked in with the sweater. A note from Annabelle said it was a gift. It was the perfect finishing touch. It kept my long hair from falling in my face but still allowed the majority to swing freely.

"Mary Clare, you are so beautiful."

"No, Mama, but you are. Is that another new outfit? We'll have to strap Richard in his chair. Better be careful. That outfit does not say, 'We're going to take this slowly.'"

Mama blushed. "You don't think the black looks too funeral homeish, do you?"

"No. I do not. This shows off your curves. I'm telling you, Mama, you may have to slap his hand before the night is over."

"That might be fun."

"I phoned Mick earlier and told him to arrive at the shop rather than the cottage. Plus, it will make the dinner seem more businesslike. Mama, why are you smiling?"

"Honey, you don't have to act around me."

"I'm not acting. This is…" I trailed off when her eyebrow raised, and she pointed her finger at me. Who was I kidding? This was not just a business dinner.

Marma Lee trotted in at six thirty-one, wearing a baggy dress and gaudy jewelry. I didn't say a word. She had yet to comment about the bra and panty set from Annabelle's, which meant she was either ignoring my humor or was seriously contemplating making the purchase, which worried me a little.

"I'm wearing this awful outfit for you, Cousin. If Mick sees me all dolled up, he might make a play for me. I'd feel terrible if that happened." She fiddled with her flat hair. "You look good, though. It's a nice change." She sat her huge handbag on the counter with a clunk.

"What's in that bag?" Oh, please. I did not need an eye twitch tonight. "It's not that awful perfume, is it?"

"No, it is not. You know me. I'm always wagging stuff around." She stepped into the dining area to admire Mama's work. "Where's everyone sitting?"

I pointed out the seating arrangement and decided I could get myself calmed if I wasn't in the same room as my cousin. As I headed to the kitchen, I heard a knock. Mama navigated to the back door.

"Good evening, Lilly. You look lovely." Richard admired her appearance. Mama's blush deepened, adding just the right splash of color to her outfit. He handed her a bouquet of pink carnations wrapped in florist's paper.

"They're beautiful." She eased them into a vase on the table then filled it with water. Now the table really was perfect.

At six-fifty, there was another knock. It had to be Mick. Rennie never knocked. I went to the door, trying not to appear nervous. My legs felt like rubber. What if they buckled under me? Answering the door on my knees would never do. I needed to snap out of it. Taking a deep breath, I slung open the door.

Sure enough, standing in the door, wearing a beige cable knit sweater and blue jeans, was Mick.

"Wow." His gaze started at the top of my head and worked its way to the sparkly tips of my new shoes.

One word. It knocked me for a total loop. I hunted for enough breath to invite him in. He looked pretty wowie himself. This guy could make a bundle modeling cable sweaters and turtlenecks.

"Come in, neighbor." I stood aside so he could enter.

He offered a bag to me. "I didn't want to arrive empty-handed, so I brought a jar of Dad's homemade barbecue sauce."

Why did he have that odd look on his face? "Thank you." He handed me the sauce and squeezed my hand in the process. I would have enjoyed it more had my mind not been wondering about Angelica. Maybe she was some big, burly aunt. Somehow, the name Angelica didn't inspire visions of big or burly. I reminded myself I had no tethers attached to my new business neighbor. He was just my neighbor. "I'll use this next time we barbecue."

"Um, Mac."

"Yes?" I turned and decided to try out eyelash batting.

"I was a little surprised to get your text this afternoon."

I racked my brain but couldn't remember sending him a text.

"You must have me confused with someone else's message, Mick. I didn't send you a text. What did it say?"

"You honestly don't know? About the picture? Will this fit into your plans? Don't get me wrong. That outfit is, well provocative. It just surprised me a little coming from you."

"Oh, dear! I sent that to you? That was supposed to be a joke for Marma Lee." Now I understood why she hadn't mentioned it to me. She had never received it. How could this have happened?

Then it clicked. Both had written their numbers and left them in the cottage for me. The handwriting was oddly similar, and both had been in pencil. I must have entered Mick's number under Marma Lee's contact information. Which meant her contact information contained Mick's number.

"I am SO sorry, Mick." After explaining the whole mix-up, I prayed silently that this would be the instant the New Madrid Fault would crack open the earth beneath me and suck me into the ground. I felt for the slightest quiver in the ground beneath me. Didn't happen.

Instead, I sucked up my inane mistake, threw back my shoulders, and motioned for Mick to follow me to the table.

Just when I thought the night could not get any worse, it did. There, sitting beside Mama's beautiful arrangement, stood that stupid sculpture. It was turned toward Mick's designated seat. Having no time to move it without being obvious, I simply glared at Marma Lee.

Rennie chose that moment to quietly enter the back door. Her signature bright colors sparkled up the room, but something was missing. After watching her for a few minutes, I realized it was her perky smile.

True to her word, Marma Lee served the meal once everyone settled in. Mama kept glancing Rennie's way. Apparently, she could stand the suspense no longer.

"Something is troubling you. Is it the book?"

"I'm sorry. I hate to be a wet blanket. Thank you." She accepted a portion of Stromboli from Marma Lee. "I've received the most upsetting news."

She reached for her napkin and dropped it. "Oh, dear. Mac, I'm a total wreck, sweetie. I shouldn't have come. Maybe I should leave." She made to push back her chair, but Mama stopped her.

"You'll do no such thing, honey. You're among friends." Sitting next to her, Mama patted her hand. "Tell us what happened. We'll try to help."

"Oh, it's awful. I hope Boomer can catch the person responsible."

"Responsible for what? What's happened?" Mama sat forward and put her arm around Rennie's shoulders.

"Saige was attacked last night. He's in a coma, and I just found out about it. Someone tried to kill him."

The next thing I knew, Stromboli was in my lap, and Marma Lee was on the floor.

CHAPTER SIXTEEN

The rest of the evening blitzed into blurry. I'm still not sure if Marma Lee fainted because Saige was attacked or because Rennie knew about it, and she didn't. Regardless, I was a mess. Literally. Luckily, my sweater survived. My new slacks did not. Tomato sauce wreaks havoc on winter white.

Mick scooped Marma Lee from the floor and deposited her on the couch. Flash and Blur reluctantly gave up their space on the couch but stood guard over her with cocked heads. Neither offered to lick her face. They did, however, nudge her when they considered her time to be up.

During that time, sweet Rennie sat with her, and I went to clean up the mess. Richard fanned her face. Mick regarded her with a cocked head, much like Flash and Blur's. He went to fetch water. She revived but only half-heartedly.

"What happened?" She might not have sounded so demanding if she could have seen her hair pooching out on both sides.

"You fainted, honey." Rennie patted her hand.

"I meant what happened to Saige?"

Rennie stopped patting and started pacing. I sidled up to Mick and wondered if he would find the subtle Italian scent of pepperoni alluring.

"When I left here this afternoon," Rennie began, "I started thinking about how abrupt I'd been to Saige when he asked me out," (to Richard's credit, he raised only one brow) "and I decided to call and apologize for my curtness. I phoned his grandmother's home, and she told me he'd been attacked during the snowstorm. She was only there to grab some clothes and was in a hurry to get back to the hospital. According to her, he stepped out to move her car to the garage, and someone clubbed him over the head. By the time the ambulance got him to the hospital, he'd lost a lot of blood." Her voice shook. "You know, head wounds bleed quite freely."

Marma Lee nodded and turned green at the same time. Richard fanned faster.

"Is he going to make it?" Marma Lee whispered.

"His grandmother said his brain is swelling, and their main concern right now is getting the swelling to stop."

"Why would anyone want to hurt Saige?" Richard scratched his hairless head. "He's new here. No one knows him."

"Maybe it was a car robbery gone bad," Mick suggested.

"I wouldn't think so." Richard studied Mick's face intently.

"Maybe I lived in Memphis too long. Sometimes violence occurs for no reason." Turning abruptly, Mick walked to the kitchen.

"Bless his heart." Mama said it softly, waiting until he was out of earshot. "Boomer told me one of the reasons he and his daddy moved back was because his mama died. She was run over by a hit and run driver in Memphis. They never found out who hit her."

"Probably a drunk." Marma Lee crossed her arms.

I glanced in the kitchen to make sure Mick couldn't overhear the troubling conversation.

"Why would Boomer tell you that information, Mama?"

"Because I asked him to find out. I'm your mother, which means I have the right to snoop."

By now Marma Lee was vertical. When she stood, Flash and Blur took her place. They woofed their appreciation and promptly settled down for a lengthy lounging session. The rest of us moved back to the dining table. Mick scraped uneaten Stromboli from the dishes.

"Leave it." I touched his back. So what if my fingers ran up and down his back. The man needed some comfort. For that matter, I could use a bit myself. "I'll make some coffee, and we'll try to get our wits about us. Would you grab Mama's cake? I'll take the cups and plates."

"I'm sorry about your friend. I hope everything turns out all right for him." He turned and wiped his hands on a rooster dish rag. His chin raised, making that five o'clock shadow impossible to ignore. His fingers caressed my shoulders and then slid down to my wrists.

My heart hammered to beat the band. "I do too. He isn't really a friend. I only met him this week." I explained his background.

"Could someone with a grudge have followed him here?" His fingers rubbed mine.

"I don't know. He did say one of his last cases hadn't gone well. He writes true crime." I relayed the story of the mother who died. "I suppose someone could blame him for the mother's death, but that seems farfetched."

I glanced at his hands, and as much as I hated to, I pulled mine away to stack the dishes. Busy hands didn't get into as much trouble.

He lasered me with those green eyes. "There's something else, isn't there?"

I nodded. "Ruby Holly asked Saige to investigate her daughter's disappearance. Ruby believes she's dead, but I guess she wants some kind of closure."

"Is this woman…" he hesitated and started again. "Does Ms. Holly seem to be a fairly stable individual?"

The question astounded me. "Of course. She's a genealogist."

A smile played at the corners of his mouth. He held his hands up. "I'm sorry. I didn't mean to insult anyone, but this incident with Saige isn't isolated, Mac. Somebody is going around town doing savage things. First he kills Smitty, and then you have two unexplained episodes here in the shop. Next, Smitty's house burns, and now Saige is attacked."

"How did you know about Smitty's house?" I wanted to tell him about the cans Boomer found, but I'd given my word I wouldn't discuss it.

"One of the customers told me about it. He said it happened last night." The coffee stopped perking, and I reached for the tray, but he stopped me. "You don't seem to understand you could be a pivotal piece of this mess. I'm worried about you and your mother. I'm not sure you're safe." He ran his hands through his hair.

Angelica. Schmangelica. Mick was worried about me.

This time I squeezed his hand. I couldn't offer any words, but I hoped the squeeze said it all. I poured the coffee into a carafe and carried it and the other serving pieces to the table. He followed with the cake. Mama cut the slices large. She knew this was a wide wedge kind of night.

It seemed impossible for the time to be only eight o'clock. Would this day ever end?

"Rennie, are you all right, honey?" Mama asked. "You still look pale. Maybe you need something more substantial than dessert. Would you like a piece of Mary Clare's leftover bread? It's very good."

"I'm okay. It just came as a fright, that's all."

Rennie's cell phone played Moon River. She answered, listened, murmured a few words of consolation, and hung up. Tears puddled in her eyes.

"What?" Marma Lee shot up like a weed on steroids. "Who was that?"

"Saige's grandmother. Saige isn't dead." She held up her hand. "I'm sorry I'm crying. I'm just so relieved. He came out of his coma and talked to his grandmother. He wanted to talk to you, Marma Lee. His grandmother thought you'd want to know. He slipped back into a coma, though. I'm sorry."

My cousin nearly knocked Mama over with a hug. "Did you hear that, Aunt Lilly? The thought of me brought Saige out of a coma."

Mama choked. "Yes, dear, I heard."

"He said something else before he slipped back into a coma," Rennie announced.

"What else did he say?" Mick asked.

"He said he smelled a woman's perfume before he was struck."

"Did he say anything else?" Richard asked.

"The attacker came up from behind, but he was sure about the perfume. That's all his grandmother could remember. She's planning to stay at the hospital until he recovers. Lilly, we need to do something for her."

Mama nodded her agreement.

Marma Lee chimed in. "I'll help. I could stay with him while y'all take her out for breakfast or something."

"I feel so horrible about the whole situation," Rennie said. It was a good thing her book was finished. Writing would be hard to do in her present state of mind.

"We'll all pitch in." Richard clapped his hands together. "I haven't met the lady, but I assume she's getting up in years. She could probably use some comforts while she's at the hospital. I'll take some books for her to read and a comfortable lounge pillow.

She'll also need money for the vending machines, and I'll send flowers from the writing group."

"I'll send Doc over at lunch and make sure she has something to eat," Mick offered. "I'll tone down my barbecues some and send plenty of tea and snacks. I may try my hand at making soup."

"Mary Clare, if she doesn't have a cot, we need to arrange one for her. The poor dear won't hold up long sleeping in those chairs. I wonder if Maybelline could take her breakfast each morning?" Mama mused.

"We could have Molly do that starting tomorrow. I'll call Maybelline in the morning and make out an order, and then Molly can deliver it before she reports for work."

We sat in comfortable silence for the next few minutes, sipping our beverages and enjoying Mama's cake. In spite of what happened around us, a bond was forged with this little group. We felt better having decided to help another. I thought about Brother Everett's favorite sermon. The gist of it was how we should all empty ourselves for others as Christ had for us. Then God could come along and fill us up again with his rich blessings. I smiled. God had his finger on the pulse of recycling long before it became politically correct.

Someone knocked at the front door. Boomer came in, his brows knit together. A collective groan sounded around the table. To say he looked a bit hurt was like saying Smitty was a bit dead.

"What did I do?" he demanded.

"Nothing. Come sit," Mama invited.

He followed her every move with a lovesick gaze. "Thank you. That's kind of you."Richard frowned.

"Why didn't you tell us about Saige?" I leaned forward and seriously thought about punching his arm.

"Because I didn't know about Saige until a few hours ago. In case you've forgotten, I was here last night when it happened."

"So when did they report it?" I asked.

"The grandmother didn't report it. She went immediately to the hospital. You know Ralph Perty volunteers there, and he called the sheriff's department from the hospital. Clarence took the call."

"Who is Ralph Perty?" Mick asked.

"The realtor across the street." Rennie pointed in the direction of the realtor's office.

"Not for long." Boomer hitched his thumb in the direction of Perty Realty. "I went over there to interview him, and he's quitting the real estate trade. He wants to open up an antique store. Said he believes with a little nudge our town could sparkle again. You may have competition, Mary Clare. Since he can't sell that old Weatherly place, he's thinking of buying it himself. The son just wants to get rid of it now since it's sat empty for so long. Ralph may just open his shop there."

I met Mama's eyes. We prayed opening Pocket Change would jump start a new wave of community pride. According to Boomer, we succeeded. Maybe the once gracious Pocket was on her way back. God was answering prayers left and right.

"Thank you." Boomer smiled as Mama placed a steaming cup of coffee in front of him. "Clarence wrote it off as a typical mugging and decided not to bother me with it. Of course, Clarence doesn't realize there's no such thing as a typical mugging in Pocket. I raked him over the coals pretty good when he finally got around to telling me."

"I'm glad to hear it." Mama sniffed and sat straight as a pole.

"His ego may sting for a while. Anyway, I haven't been to the hospital yet to interview the grandmother, but Clarence said the guy is in a coma. Doesn't sound good."

"His grandmother just phoned here," offered Mick. "She said Saige told her he smelled a woman's perfume before he was hit."

"A woman's perfume?" Boomer repeated, sipping his coffee. "Clarence believes the doctor is pretty concerned. The blow to his head was severe."

We knew all of this. Boomer was belated.

"We've come up with a plan to help out." Mama made announcements like she made cookies. Like a cheerleader. "Starting tomorrow, we all have an assignment. We want to help Saige's grandmother as much as we can."

"That's thoughtful." Boomer all but crooned. "You're a considerate woman."

Richard sat with the same frown on his face. The only difference in his appearance was the not-so-healthy redness on the top of his head. "She's quite thoughtful." Richard's tone had a decided edge to it. It was time for a diversion.

"Let's sit by the fire." I gathered up cups and saucers and hoped the fire would lull the group into a happier frame of mind. Chairs scraped, and our herd migrated to the other room. Flash and Blur hadn't moved an inch. I had to lure them off the couch with ice. They loved ice cubes. Marma Lee and Rennie nabbed spots on the couch. Everyone else chose easy chairs and sank down. I held back. "Boomer." I motioned for him to stay in the kitchen.

"Yes, Mary Clare?" He sounded tired, but I really needed to know.

"Why did you come by tonight? You could have told us about Saige tomorrow."

"Because I knew you'd be anxious about what I told you this afternoon." He ran his hand over his eyes. "I know I made you promise not to discuss what I told you."

"I haven't." I jerked my chin up. "What did you find out about the cans you found?"

He took a sip of his coffee. This whole conversation was taking way longer than necessary. I began tapping my foot.

"I searched Smitty's property this afternoon and found a couple of items. One was a gas-soaked rag." He stopped to take another long sip from his coffee cup. At this rate, Richard would have time to grow a new head of hair before I found out the rest of Boomer's story. "I suppose you want to know about the paint can too?"

"That would be nice." I gritted my teeth. First thing in the morning I would call my dentist and ask about caps.

"The can hasn't held paint for a long time, but it wasn't empty."

I shifted my weight then led the way to the cozy area. "What was in it then, if it wasn't empty?"

"A hairbrush." Boomer leveled his gaze at me then took in the rest of those assembled. "You'll all find out soon enough."

"Why would Smitty have a hairbrush in an old paint can?" I asked.

"Evidently, he hid it. Didn't think it would be found."

"Why hide an old hairbrush?" Mama asked.

When he set his coffee cup down and rubbed his face I knew things were about to get interesting. "The hairbrush inside the paint can belonged to someone else. The owner's name was inscribed on it. I've had it examined and its ownership verified."

"Who examined it?" I had a sneaky feeling I knew the words that were about to fall out of Boomer's mouth.

"The owner's mother." Boomer inhaled half the room's oxygen. "She confirmed the hairbrush belonged to her daughter, Cora Ann Holly."

CHAPTER SEVENTEEN

Stunned would be a good word to describe my reaction. "Are you sure?"

His withering expression was comparable to mine. "Ruby identified the piece and even showed me the matching comb in Cora Ann's room. The brush was more tarnished, but they are a matching set. You know, Ruby's believed for years Smitty had something to do with Cora Ann's death."

From there the evening took a nosedive. Fatigue and worry sent bodies scurrying home. It was after nine o'clock when Boomer, the last to leave, slogged to the door.

"Lilly."

"Yes." Mama placed glasses in the dishwasher.

"I'd rather you stay with Mary Clare in the cottage until this whole thing blows over." Mama nodded and reached for my hand.

Boomer looked around the kitchen. Mick had cleared the table, but the dishes and leftovers still needed cleaning and storing. Rolling up his sleeves, Boomer moved away from the door and went to work helping Mama load the dishwasher.

I stared. "What are you doing, Boomer?"

"Six hands are faster than four. The quicker we get this mess cleaned up, the faster you two can get to the cottage. I intend to escort you there and check it before you go in."

"That's not necessary," I insisted. "It's not that far away."

"Neither was the car Saige went to move. We aren't taking any chances. For a self-proclaimed gadget girl, you still don't have a security system out there, Mary Clare." He shook his head. "I'm sorry, ladies. Guess I'm just tired and cranky. We'll make sure Flash and Blur go to the bathroom before you go in. I don't want you opening the door during the night. Understood?"

I nodded, and although I would never admit it, the whole situation began to spook me. I had to be careful from now on, and I had to think of Mama. I didn't want to think someone we knew could be a killer, but the possibility was a distinct one.

"Boomer, do you think what happened to Saige is connected to Smitty?"

He shrugged. "I don't know. As a sheriff, I have to look at everything with a critical eye. It's hard for me to swallow these incidents as coincidental."

We finished in the kitchen, and Boomer checked the doors and windows and deemed them secure. Picking up Marma Lee's uglier-than-squished-squash sculpture, I stashed it in an inconspicuous place beside the fireplace. Tomorrow, I'd throw the thing away. I returned to the kitchen and flipped off the lights. The five of us made our way to the cottage. The wind picked up, and the temperature plummeted.

Mama and I shivered. Boomer took off his jacket, and we both huddled beneath its warmth. Like the excellent dogs they were, Flash and Blur puddled and pottied in record time. They returned to huddle with us on the newly delivered hay bales. Within minutes, Boomer gave us the all clear sign and ushered us into the cottage.

"Here's your coat." Mama smoothed the collar down once he had it on. "I know you must be tired. You've been going all day."

She reached up and patted him on the cheek. I thought he would keel over. She, of course, had no idea her actions were causing such turmoil. Maybe I should sit her down and tell her. No, that was Boomer's place. I was staying out of this one.

"It's all right." Boomer recovered quickly. "It goes with the territory."

"Would you like to stay for a while?" She had no idea what she was doing to the poor man.

"No. I should be getting over to the hospital. I want to see if Saige has regained consciousness."

Mama's scowl spoke volumes. "Couldn't you let that nincompoop Clarence go to the hospital for you?"

"I don't trust Clarence completely. Not just yet. I'm sure he'll come along, but this is too important. I'll have him patrolling, though. I'll send him over every hour and tell him to look for suspicious activity. It'll be good practice, and it should keep him out of trouble."

"What if something does happen?" Mama looked around. "Will he be instructed to handle it on his own?"

"No. He will be instructed to call me."

After Boomer left, we decided to call it a night. I lay awake listening for sounds. The lack of anything out of the ordinary began lulling me to sleep. I tried to stay awake by pondering Mick's theory of a madman in our midst committing random acts of violence. Something about that didn't ring true. My eyes began to droop, and my thoughts clouded over. As I dropped off to sleep, two thoughts floated to the surface. I still hadn't found out about Angelica, and someone didn't want Saige investigating Cora Ann's disappearance. I should be the most worried about the latter, but it was the elusive Angelica that made me wake with a frown the following morning.

The day dawned brightly, and then it changed its mind. A slow rain began and washed away the rest of the snow. By the time Molly arrived, the only evidence of our bizarre October blizzard was one little patch of snow in the front yard and a wicked chill. She hurried in the door, wiping her feet.

"Good morning," she called from the foyer. She stashed her umbrella and waved goodbye to her ride.

"Is that your mom?" I pointed toward the retreating car.

"Yes, ma'am. She'll bring me to work until I can save up enough to get a car. I've got my eye on a good used one in Jonesboro. It's red."

"Red's a great color. Would you like to use Old Blue until you can get one of your own? They say if they aren't driven, they get lonely. You can use it to get to and from work and to make deliveries."

"Oh, Miss Casteel, that would be wonderful. This is the greatest job. When will the costumes be finished? Do you think my outfit will be ready for open house? We are still opening on time, aren't we?"

"Yes, we are, and you'll be happy to know the costumes are ready to pick up. As a matter of fact, I need you to do a few errands before getting started downstairs." I explained about the breakfast orders for Saige's grandmother.

"I'd be happy to do that. Do you want me to run by the nursing home after I've delivered the food and get the costumes?"

I nodded. "Plus, it will give you a chance to get used to the car. It has a mind of its own. I'm anxious to see the costumes too. The mystery characters are coming this afternoon for a briefing. They can try them on and practice parading around. Uncle Ardmore will be here. He's coming as Uncle Sam."

Molly grinned and reached for her coat and umbrella. "I like him. He doesn't say a lot, but when he does, it pays to listen to him." She headed for the door. "I'll leave for Maybelline's. Is she expecting me?"

"Yep. I told her to keep a lookout for you each morning until Saige is dismissed."

"If it's all right with you, I'll deliver the food before coming to work. It'll be hotter that way."

"Not to mention faster. Give Saige's grandmother my best, and tell her we're praying for them."

"I'll add them to our prayer list Sunday." She popped the umbrella and ran to Old Blue then pulled out of the parking lot and headed toward Maybelline's Diner.

I sat at the desk in the foyer and tried to reconstruct my to-do list. I'd written three things when the door opened, and Ralph and Newton blustered in. Ralph looked mad. Newton, as always, seemed on the verge of hysterics.

"Mary Clare," Ralph barked, "I need to know where Ethel is." Newton cowered behind him.

"Why?" Ralph wasn't my uncle or my employer, and he didn't intimidate me in the least. Newton stared at me with fleeting admiration. He almost smiled.

"Because I want to buy that lot of Smitty Small's. That's prime land out there."

"It's two miles from the dump. What's so prime about it?"

"It's being rezoned as commercial." He dripped on my floor. He was not making himself welcome. I glanced at his nephew. For Newton's sake, I silently said my old standby prayer. Twice.

"Nobody knows where Ethel is." I refused to be bullied around by this irritating, overbearing jerk.

"Boomer said she was released, and since you seem to be her sympathizer, I figured she'd call you."

"Nope. Haven't heard a word."

Apparently, he decided to change tactics. Leaning on the desk amiably, he propped his chin on one fist. "Mary Clare, I want that land. I'm trying to build a business for young Newton."

"Of course, you are."

He favored me with his signature cheesy smile then strolled

out the door and down the steps before Newton had a chance to finish the sneeze he'd started.

"What's with him?" I asked his nephew.

"He's in a really rotten mood. We lost a sale. He showed a house to a couple and knocked something off a shelf. It broke, and the owner's madder than an old wet hen."

"Is that the great big house out on Highway 63?"

"That's the one. Our listing time was up, and she changed realtors yesterday. It sold the same day. It went for two hundred fifty thousand dollars. Uncle Ralph lost a huge commission."

"No wonder he's riled." Maybe I needed to share my old standby prayer with Ralph. Sounded like he needed it.

"I planned to ask him for a raise this week. Think I'll wait." Newton shrugged and headed for the door. With slumped shoulders, he hurried down the steps and across the street to Perty Realty. Bless his heart. He was everything his uncle wasn't… humble, homely, and honest.

I would call Boomer today and ask if there was any news about Ethel. If anyone had a right to profit from Smitty's land, it was her.

I'd written my fourth item on my list when Rennie came in the door. She looked like death warmed over. Dark circles decorated her sallow complexion. From the looks of her, she hadn't slept any better than I had. "Good morning."

She hung her dripping raincoat on the hall tree and managed a wan welcome. "I just came from the hospital. Saige's condition is worsening. They've moved him into the intensive care unit. I saw Molly. She delivered breakfast to Mrs. Nichols in the waiting room. It thrilled that old woman to tears."

Mama came in with a spatula in her hand. "I thought I heard voices. Was someone just here?"

"Newton and Ralph. Ralph wants to locate Ethel so he can buy Smitty's land, but nobody knows where she is. Boomer said her disappearing like this just makes her look more guilty."

"I don't believe she killed him." This was the first time Rennie had offered an opinion on Ethel's innocence.

"Why?" I asked.

"Because she seems like a smart lady. Too smart to move to town, ask for help, and then kill him off when he refused. It's too convenient and way too obvious."

"Right now, my mind is so muddled it hurts." Mama rubbed her temples. "Maybe I need something to eat. C'mon in the kitchen, girls. Let's have breakfast."

We followed the smell of bacon and sat at the loaded table. "Mama, I thought you were fixing toast?"

"I did." She pointed to the middle of the table where a stack of eight pieces leaned precariously beside the peanut butter jar. Along with the toast sat an array of two meats, scrambled eggs, and three kinds of jam. "Dig in."

Amazing what a calorie-laden breakfast can do for a gal.

Molly came into the kitchen. "I brought the costumes in and put them in the main room. I peeked. They're really cool. I'll clean up in here, and y'all can go check 'em out."

That got us moving. Rennie was scheduled to appear as Miss Marple. We found her costume on top, complete with knitting basket and hat. Richard arrived about one o'clock and offered to take charge of placing the mums that Uncle Ardmore and Junior had delivered. He excused himself and returned thirty minutes later with two mystery bags. From one he pulled several large, brown paper bags. The other held burlap ribbon. We watched as he placed each pot of mums in a brown paper bag, wrapped a burlap ribbon around the outside, cinched it into a long knot, then set the arrangements throughout the shop. He saved the biggest mum, an orange sunburst, to put in the cottage.

"What made you think of brown paper bags and burlap?" I admired his work. It added a rustic contrast that blended well.

"I used to do this in my restaurants. It's inexpensive and occasionally I'd give them as gifts. Customers loved it."

"That's a great idea. We'll have everyone sign up tomorrow for a free plant to be given away at Thanksgiving. Will you man the guest book and see that everyone signs up?"

His smile answered my question.

The rest of the day flew by. Richard installed the door on my office and even primed and painted it. Everything was taking shape. Only one burr was in my saddle. Mick hadn't put in an appearance, and he knew we were opening tomorrow. Traffic in his shop had been minimal today. Maybe last night's escapades convinced him to stick with someone less troublesome. Someone named Angelica, for instance. It hurt that he hadn't even bothered to call.

The telephone rang. With relief I reached for the phone. It had to be Mick calling to apologize. I'd play it cool and assure him everything was under control. I squared my shoulders and prepared to exude professional aloofness at the sound of that beautiful baritone voice. Only his voice sounded quite feminine. It sounded a lot like Marilyn Monroe.

CHAPTER EIGHTEEN

"Miss Mary Clare Casteel?" The caller purred like a hairball afflicted cat.

"Speaking." Was this caller another kook asking for money? I tried to recall the circus story when the caller continued.

"Miss Casteel," she breathed, "my name is Angelica Floray." A lengthy pause took up the better part of a minute. At this rate, the conversation could run into the evening hours.

"Thahhht's niiiiice." I tried to get into the swing of things. I missed altogether. I sounded more like Dracula.

"I'm an old friend of Mick Walkers." Either this woman had some serious lung issues, or she was overheating. I looked at the caller ID. Why did this number seem so familiar?

"What did you say your name was?" I waited through four Mississippis for her response.

"Angelica Floray. I was told he might be at your establishment. Might I speak with him?" Her sigh could've blown the feathers off a flock of geese. Maybe she had asthma. I waited for her to go on. She didn't. Had she expired? Maybe the phone was dead. I tapped the receiver.

"Hello?" Rustling on the other end. "He isn't here," I informed her. She exhaled one last time, thanked me, and hung up. So, Angelica was an old friend. This was the woman who'd sent Doc scurrying over to give Mick a message the day Barlow was taken for questioning. Had Mick left word for Doc to alert him immediately if she called?

Lightning struck.

A. This was the A. from Mick's mystery caller the night he'd accidently left his cell with me. If I hadn't been so tired, I would have caught the connection before now. I'd bet my last Snickers bar on it.

Rushing outside, I was in time to see a sleek blonde exiting Mick's shop. Tossing her shoulder-length mane, she slid into a Mercedes and snailed her way past Pocket Change. Chatting on her phone, she was oblivious to the nonchalant figure on the porch straightening a hay bale. Her vanity plates read Angel I. I went directly to the telephone and punched in Boomer's office number. Clarence answered.

"Sheriff's office." I pictured him sitting ramrod straight.

"Clarence, this is Mary Clare Casteel. I need to talk to Boomer right away. Is he there?" Surely he could dig up some information on this mystery woman. What were police computers for? Maybe he'd find she was an escaped mental patient with a penchant for Marilyn Monroe.

"No, ma'am. He's gone to Jonesboro and won't be back until tonight."

"What's he doing in Jonesboro?"

"That's official police business, ma'am, and I'm not at liberty to divulge that information. If you'll tell me what this call is concerning, I'll pass it along to the proper authority."

"I'm not at liberty to tell you." I could starch up my voice too. Then I hung up. Two could play that game, and what was that crack about passing it along to the proper authority? We both knew that was Boomer. Someone needed to dry Clarence off behind the ears. I needed to brood but didn't have time. It was already five p.m., and not everything on my list was finished. The rain stopped, but the sharp wind from earlier refused to die down. I would have to hold my breath. Moisture and cold air could mean snow, which would put a serious cramp in tomorrow's festivities.

Molly had left at four p.m., trailing behind her mom in Old Blue. Both were ecstatic and grateful. I'd break the news at Christmas that Old Blue was hers to keep, but first I'd book it into a shop to get a new red paint job and have it detailed. I liked having money. It was fun.

Mama, Rennie, and Richard had disappeared before Molly left. Now, the threesome came waltzing through the front door with takeout cartons peeking out of white plastic bags. My stomach rumbled.

The ice clinked as I dropped the cubes in glasses before filling each with tea. Richard placed the cartons on the table while Mama located plates and silverware. Rennie grabbed the napkins. The smells wafting from those innocent-looking little containers teased my nose and had my mouth watering. "Richard, will you say grace?"

"Be glad to. Father, we thank You for blessing us with precious people, warm friendships, and the opportunity to share this meal. Amen."

"Amen," we chorused.

"Where did this come from?" I asked, peering in the first carton. It contained mashed potatoes with gravy. Meatballs, steamed asparagus with a creamy sauce, and corn rounded out the meal. Rolls were wrapped in separate foil.

Mama beamed at Richard with pride. "It came from the secret recipe files of Richard Lorch."

"When did you have the time?"

"When I have extra time on my hands, I make up portions and freeze them." He shrugged.

I chased a meatball across my plate and popped it into my mouth. Yum.

"Poor Marma Lee." Rennie pushed a renegade beet around her plate. "She's missing out."

"She'd better have a good reason for not showing up today." She could be replaced as a buyer. Come to think of it, I could hire a nicer cousin too.

"Oh, honey. I completely forgot to tell you. She's at the hospital keeping Mrs. Nichols company." Rennie's face turned red. "She told me to tell you she wouldn't be here. I declare my mind just isn't working right."

"It's okay. I'm glad she's there. I can't for the life of me understand why he wanted to contact her, of all people."

"Love is blind," Richard quoted.

I popped the last bit of roll into my mouth. "I wonder if she's coming tomorrow." I planned on her helping behind the counter. "That reminds me, I need to update our Facebook status, send out tweets, and remind the mayor's secretary to post the opening on the town marquee. Plus, I need to run out to the cottage and get our promotional stuff. We need it within reach when our customers check out. We'll let them choose their item. I bet the bracelets go first."

Hearing the front door slam, I hurried to the main room, expecting to see Marma Lee. Instead Mick greeted me. My hands automatically flew to my hair. I'd tied a bright triangle scarf over it this morning to keep it out of my face. It was red and probably matched my face. He, on the other hand, sported a suit and tie. I felt like a mud pie beside Neiman Marcus brownies. I really needed to stop equating things with food.

"I ignored the closed sign and barged in." A sheepish look sat on his insanely handsome face. "I would have been here sooner, but there was business to take care of." With one quick scan, he took in the room around him. "Looks like you're all set. Your do-rag's cute."

I ducked my head. "We're nearly there. Come on in. Richard made dinner."

"No, I don't want to intrude. I just wanted to make a delivery." Stepping outside, he came back hauling the gorgeous plant I'd admired at the nursery. It stood nearly as tall as the door frame.

"It's beautiful," I exclaimed.

"I can't take credit. It was Marma Lee's idea. She noticed you eyeballing it and thought you might enjoy it in the shop."

Drat. I could never stay mad at Marma Lee for long.

I indicated the spot for the plant, and Mick lifted it with ease, refusing to let me help. "I haven't exactly made myself useful today. The least I can do is move this plant."

I dawdled, admiring the plant's shiny leaves. I had to tell him about Angelica's phone call.

Didn't I?

It would be unethical not to mention it.

Wouldn't it? I glanced at the clock. It was seven-thirty p.m. and dark as tar outside. I still hadn't put out the red carpet I'd bought or trimmed the outside of the bay windows with fall garland. I headed for the storage closet to drag the carpet outside. In an instant, Mick was at my elbow.

When I told him my plans, he shucked off his suit jacket and rolled up his sleeves. Next, he lugged the runner out the door and positioned it down the steps. I retrieved my work jacket and ran next door to get Mick's. We turned on the outside lights and went to work. He secured the rug to the wood and by eight-thirty, we were finished and admiring our work. Enough garland was left to twine around the banister of the steps.

"It's perfect. You don't have anything to worry about tomorrow. Pocket Change will be the talk of several towns. I wouldn't be surprised if you don't have news coverage. I'm proud of you."

That did it.

"I had a telephone call today."

"You did? Was it the governor?"

"No. I thought it was Marilyn Monroe, but she's dead, you know."

Silence.

I forged on. "Her name was Angelica Floray." I did my best to imitate the breathless blonde.

"Why did she call?" Mick rubbed the back of his neck.

"She wanted to talk to you, and someone told her to call here."

"Probably Dad. When I left this morning, I told him I planned to help you today."

I'm sure the confusion on my face came as no surprise. "You just got here. But," I held up both hands, "you're a busy man. I didn't expect you."

"Yes, you did, and I let you down. I had an errand to run." I leaned inward to hear the rest of his explanation.

He backed away. "I can't tell you about it, Mac. It's personal."

That stung. "I see. Well, you should contact Ms. Floray. She seemed disappointed at your absence."

"I'll bet she was."

"She didn't leave a number. I'm sorry. I didn't think to ask for one."

"I have her number." A nasty edge lodged in his laugh.

"It's cold. We should go in."

Mick snatched at my wrist. "It's not what you think."

"Well, obviously, you don't care to explain it to me." I tugged my wrist free and scurried up the steps and into the shop. He didn't stop me. His silence was deafening.

"Goodnight, Mary Clare." Already, he was striding across the parking lot toward his shop.

"Goodnight, Mick." The wind caught my words and tossed them right back at me. My heart hurt as I watched him enter his door. I leaned against Mabel-the-tree. Would I ever learn?

Rennie and Richard were pulling on coats when I returned. Rennie assured Mama she'd arrive bright and early to get the "characters" in costume and in place. Six anxious mystery buffs had met with Mama earlier. Each departed, happily toting their costume for opening day. Mama gave them lessons on "direct discretion." She was quite proud of the term she'd invented to inhibit shoplifting.

If all else failed, the roving eyes of the portraits would catch the shoplifters. I'd caught a glimpse of Clarence patrolling when Mick and I worked outside. I wondered if Boomer was still in Jonesboro. It seemed strange he hadn't put in an appearance either. It was enough to give a girl a complex.

The phone rang as I was coming up from the Children's Chamber. I picked up the receiver with shaky hands and was surprised to hear Ralph's voice instead of Mick's. "Mary Clare, I just had the strangest telephone call from Ethel. I'm trying to decide if I should notify Boomer."

"Ethel Glacier called you?"

"Yes, she did. She was quite friendly. We chatted for nearly thirty minutes before she finally told me what she wanted. Do you think I should call Boomer?"

"He's out of town. Did you get her number?"

"No. She called me here at the realty office, and the caller I.D. tagged it as unknown. She wants to meet me tomorrow to discuss some rental property I have. She's staying in Little Rock right now."

Why hadn't I thought of Little Rock? Of course, she'd return to the place where she was most familiar. That had been her home for years.

"What time are you supposed to meet?"

"Eight o'clock at my house. I guess she doesn't want to see a lot of people. I told her that was fine." He sounded tired.

"Are you okay? You sound odd."

"I'm discouraged. Property isn't moving lately. I'm sorry

about my gruffness this afternoon. Sometimes I get that way when I'm worried."

Well, great. Make a girl feel guilty, why don't you? "We're all like that sometimes."

"I'll try to get by tomorrow for the opening." Ralph sounded like a lost little boy. "Break a leg."

"Thanks. Don't worry about Boomer. I'll tell him about Ethel. He may want to question her. Get some rest."

"That's good advice, but I'm down to volunteer at the hospital for a few hours. Maybe I can grab some sleep after that. Goodnight, Mary Clare."

"Goodnight." I hung up the phone and peeked out the window. Sure enough, Ralph's office light went black. I watched him hurry to his car. Monteen and her virtual mountaineers would close down in an hour, and then all would be quiet in our little neighborhood.

I dialed the sheriff's office, but the line was busy. I dialed Boomer's home phone, but no one answered. His cell switched directly to voice mail. I didn't like the idea of having this message recorded. I'd call again later or try to catch Clarence on patrol. Obviously, Boomer must still be in Jonesboro. I went searching for Mama. I found her standing upstairs in the Christmas room.

"Hey, Mama. What are you doing?"

"Thinking about your daddy. I wish he could have lived to see this. He'd be so proud of you."

"You still miss him, don't you, Mama?"

"Yes, I do. Maybe I always will. Your first real love never leaves your heart."

"You're blessed. Some people never know that kind of devotion."

"Not everyone finds love as soon as your father and I did, but the age doesn't matter. What matters is they find it." She was right. She was also a romantic. Maybe some of us didn't have a soul mate out there. Maybe all I could hope for was a soul buddy.

"Mama. Ralph Perty called."

"What on earth did he want?"

I told her, but she wasn't as surprised as I'd been. "It's wise of Ethel to come back," Mama said. "Otherwise, people are going to talk. You know how small-town gossips are."

I nodded. "At least this way, she won't appear to have run away. I have to admit, it made her look guilty."

By this time, we'd checked every entrance. I turned the lights out upstairs as we worked our way to the main floor. Flash and Blur appeared at our heels. They were ready to tackle anyone out of the ordinary. The fact that our only defense was two lick-happy dogs didn't deter us. We locked the back door and headed for the cottage. The dogs finished their nightly constitutional and hurried to the door where we were waiting under the dim porch light Boomer instructed us to leave on. Now, I was glad of the illumination. We were to leave it on all night. I probably should have left the carriage lights burning at the front of the shop, but I didn't want to backtrack.

By ten p.m., bodies and beasts were tucked in bed.

Eleven o'clock rolled around, and still I lay awake. I'd forgotten something, I just knew it. Something I would need tomorrow. I sat up in bed.

I'd forgotten to go to the bank and get money. People would start arriving at nine a.m., and I'd have no money to make change. The ATM would only allow me to withdraw so much, and none of those would be single bills. For an instant I thought of calling the bank president and rousting him out of bed. Bad idea. I chose to pace instead.

"Mary Clare." Mama grumbled from across the hall. "Why are you awake? We have a big day tomorrow." She yawned loud enough I could hear it from across the hall.

I opted for out-and-out wailing. "I forgot to get money for

tomorrow! It was on my original list of things to do, but I never found my list."

"Is that what you're worried about? Rennie and I went to the bank this afternoon. We have plenty of money for tomorrow. It's in the safe, sweetheart."

My shoulders unknotted, and my nerves stopped jingling. "Mama, you are such a blessing."

"So are you, dear. Now get some sleep." She instructed the dogs to lie on me and keep me in bed. They did their best to accommodate. My mind, however, insisted on fretting. As hard as I tried, I hadn't been able to recreate my list, but I was sure there were chores left undone. No matter how hard I concentrated, I couldn't pull it up from the depths of forgetfulness. I did, however, succeed in counting four hundred thirty-nine Bar-B-Que sandwiches before nodding off.

I might have slept right through the rest of the night had it not been for the pounding on the cottage door. If my bleary eyes could be trusted, my bedside clock read two-thirty a.m. I hurried downstairs, pulling on my robe. It never occurred to me to flip on a light. It never occurred to me to look out the window before wrenching the door open. I stared into the eyes of Clarence Leonard. His gun was drawn.

I was speechless. Deputy Leonard stood with lips pursed and squinted into the darkness.

"Is that your mama coming down the stairs, Miss?"

"Yes, it is. Why are you pointing your gun at me?"

"Oh, sorry." He lowered the gun. "Are you two alone in the house?"

"Of course, we are." I flipped on the living room light. Mama stood her ground at the bottom of the stairs. "It's okay, Mama. It's just Clarence."

"Make him give you his gun, Mary Clare. I don't trust him."

"I'm sorry, ma'am. I can't do that. The two of you may be in danger. You need to come with me right away."

"What!" We yelled in unison. "Why?"

"Because Boomer told me to take you with me to the police station. He's inside your shop right now."

Mama and I rushed to the window. Sure enough, every light in Pocket Change blazed. "Why is Boomer in our shop?"

"Please come with me, ladies. I'm not to relay any information until you are secured at the station."

"We're not moving." I crossed my arms.

"If you don't tell us what's going on, I'll tell everyone in town Boomer won't let you have any bullets," Mama threatened.

"That's not true," the deputy spluttered.

"Won't make any difference." Mama was adamant.

Clarence shuffled his feet. "I'm really not supposed to tell you anything." He lowered his voice. "It could get me into a lot of trouble."

We glared him down.

"Okay." He kind of reminded me of a deflating balloon.

"That's more like it." Mama jutted her chin in the air. "Now, let's have it."

"Someone tried to burn down your business tonight." I heard the gulp in Clarence's voice.

I remembered the other items on my to-do list. Install motion lights and call the security company. I had to do a better job of keeping up with my lists.

CHAPTER NINETEEN

In defense of Deputy Clarence Leonard, he acted calmly. He kept his composure while we fell apart. We asked for the bombshell. He obliged. It wasn't his fault we were coming unglued. The stress of the last few days had left stretch marks. Mama bounded up and down the stairs looking for her shoes. I checked the fridge for my watch. Mama found her shoes and then asked Clarence if he'd seen her favorite bra. Muttering, she ascended the stairs, only to return a few moments later to announce she'd found it. Deputy Leonard chose to step outside. He was wiser than I'd given him credit for.

After ten minutes, we were dressed and leading the dogs out the door.

"I wasn't instructed to take the dogs, ma'am."

"The dogs are going." Mama clicked the leashes onto collars and stood ready.

"Yes, ma'am. The dogs are going." He put Mama in the front. I climbed in the back with Flash and Blur. They didn't like the cage in front of us any more than I did. They barked. I whined. Deputy Leonard backed out of the lot and turned on his siren. The dogs went crazy.

"Turn that contraption off," Mama shrieked.

"Yes, ma'am." He flipped the switch, and it died a slow, distressing death. As we passed the front of the shop, I caught a glimpse of Boomer on the porch. He examined loose hay and what appeared to be charred corn stalks.

Within minutes we were inside Boomer's office. It was nearly three-thirty a.m. when Boomer finally made an appearance. The dogs had fallen asleep in one of the empty holding cells.

"What's going on, Boomer?" I tried to stomp my foot, but it was asleep.

Boomer looked at Clarence. "Did you tell them?"

"He said someone tried to burn down Pocket Change," I blurted, before Clarence had a chance to answer. "He won't tell us who, when, or why."

"That's because I told him to get you to safety as soon as possible, and we don't know who, when, or why. We weren't sure what the situation involved, and we wanted to remove you from the premises." He lowered himself into his chair. It groaned under his weight.

"He scared us nearly to death." Mama's indignation blazed all over her cheeks. "His banging on the door nearly gave me a heart attack."

Boomer scowled and leaned forward until his chair begged mercy. "It would have been worse if someone burned down your business and your cottage. I realize neither of you are happy to be here. I also realize your nerves are shot. What you don't realize is Clarence is probably the only reason you still have a business and possibly a home. He spotted the arsonist at the front of the shop. When he engaged his lights, the guy took off. If the hay hadn't been damp from the rain, it probably would have been too late. You owe a debt of gratitude to my deputy."

Mama and I looked at each other then down at the floor.

When I lifted my head, Boomer was watching us with raised eyebrows. Clarence sat nearby, studying the shine on his shoes.

"I'm sorry, Clarence." I looked him straight in the nose. "None of this is your fault."

"I'm sorry I called you names." Mama's whisper fluttered out with shame.

"You didn't," Clarence replied.

"Oh. I meant to. Wait, that didn't come out right. I…"

Clarence stared at her and then at Boomer. I could tell he thought a transfer might be nice. Finally, he nodded and excused himself. "I'll go back to the shop."

Shaking his head, Boomer said, "Park your car at Mutt's grocery, and go to the cottage on foot. The lights are off, but I told the other officer you'd be back. He's expecting you. He's doing surveillance at the shop."

"Yes, sir." Clarence saluted.

"There are some lovely cookies on the counter, young man. Feel free to help yourself." Mama believed cookies cured everything.

We watched Clarence exit. The magnitude of the situation began to sink into my muddled mind. "Boomer, what happened?"

"I had an emergency in Jonesboro." He cleared his throat. "I left Clarence in charge with instructions for what to do and where to patrol. I didn't get back until almost one o'clock in the morning. I called him. He said everything appeared to be fine. An hour later, he phoned and reported a suspicious figure fleeing from your front porch. I instructed Clarence to get the two of you off the premises. I'm sorry he frightened you, but we had to make sure you were safe."

"Why on earth would anyone want to burn down Pocket Change? Do you think someone would have burned the cottage with us in it?" I shivered. "Are you going to shut us down?"

The smell of coffee filled the air, and he didn't answer for a long time. We were in a quandry. Taking a deep breath, Boomer poured the coffee and brought each of us a cup. This time we accepted gratefully.

"What time do you open?" He took a tentative sip of the scalding brew.

I looked at the clock on the wall. "In five hours, but the employees will arrive about eight. Rennie may get there earlier." I took a sip of the brew and winced. Bitter coffee to wash down bitter news.

"I know you've got your heart set on opening today. But the truth is I don't know if it's safe. A window was broken out. Someone threw a gasoline-soaked rag inside. Same kind of rag I found out at Smitty's place."

All our time and effort would have been lost. The treasures in the shop would have been reduced to ashes. Mama tried to hold her composure, but her coffee cup shook. She set it on Boomer's desk with a clatter.

Boomer jumped to his feet. "Lilly, are you okay? Would you like to lie down? Those cots are real comfortable." Flash and Blur wagged their rears in agreement. "You want me to call a doctor?"

"No." Mama gritted her teeth. "I'm fine. I'm just very, very angry."

"Oh, I understand, Lilly." Boomer seemed relieved to deal with anger over hysterics.

Mama looked Boomer square in the eye. "I don't understand why someone is doing this, but I do know we can't sit around and wait for them to accomplish their goal."

"I agree." Boomer hovered near her. "If you continue with your open house, there would be conditions. I'd place two men on the premises. They'll wear plain clothes, and they won't bother any of your customers."

"Could they stay in the office with the surveillance cameras?" I asked.

He rubbed his jaw. It made a scratching noise. "One could. The other would monitor the perimeter. They could change every hour."

"Where will you be?" Mama asked.

"I'll be questioning Boyd Barlow in about two hours." He glanced at his watch.

"Why Barlow?" I asked.

"Because I'm beginning to think you might be right about him. I could have sworn I saw his car pass while I searched your shop. There's nothing illegal about that, but why would he be out at that hour?"

"Are you certain it was his?" I asked.

"No, but I'm going to check it out anyway. I also need to see if Saige has regained consciousness, and I had a message from Ruby Holly. She wants to meet with me today."

"Why does Ruby want to talk to you?" I inquired.

He shrugged. "She wouldn't tell Clarence. She said it was important she see me today."

"You may want to make time to question Ethel Glacier."

"Ethel?" Boomer's head jerked up. "You've talked to Ethel?"

"No, but Ralph did. She's been in Little Rock and plans to meet with him this morning at eight o'clock at his house. She requested a private meeting before business hours," I explained. "She's looking for a place to rent."

"Will wonders never cease?" Boomer straightened and cocked his head. "Did she tell him why she disappeared?"

"I don't know. That's all Ralph told me. My guess is she got scared and needed time to think."

"Okay." Boomer added yet another appointment to his pad. "I'll start with Barlow at seven o'clock in the morning and go to Ralph's house afterward. Ruby may have to wait until this afternoon."

"Boomer," Mama interrupted, "when do you plan to sleep?"

"When this mess is over. It's okay. I do worry about

Clarence, though. He's not used to eighteen-hour days. The poor guy may change his career before it gets started."

"We haven't exactly given him much support," I confessed.

Mama stood. "Boomer, may we go now? We really do need to get back."

"Sure. Y'all get Flash and Blur out of cell number one, and I'll drive you. Give me a few minutes. I'll warm up the car."

Within minutes we were back home and trudging up the stairs. It was five-fifteen. I set the alarm for six-thirty and fell on the bed fully clothed.

In what seemed like two seconds, the phone alarm beeped, and prancing dogs yipped in my ear. I moaned and rolled over. Sure enough, the alarm monster read six-thirty. I stumbled around and found my slippers. Mama's bed was empty, and I could hear clattering in the kitchen.

"Mary Clare, are you up?" she hollered.

"I'm up. I'm not awake, but I'm up. Why are the dogs so hyper?"

"I fixed each one a pancake. You want two or three?"

"None. I want to check the shop. There's no telling what kind of mess we may have to clean up. I'll be down in a few minutes." I hurried into the bathroom to shower.

I pulled on new khaki slacks and a warm sweater and slipped my feet into loafers. A quick tug of the brush through my damp hair was all I could muster. The last thing I grabbed was the bibbed apron from the closet. As I cinched the perky red accessory around my waist I began to feel the exhilaration I'd been expecting since winning the money. I would not allow our proud moment to be tarnished by all the weirdness of the last several days. I couldn't wait to see the pretty apron being worn by the other employees. Hopefully, the Pocket Change crest would become synonymous with integrity, fairness, and quality. I rushed down the stairs with the hyper hounds at my heels.

"Are you sure you don't want something to eat, honey? It may be a long day."

"I'm sure. I just hope we have customers. We may have plenty of time to eat."

"You worry too much. Trust in the Lord, Mary Clare." She shoved a paper cup and a bag full of promotional goodies at me. I hoped there was a full day's worth of energy in that cup of orange juice. "We'll have a glass of juice to tide us over."

I was amazed by her composure, until I saw the kitchen. Cooking and baking had always been Mama's therapy. From the looks of the cottage kitchen, she'd cooked her way through four skillets and three stew pots. Tidy piles of scones stood on the counter. Cider filled every available pitcher.

The crisp air and overcast sky taunted me, but the weatherman promised the wintry precipitation was supposed to hold off until tomorrow. Maybe the weather, at least, would cooperate. We strode to the shop and went in through the back door.

"Morning, ladies." Boomer grunted a greeting.

Fortunately for him, most of my juice was gone. Otherwise, he might have been wearing it. "You're not supposed to be here." I yelled to make myself heard above the pounding of my heart.

"Sorry. I should have parked around back so you'd see me."

Mama clutched her chest. "Boomer, why are you here? Aren't Clarence and his helper supposed to be on duty?"

"They were on duty up until an hour ago. I caught a little shuteye on the couch in your office until they left. I hope you don't mind. I sent them home for two hours sleep. They'll report back at nine a.m. sharp." He rose slowly from the kitchen table. The man had to be exhausted.

"Why don't you go back to sleep for a couple of hours? I'll wake you at nine."

"Thanks, but I want to get the jump on Barlow. I'm already a little later than I'd planned. The early bird catches the worm, you know."

"How appropriate," I said.

He glanced toward the front. "I've checked everything out. Clarence taped cardboard over the broken window. It's on the side by the garage, so it shouldn't be real obvious from the front. You may want to set a plant or something in front of it until the glass guy can fix it. Um." He hesitated.

"What?" I felt dread inching up my backbone like a caterpillar.

Boomer examined the ceiling, the floorboards, and even his nails.

"Well, you know that window goes almost to the floor. It's possible a critter could have crawled inside before the cardboard went up." He continued to look around. "I didn't see any footprints, though."

"What kind of critter?" I eyeballed the immediate area.

"We do have a lot of racoons in the area. Wouldn't be the first time one tried to set up residence in somebody's house."

"Thanks." I felt much better as I rolled my eyes.

"Sorry. Just want you to be prepared for whatever."

I was not now, nor would I ever be, ready for a raccoon. I'd have to alert all the workers and volunteers to be on the lookout for shoplifters and bandits.

Boomer left, and Mama ordered me to get to work. She went in search of baskets in which to put the assortment of bookmarks, magnets, bracelets, and other promotional items. We carried them to the checkout counter and placed them neatly beside the massive brass cash register.

It had taken three men and two fussy women to lift it to the counter. Marma Lee located it in Tennessee at an old variety store auction. Seventy years old, it still shone like new. Computers may be necessary for the office, Smartphones might make my life easier, but this gorgeous hunk of history made me fuzzy with happiness every single time I looked at it. This beauty was the focal point of the twelve-foot oak counter. It held its place of distinction with pride.

For the next hour, we set up the refreshments. I looked for masked critters and caught Mama doing the same, but she wouldn't admit it. She claimed the idea of a raccoon climbing in the window and us not seeing evidence of it bordered on the ridiculous. Still, I saw her pulling up the tablecloth on the refreshment table and peeking under it.

By the end of the hour, the kitchen counter held enough goodies to feed a shopping army. Whiffs of cinnamon cider wafted from a cherry sideboard. Marma Lee arrived promptly at seven-thirty and began lighting candles, her specialty. No one mentioned her dumb sculpture, and I didn't offer any explanations. Later, I'd throw the thing away.

When Molly arrived, she headed to the Children's Chamber and began the "chamber" music. Recordings of Halloween resonations echoed eerily up the stairs. Soon, the faint sounds would hopefully be lost in the hubbub of excited customers. My only worry about the downstairs area was the still-not-caulked phone booth. Another thing on my lost to-do list..

The mystery moguls bustled through the entrance. Each picked up silver trays from the kitchen. Hercule Poirot hosted the cider bowl. Hercule looked strangely familiar. His was the only character to look a bit odd.

"Mama, is that Richard?"

"Yes it is. Doesn't he look debonair?"

"I always thought Hercule was on the short side."

"You're right. That's why we have Richard serving the cider. His pants are five inches too short. We threw a white towel over one of his sleeves, and Marma Lee told him to keep the other one behind his back. Unless he needs to pour, of course."

"What happened to the man who was here yesterday? I thought he was playing Hercule?"

"He came down with the flu. Don't they all look amazingly authentic?" In addition to Hercule Poirot, we had Miss Marple, Alfred Hitchcock, Shawn and Gus from Psych, Jessica Fletcher, Richard Castle, Nate-the-Great, Sherlock Holmes, and Dr. Watson.

I nudged Mama as Marma Lee flitted by in a tight-fitting suit and seamed hose. "Why is Marma Lee in that getup? She's supposed to help at the register."

Mama shrugged. "When I questioned her about it, she said she wanted to look like one of the "dames" in the gum shoe books. I told her what I thought she looked like. You know, sometimes she doesn't appreciate candor."

"I hope she didn't go to the hospital in that garb. If poor Saige did revive, that would throw him right back into a coma."

It was eight forty-five. I glanced at the front door. The back door opened. In walked Clarence.

"Good morning," I chirped. "Would you like some cider or something to eat?"

"No, thank you, ma'am. I need to get to my post."

"Come with me. The cameras are set up in the walk-in-closet inside my office."

He kept pace behind me, straight-faced and serious. With all the preliminary activity, no one seemed to notice him.

"Would you mind placing some of Pansy's cards by each of the mums? I almost forgot."

Rennie nodded as I plopped a handful beside the guest log.

"I'll be happy to. Everything is ready to go." She lowered her voice. "Lilly told Marma Lee, Richard, and me what happened. They," she bobbed her head toward the babbling group of mystery characters, "don't know about it. Might be wise if you didn't mention it. It might put them out of sorts."

I nodded and glanced around.

Rennie cleared her throat. "I hope you don't mind, but I asked Mick to clean up the mess on the front porch. He came in about thirty minutes ago wanting to know how he could help. I suggested porch detail. There was only one hay bale badly damaged. He rearranged the others and they look pretty good."

"I didn't ask him to help."

"He mentioned that." Her voice went soft. "Still, he wanted to do something. He insisted he'd be happy to help load merchandise too."

"That was thoughtful."

Rennie patted my hand. "It's a start."

I never had a chance to see Mick. The first car arrived promptly at nine a.m. We all froze then dashed to our places. This was it.

For the next several hours, we didn't have a chance to even acknowledge one another. Mama and I were kept busy at the counter. Marma Lee, aka "doll face," wrapped as we rang up purchases. Books flew off the shelf at an alarming rate. I'd need to place another order first thing Monday.

Two English buffets, three chairs, and our entire dining room suite were loaded into a van. The cherry sideboard, holding the cider, sold at eleven o'clock. Richard and Mick neatly transferred all of Richard's paraphernalia to a hutch. Karen Kingsbury's shelf had only one lonely book left, and Mitford was a mess. At least the three remaining books were. They were upside down and backward. Jan Karon would have been delighted. The Amish books sold like hotcakes, and according to Molly, Sheila Turnage's display emptied within two hours. Every techie tidbit and cutting-edge invention found its way to the cash register. O'Hare's would have been proud. If I'd had time, I would have moon walked.

No time.

By noon, my head swam. Rennie continued to meet and greet graciously as people from everywhere poured into the store. The main attraction, however, seemed to be behind the cider kettle. Groups of mature women clustered around Hercule.

"Just look at Verna May Peabody." Mama's jaw clenched as she stuck a scone in my mouth.

I removed the scone and smiled at my customer, an Aunt Bea look-alike. Her purchase, a beautiful broach boasting ruby stones and turquoise, demanded my attention. Marma Lee wrapped it delicately and tied a ribbon around the handle of the bag. A happy and satisfied customer sauntered toward the door.

Marma Lee pointed to the array of promotional items. "Don't forget your goodies, Toots." Marma Lee's husky voice bordered on the bizarre. She carried this role-playing a little far. The woman just coughed, took two steps back, and nabbed the last bracelet.

The infamous Verna May was indeed making a spectacle of herself. Not a bookmark could have been wedged between her and Richard, despite the fact he kept trying to ease away from her.

"Look at that," Mama hissed.

The noise ebbed to a comfortable level, which meant we could hear Verna May's high-pitched voice. She flirted outrageously with Richard and bullied any woman away who came within arm's length.

The front door opened, and Clarence's replacement strolled across the floor and quietly slipped into the office. Like clockwork, Clarence came out and headed for the back door. Noticing the commotion at the cider hutch, he stopped to listen and observe. He turned to look at Mama. Marching over to the table, he genially asked Richard for a cup of cider.

"Good afternoon, Ms. Peabody," Clarence greeted.

Verna May blushed. She wasn't used to having two males in such close proximity.

"Why, hello there." Her flamboyance made the china dishes rattle. "Are you new in town?" She squinted and batted both eyelashes at the same time. The movement was magnified threefold by her thick lenses.

"No, ma'am. I'm Deputy Clarence Leonard. Don't you remember me? I helped you when you called for assistance. You remember? When you got stuck in the bathtub." Clarence delivered this announcement with a straight face. "You probably don't recognize me out of uniform. Nice to see you, again, ma'am." He took a sip of the cider and set his cup on the table. Turning toward Mama, he winked and marched out the back door.

Within minutes Verna May Peabody left the building, the gaggle of giggling women cleared out, and Mama beamed. Deputy Clarence Leonard had been upgraded to hero status.

Boomer walked in the front door with a grim face. Behind him were two uniformed officers, whom I recognized from last week. Either Verna May was having us arrested or something was terribly wrong.

"You watch the counter, Mama. I'll be right back." I followed Boomer into the office. He shut the door and told me to sit down. I did. The officers stood by the door.

"Mary Clare, I have some bad news."

"What is it?"

"I tried to interview Barlow this morning. He wasn't there. The business has a closed sign on the door, and no one answered."

I listened to the information and nodded. This was a definite kink in the investigation, but it didn't warrant his somber expression. I told him so.

"That's not the worst. I left there and went to Ralph Perty's house. That's where I've been most of the day." He dropped his head.

"You've been questioning Ethel all day? Isn't that a little excessive?"

Boomer shook his head. "We didn't find Ethel." He took a deep breath. "We did find blood, a great deal of blood. We have reason to believe Ralph Perty's been murdered."

CHAPTER TWENTY

"Ralph's dead?" I was dumbfounded.

Boomer nodded. "We found a knife. The police are searching the grounds for his body. I'm sorry to have to tell you this now, but you needed to know."

"This whole ordeal is too bizarre."

"We believe Ethel and Barlow did this together. It all boils down to greed."

I thought about taking up hand wringing. "Ethel seemed like such a gentle person. Boy, did I call that one wrong."

"You weren't wrong about Barlow. If he is the mastermind, that would explain why he wanted rid of you. You've said all along he was guilty. Your insistence almost got your building burned down."

Using the security cameras, I scanned the room for Mick's face. His arm around my shoulder would feel really good about now. But Mick wasn't here. "What about Newton? Does he know about his uncle?"

Boomer nodded again. "We notified him a few minutes ago. He took it pretty hard."

"Why would Ethel kill Ralph?" I grasped to make sense of this.

"Revenge. It wasn't common knowledge, but Ralph is the one who turned her in. From his store window, he saw her talking to Smitty on the night of the murder. He bragged about it later. Worst mistake he ever made. Word must have gotten back to her."

I remembered watching Ralph's lights go out after our conversation last night. I had a perfect view of his office from the shop. That meant his vantage point from the realty office was just as clear.

"Then why would she call and ask to rent something from him?"

"That was a ruse. Newton said business stinks right now, and let's face it, Ralph likes to turn a dollar. He had no qualms about renting to her as long as he made money from it. Besides, by then she'd been released, and he probably thought she'd been cleared. I'll patrol tonight. Barlow and Ethel are still at large. I seriously doubt they're anywhere near Pocket, but I don't intend to take any chances."

Boomer left with the two officers. Clarence resumed his vigil, and the rest of the afternoon progressed without any more mishaps. At five, we were assisting the nursing home residents, who'd come to celebrate the grand opening, to their waiting van. We presented each with thank-you baskets. Inside were perfumes, stationery, candies, books, and symbolic gold thimbles for the work they'd done in designing and creating the mystery characters' costumes. We'd also enclosed a hundred-dollar bill for each person. They were delighted.

With the exception of Boomer's news, the day went well. Parents and kids loved the Children's Chamber. Molly beamed as she came up the stairs. She'd distributed almost all the free yo-yos and bookmarks and read over thirty books at the reading bar.

"Uncle Ardmore came up, said he'd found shiny stuff in the

phone booth, and handed it to me." I took it from her extended hand and dropped it into my apron pocket. Aside from the one I'd kept for myself, it was the only survivor. The bracelets and paperweights were the first to go.

I handed Rennie the keys, and she locked the front doors, flipping over the closed sign as she did. We all crashed on the nearest surface. Richard and Mick carried in bar stools from the kitchen. The dining table and chairs were now sitting in someone else's house. We would have to bring more furniture from the storage shed before Monday.

Mama floated around the room distributing leftover scones, cookies, and cider, and no one said anything for a long time. When the tray was empty and every cup was filled, she went to Richard, who immediately gave up his seat, opting to stand near her.

Mick kept his distance. I had to admit, he'd been a trooper today. I completely forgot to clean up the singed mess from last night's escapade on the porch, and having someone to load furniture hadn't even entered my mind.

I wanted to approach him but didn't want to appear forward. Besides, there were other concerns. The little niggling worry I'd kept at bay all day nudged my brain. What if Ethel and Barlow returned? Revenge was an ugly and consuming thing. If they killed Ralph, why not me? I shoved the thought right out of my mind. However, I did make a decision. I would make sure Mama wasn't in any danger. She didn't know about Ralph. None of them did.

First, I'd complete my day on a positive note. I went to the office to get my surprises. When I returned, everyone straggled toward the back door, but I headed them off at the pass. Handing each a card and dispensing hugs, I thanked them for making the grand opening such a success. The mystery characters were the first to discover the contents. Inside each envelope nestled a hundred-dollar bonus for a job well done. Pocket Change was off to a good start.

Molly trailed behind the other employees. She held back and held out the hundred-dollar bill. "I don't think I should take it."

"Why?" Inwardly I groaned. Here it comes. She's taken another job.

"Marma Lee told me the phone booth was supposed to be sealed. If I'd been watching more closely, no one could have opened it. I'm just glad it was Uncle Ardmore and not a child. I'm sorry, Miss Casteel. Maybe this hundred dollars will pay to have it fixed."

"Oh, Molly. Marma Lee's wrong. The booth was supposed to be sealed so no one could get in, but the job wasn't finished. It's not your fault. The fault is mine for not remembering to get it sealed." I pushed the money back toward her. "You deserve it. We're blessed to have you with us and please, from now on, call me Mac."

Her face relaxed in relief. I'd throttle Marma Lee when I got my hands on her.

Mama started to the back door. "I'll start dinner." Her shoulders slumped. She was tired.

"We're ordering out, Mama. I'm in a pizza kind of mood tonight. How about y'all?"

Within minutes Richard called the order in. We tidied up and turned out the lights. Richard and Mick locked up. We opened the back door and were met by a blast of winter. Everybody scurried to the cottage. No one noticed when I unplugged the landline. I prayed everyone's cell was still turned off. I'd asked them to do so when we opened up this morning. Now, we deserved a few hours of uninterrupted down time. I deliberately left the television off. At this moment, there was no need for my friends to find out about today's tragedy.

Excitement over the success of the day replaced fatigue.

Mick shared tidbits of what customers said about the business. I couldn't help but notice how many times he looked directly at me with eyes shining with something I hoped wasn't just friendly goodwill. He seemed determined to make up for his absence the day before. Marma Lee was the only one to complain.

"Do you suppose women really used to stand around in stiletto heels? My feet are killing me." She kicked off the offensive shoes and massaged her red toes.

"You weren't supposed to be in costume. If you'd worn what you should have, you would have been comfortable." I shook a napkin at her.

"I wanted to stand out."

"You did," I assured her. "One of the nursing home residents wants to fix you up with the guy across the hall from her. She said he'd think you were the bee's knees."

The food arrived, and Richard offered up grace. We ate on the floor around the coffee table. There was plenty of room at the table, but no one wanted to leave the coziness of the fireplace. Richard hopped up and down, acting as waiter. Marma Lee's look of admiration spoke volumes as did Mama's gleam in her eye. When the only thing left was a string of cheese stuck to the top of a pizza box, we gathered in the kitchen. As we'd done all day, we worked as a team to clean up.

By seven-thirty, everyone's steam was gone. Marma Lee borrowed a pair of tennis shoes and called it a night. Richard bid a fond farewell to Mama and even gave her a quick peck on the cheek.

Mick lagged. "Boomer told me what happened."

Alarmed, I checked to see if Mama had heard. I wanted to break it to her myself. I heaved a sigh of relief. She and Rennie were outside, no doubt sniffing for snow.

"It's not safe for you to stay by yourself." Concern etched lines over his handsome face. Part of me wanted to run my fingers across his brow and smooth away the lines of worry. The other part was thrilled they were there.

"Boomer will be patrolling all night." I fidgeted. "Besides, Ethel and Barlow are probably in another state by now. It's too dangerous to return, and I'm no longer a threat. I'm sorry they had to hurt Ralph before they left."

"That's just it. They weren't forced into killing him. They killed him out of vengeance. They had a vendetta against him. They have one against you too."

I shrugged it off. "I'm fine. I'll be extra careful." I hoped I sounded more confident than I felt.

He gazed at me for a long time. "Angelica left last night."

"Oh."

"I called her after I left Pocket Change. I told her it was over. I've told her before, but she can be very persistent. She hears what she wants. When we met a few years ago in Memphis, she worked as an interior designer, and Dad and I did some consignment work for her. She seemed exotic to a small-town guy."

He couldn't possibly imagine how this bruised my already aching ego. "She's still exotic. You might find you miss that."

"I like integrity and truth. Those aren't qualities she's familiar with. I owe you an explanation about yesterday. Angelica knew it was the anniversary of my mother's death." His eyes were full of leftover pain and loss.

I felt like a complete fool. "I'm sorry. I didn't realize."

"Angelica thought she'd breeze into town, and I'd be grateful and take her back. She didn't know I usually spend the day alone. I go visit Mom's grave and just get lost for a while. I'm afraid I'm not very good company when this date rolls around. I should have told you all this. I'm sorry."

"Angelica's very beautiful." I thought I could hear the thud of my heart dropping to the ground.

"Not as beautiful as you." He cupped my cheek in his hand. "I'll be happy to stay here. I'm worried about you. Maybe it's because of what happened to Mom, but I have this," he hesitated, trying to pluck just the right word out of his brain, "dread."

The word came out slow and flat. Dread, dead. Sounded a lot alike.

"I'd like to stay." His weary smile tugged at my heart. "I'll be quiet as a mouse. You won't know I'm around." He stepped close enough so that no one else could have heard the intimacy in his voice. "I want to make sure you're safe. Let me do that for you." He pulled me to him, and I could feel the strong and steady rhythm of his heart.

I closed my eyes and breathed in the scent I'd come to adore.

Even as strong as my faith was, I knew not to put myself in a situation that would give people like Verna May Peabody fodder for future rumors. I didn't want that for Mick, and I didn't want it for me. If we were to move forward with a relationship, I didn't want it to start out tainted or tarnished by inappropriate gossip.

I stole a look at his face. "I have your number if I need you. I'll be fine. And this time I have the correct number. I fixed my goof in my phone."

He smiled then tilted my chin and gazed into my eyes. "If you won't let me stay with you, then I'm staying at my shop tonight." He stood back, and I swayed a bit from the sudden release.

"Go get some sleep." I placed my hand on his arm. "I appreciate all you did today. It means a lot, and thank you for explaining about everything."

Retrieving his jacket from the back of the chair, he reluctantly headed for the back door. "Please, Mac. If you hear anything, if you just want to talk, call." The unsteadiness of his voice sent shivers down my spine. But not in a good way.

"I'll be fine. Why don't you come for breakfast about nine? I'll make it exotic," I teased.

He took my hand. Together we walked to the door, fingers

laced together, our steps slow. I reached for the doorknob. He reached for me, then I was in his arms. His kisses were tender, slow, loving. When he raised his head, he ran his hands through my already mussed hair. I trembled and wished I could cuddle in his arms until all this mess with Smitty was over. He opened his mouth to say something, changed his mind, shook his head, and walked out the door. For one wild, hairbrained moment, I thought about chasing him down and dragging him back. Instead, I bowed my head and prayed God would watch over him and remove his heartache and worry. I wasn't sure if he was truly worried about me or still mourning the anniversary of his mother's death. Either way, I wanted God to help him. I marched into the front room. Mama and Rennie were talking excitedly.

"Honey, that's a wonderful idea." Mama clapped her hands together.

"We really should. I'm sure she and the nurses would appreciate them." Rennie's grin spread from one triple-pierced ear to the other.

"What are you two plotting?"

"Honey, Rennie and I are going to take the rest of the refreshments and cider to the hospital. It will do Mrs. Nichols good to have some company, plus we can check on Saige while we're there. Do you mind?"

"That's great." I plastered a smile on my face.

Mama looked at Rennie, a twinkle in her eyes. "We thought we might drop in on Richard if we finish up in time."

I shook my fork at her. "Lilly Casteel. You're spying. What are you going to do if you find Verna May Peabody there?"

"Honey, I'll just throw her in the bathtub."

I helped them load up the leftover refreshments along with cups and napkins. Snow began drifting to the ground. "How long you think you'll be gone?"

"We'll be back by midnight, Mother Mac." Rennie saluted.

"Tell Mrs. Nichols I'm praying."

"We will, sweetheart. Now, don't wait up. I know you're tired, and I'm a big girl."

I hugged her. "Okay, Mama. I love you."

I hugged Rennie. "Keep your eyes on her. Don't let her out of your sight. I'll explain later."

She gave me a quizzical look and glanced at Mama to see if she'd heard. Mama, however, sat in the car playing with the radio.

Rennie's eyebrows came together. "Is everything all right, Mac?"

"I think so." Mama honked the horn. We both jumped. "Boomer will be patrolling tonight. Everything will be fine. Drive carefully." I opened the driver's side door for her.

Rennie put her car in reverse and waved a hesitant goodbye.

Chiding myself for my over-active imagination, I walked in and straightened the already tidy kitchen. Still wearing my apron, I decided to dust and sweep, but my heart wasn't in it, and my energy reserve petered out. With a sigh, I turned off the lights and sat by the flickering fire, thinking about Mick. Angelica was gone. He told her it was over.

He called me beautiful.

That was the last I remember. When I awoke with a start, something pinged on the window. I jumped up from the rocker and peeled back the curtain on the front window. The yard was white, and the sleet was back. A thin layer of ice was already evident on the tree limbs. Remembering that I'd disabled the phone, I hurried over, plugged it in, and called Rennie. She answered on the third ring.

"Hi. Is everything okay?"

"Everything is fine. Are you going to tell me what's going on? I told Lilly the roads were too slick to drive on, and I brought her to my house. I've been trying to call you for the last two hours. Your Mama fell asleep the minute we came in. I promised her I'd get hold of you before I tuck in for the night."

"I'm sorry. I unplugged the landline while everyone was here and forgot to plug it back in. My cell's upstairs. Everything's quiet here, so go on to bed. Thanks, Rennie."

"Won't you tell me what's going on?"

"In the morning, I promise. I have to go. Flash and Blur need to go outside."

"Okay. We'll get there as soon as we can in the morning."

"Mick's coming over for breakfast at nine. We'll have a party."

I hung up the phone and hurried to the dogs, who were prancing and whining as I clicked on their leashes and opened the door. They scrambled outside and trotted to the side of the house. Within minutes they were back, supreme relief shining on both faces.

"Let that be a lesson to you. Pizza and pumpkin cookies are not recommended doggy foods." I bent down to nuzzle their foreheads. "Let's go to bed." They understood the word "bed" and bounded up the steps. I extinguished the fire and followed them.

Within minutes, a neat little heap of clothes lay on the chair in the bathroom. After a hot shower, I threw on my favorite pair of flannel pjs, picked up my work clothes, and carried them to the hamper in the hall closet. I slung the apron over my arm and dumped the rest inside the wicker basket.

By the time I walked to my bedroom, my tail feathers were definitely dragging, but I was determined to go empty out my apron pockets before hitting the bed. Out came the day's accumulation: a paper clip, a penny, a pencil, and two bracelets. I knew the minute I placed the bracelets on the bedside table something was amiss. One of the bracelets was not a Pocket Change giveaway. It was gold, expensive, and engraved. In the flurry of the day, Molly probably just glanced at it and assumed it was one of the giveaways. Neither she nor Uncle Ardmore realized it wasn't.

It hit me like a hammer. "Shiny stuff." That was what Uncle Ardmore had been talking about the day he and Junior delivered the mums and hay. He'd looked at the floor of the phone booth and declared "shiny stuff." The bracelet must have been what caught his eye. Sitting on the edge of the bed, I held it by its sturdy chain and flipped it over, examining it under my lamp. The identification bracelet had curly initials proudly engraved on the back along with a short but personal message.

Flash and Blur settled on the loveseat under the window. They watched as I gave the bracelet my full attention. I used the pencil I'd pulled from my pocket when turning the bracelet over. If I'd learned one thing during this mess, it was to be mindful of fingerprints. Molly handled it, and so had Uncle Ardmore. I didn't want to smudge the prints any more than they already were.

Not sure what to make of it, I trotted downstairs and rummaged around in a drawer until I found what I looked for, a plastic Ziploc bag. What had people ever done without Ziploc bags? I padded back up the stairs, placed the bag on my table, and switched out the light. Sometimes thoughts come easier in the dark.

I listened to the sleet hitting the window. By morning, the entire town would be glazed. Tomorrow would be Sunday, and everyone would breathe a sigh of relief at not having to travel any farther than church.

The bracelet troubled me. I should know the initials. They were important. I reached for the phone to call Boomer. The line was dead. No doubt the ice broke a telephone line somewhere. I reached for my cell, but the charge was empty, and I had no idea where the charger was. The idea of sitting in the car while it charged made me shiver, frown, and then shiver again. But I missed my phone. I'd gotten way more attached to that thing than I'd realized. The empty pillow where it usually rested when I slid into bed each night looked forlorn. It was almost like a person was missing on the other side of the bed instead of a machine. I pulled the down comforter around my shoulders and nestled. Before long, I felt two thuds. Flash and Blur joined me. We all listened to the splinking sound at the window. The clock read one-thirty a.m.

Then it hit me.

If I hadn't been so tired, I'd have recognized those initials sooner. I jumped out of bed and in my haste grabbed only my shoes and my keys, leaving my dogs and my coat behind. I had to get to the Children's Chamber. Unless I was mistaken, something important waited in the phone booth. I was pretty sure I knew why Smitty hadn't caulked it.

Slipping on the icy ground, I reached the kitchen door and turned the key in the lock with clumsy fingers. Scurrying across the kitchen, I was through the main area in seconds. Hurrying down the stairs leading to the Children's Chamber, I stopped only long enough to flip on the lights. They still didn't work. What a time for a power outage. There was no illumination on the stairs or in the Chamber.

Continuing at a snail's pace, I reached the bottom of the stairs. Stumbling over to the reading bar, I rummaged around until I found the flashlight. The bright beam lit up the room. In three long steps, I reached the phone booth and yanked open the accordion door. I knelt down to the floor, remembering the day I kicked it. Something had jiggled, but I dismissed it. It must have been the bracelet, and I must have dislodged it from its hiding place. I groped behind Superman and felt a cylinder. I'd been right.

Easing the flashlight down, I carefully pulled out the missing caulking gun using my pajama sleeve. I saw Smitty's initials scratched into the side. This had to be the same caulking gun Mama saw on the cabinet. Smitty bought a new one to use because he'd used this one to hide the bracelet in, but I'd dislodged it, and the bracelet had come out of its hiding place.

Returning to the bar, I grabbed a dusting rag and flipped open the compartment that should have held the caulk. Instead, there was a piece of paper rolled up and secured with a piece of carpenter's string. It was the type Smitty used, and here was the tool Smitty relied on. No one would think anything about the caulking gun in the phone booth. He'd planned to seal the door shut. Had he placed the paper in the cylinder as insurance? He must have bought the new caulker to complete the bathroom, which he never got the chance to do. Thankfully, Uncle Ardmore had only picked up the bracelet. The note inside was intact and so were the fingerprints.

Should I unwrap it? I knew not to cut the string. If Boomer were here, I could ask him, but if Boomer were here, he wouldn't let me see it. He'd whisk it away as evidence. Carefully, using my thumbnail, I removed the string. Sometimes it was best to do the deed and then beg forgiveness.

What I read confirmed my suspicions. I wondered if I could make it to the police station on the icy roads. Carefully, I re-rolled the paper and stood, cradling the caulking gun in my hand as I replaced the paper. Then, aiming my flashlight toward the stairs, I started up. It wasn't until I was at the top, that I noticed a chill in the air, even though I'd turned the heat up before closing up. I turned to look at the window covered with cardboard. The cardboard was missing, sleet pelted my floor, and there were creaking noises coming from my office.

CHAPTER TWENTY-ONE

Too late I doused the light. No doubt, the person I heard stumbling from my office already spotted me through the two-way mirror. I was at a disadvantage. On top of that, I felt a distinct tickle in my nose.

My sneezes aren't dainty. They sound like a Nascar muffler malfunction. It was enough to give my pursuer pause, however, which was exactly what I needed. Thank you, God, for tickling my nose.

I threw the caulking gun in the direction of the nearby bathroom and darted behind the checkout counter. Surely the sound of the metal would confuse the intruder. My eyes were getting the hang of the darkness, and I scanned the shelves to see if there was anything within arm's reach that would help me defend myself. Feather dusters and twine were my only choices. Fat lot of good those would do. I tightened my grip on the flashlight and hoped for the best. Maybe the sound of the rolling tool would scare the person away. Why in the world had I let my cell phone lose its charge?

Crouching, I listened for an opening door and retreating foot-steps. None came. Frantically, I tried to think of a plan. The information in the letter confirmed Smitty's murderer, but the killer didn't know about the note, only the bracelet. Had Smitty told the killer about the bracelet and demanded money? That would explain Smitty's expectance of a sudden windfall and the murderer's multiple trips to Pocket Change after Smitty's death. When he didn't find the bracelet on Smitty, he must have figured out the bracelet was hidden in the shop.

The only thing I knew for certain was the killer wouldn't fret over another murder. Silencing me would be a top priority. Chilling reality hit hard. This was someone in my world. Someone who'd appeared helpful, caring, and vulnerable. Anger began to replace the fright I'd felt moments before.

I could either stay here like a sitting duck or make a run for it. Taking a ragged, silent breath, I opted for the latter. Gripping the flashlight, I moved stealthily to the end of the bar and peered into the darkness. No one was in sight. Straining my ears, I heard an unusual sound coming from near the bay window. Had he run into the ficus tree?

Hearing another thud, I heard him descending the steps. Crouching low, and running as fast as possible, I made a mad dash toward the kitchen door. My hand was on the doorknob.

"Mary Clare."

The singsong voice stopped me in my tracks. I shielded the flashlight behind my back. It was my last hope. I pivoted to face the person who'd killed Smitty Small.

"Why?" My voice shook.

"You know why." The voice floated to me and chilled every bone in my body.

"No, I don't."

"I think you do, and that's regrettable. Things could have remained so uncomplicated. So…nice. You ruined everything." The voice was too near and way too familiar. My heart wanted to break.

Movement stopped, but even in the darkness, I caught a

glimmer of metal. It wasn't the caulking gun. Caulking guns didn't have sharp tips that can slice.

"Don't worry. You're safe for the time being. Why, you never know what could happen." The dry laugh reminded me of sawdust and sandpaper. "I may get sentimental and not hurt you at all. Let's go into the Cozy Area. You can light a fire and sit. It's drafty in here with that window out." I looked at the cardboard on the floor. Easy entry.

"I know we don't have to worry about your mother. She's with Rennie. My goodness. Things certainly are working out well. Sit in one of those cushy chairs and tell me where the bracelet is."

Hesitating would only make things worse. I took a step, easing the flashlight in front of me.

"Don't you find that flashlight cumbersome? Drop it." Curt and commanding.

My heart sank. I allowed my last hope to clank to the floor. Words from an old song flitted through my brain. Mama sang them after Daddy died. "God will take care of you. He will take care of me." I headed toward the fireplace.

"Light it."

Leaning over, I turned the knob. The gas flame leapt to life.

"Sit down." I perched on the chair to the right of the fireplace. My gaze never moved from the knife.

"You like my little whittler." The light from the fire cast a menacing look on the face across from me. "It comes in handy for everything from carpentry work to motivating people."

"Why didn't you use it to kill Smitty?"

"Too messy. I'm a neat person by nature. A place for everything and everything in its place. I only use this," he held up the knife, "when it's absolutely necessary. This," he said, tugging at a tie, "is what I used to kill Smitty. You've seen me with it on. You never suspected."

"No. You fooled me."

Gone was any semblance of sincerity. A cold, hard stare replaced the friendly smile.

I'd been so foolish. *Dear God, help me.*

"Yep, I take pride in that."

"Why did you kill Smitty?"

"Why should I tell you?"

"Because I'd like to know before you use that tie on me." I folded my arms. "That is what you're going to do, isn't it?"

"Yes."

Suspecting was one thing. Confirming another altogether. Sadness swept over me. I'd never see Mama again. I'd never pet Flash and Blur, and I'd never have another argument with Marma Lee.

Marma Lee…

"In that case," I said, settling on the chair, "I'd like to hear the whole story."

An odd expression crossed his face, and he nodded. Apparently, he was in the mood to brag. "All right. I'll tell you. You need to understand this entire situation is your fault."

I opened my mouth to argue, realized it wouldn't be prudent, and shut it.

He continued. "Smitty died because of something he found on this property."

"The bracelet?"

"No, the body."

"What body?" I was pretty sure I could guess the answer.

"Cora Ann Holly's body. I murdered her."

"Why?" I asked incredulously. "She was just a girl."

"She was twenty-one years old. She wasn't a kid," he spat. "She thought she could trick me into marrying her if she got pregnant. I am no one's puppet. I will not be manipulated." He shouted and hit the chair arm. I jumped and waited for him to calm down. After what seemed like enough time to complete a wash cycle, he composed himself and crossed his legs.

"You buried her on this lot." I urged him on.

"When my dad died, he left me the realty business. This lot was the perfect hiding place. The agency was right across the street. I could keep an eye on it. Everything was fine and had been all those years until you talked Newton into selling the lot to you."

"That's why you were so mad. It wasn't the price at all, was it?"

"No. Still, I kept my fingers crossed. It's a big lot. If you hadn't built that stupid cottage in the back, Smitty would never have found the body."

"Smitty found the bracelet on Cora Ann."

"He must have. I didn't realize she had it on. I guess she was going to give it to me for my birthday. I assumed it was hers. I took her purse and went through it, but I was careful not to leave prints. I dumped it in front of that preacher's house so it would look like she'd been abducted. I took the hairbrush because I thought it might come in handy some time." He chuckled. "It did. Now they think Smitty killed her. I'm glad I held on to it all these years.

Finding that little piece of 'evidence' must have thrown Boomer for a loop. I put it inside an empty paint can I'd used on the old Weatherly house. Then I stuck it in Smitty's shed the night his house burned. I figured the police would find it eventually, but if they didn't, I knew some snoop would. With her initials on it, even an idiot could connect the dots."

"Why did you burn his house? Did you think the bracelet was there?"

"No, but I was afraid maybe he'd written something incriminating. I couldn't take any chances."

I thought of the caulking gun and the note Smitty placed inside, explaining that Ralph murdered Cora Ann. Obviously, Ralph knew nothing about it. "How did you know the bracelet was here?"

"Smitty told me. He called and said to meet him out in the shed with money. You and Lilly were gone, so the timing couldn't have been more perfect. Smitty was an idiot. When he realized I didn't have the money with me, he turned his back to walk away. I put the tie around his neck and started pulling. He thought I'd stop once he told me where the bracelet was. When he said it was downstairs in the basement, I figured it would be easy to find. I didn't realize there was a stupid amusement park down there. I killed him before he told me exactly where to look."

I drew a deep breath. "Then you stuck him in the casket."

He snorted. "Too good to pass up. Kind of poetic justice, eh? You messed things up by buying the property. Seemed perfect for me to mess up your grand opening and your ridiculous prize casket."

"What about Ethel? Was all that blood they found at your house hers? Is she dead?"

"No. I swiped three liters of blood from the blood bank at the hospital. I volunteer my time there. Rumor had it the hospital wanted to expand. I own the land adjacent to it, and I wanted to get in good with the staff and directors. They were short staffed, and as it turned out, it gave me access to a lot more than just the directors," he bragged. "Getting the blood was a snap."

"Is Ethel dead?" I repeated.

"She will be when I finish here."

You'd think the man was discussing a toe fungus.

"I have her money," he bragged. "Once she was cleared, she accessed Smitty's accounts. I made her withdraw all of it. She came to me when she was released from jail looking for a place to rent. Can you imagine? She said she needed time to think things through." He chuckled. "Talk about luck landing in my lap. I grabbed the opportunity. We took a little trip to the bank, and she withdrew everything. I have quite a nest egg. Now everybody thinks I'm dead, so I'll just disappear. By the time they figure out what has really happened, I'll be long gone. The realty business stinks. It's dried up, and now, I've tied up every loose end." He sighed contentedly.

"So, she never went to Little Rock, and that whole scene in the foyer about asking me where she was in front of Newton…" I trailed off.

"That was brilliant, wasn't it? I made that whole story up, and you fell for it. You're more gullible than I thought."

"I should have known something was wrong when you said she talked to you for thirty minutes on the phone. She doesn't like to talk on the phone any more than I do."

"That is not something you'll have to worry about much longer." He looked at me expectantly. "Now, it's your turn. Where's the bracelet?"

"You haven't told me about Saige yet." I hedged. "He told Mrs. Nichols he smelled a woman's perfume before he was struck."

"Oh, that." He chuckled again, laying the knife across his lap. "That was a bit of an accident. Now don't get me wrong, hitting him wasn't an accident. The way I smelled was an acci-dent." He scratched his chin.

"I wanted to get rid of him permanently because I'd done some checking. He has the reputation of being a bulldog. The guy doesn't give up until he finds out exactly what he's after. I didn't want him sniffing around, so I decided to delete the dilemma. I didn't hit him hard enough. I regret that. Doesn't matter now. Everyone will assume it was Ethel. As for the perfume smell," he explained grandly, "I'd been showing a house that day. I knocked a bottle of high dollar perfume off a shelf and broke it. I got the junk all over me trying to clean it up. The old battle-ax threw a fit and withdrew her listing."

"What about Ethel's button? How did that end up inside the crime scene?"

"You certainly are inquisitive, aren't you?" He frowned,

flicked the knife's edge on his pant leg, and continued. "The button was in Ethel's purse the day we came over here to tour. When her purse fell over, I spotted the button and an opportunity. She thought I was being helpful." He sneered. "When I offered to pick up all that junk, I nabbed the button and tossed it inside the shed that night then told Boomer I'd seen her in the shed with Smitty. Any more questions?"

We both heard the sliding sound at the same time, but I saw the reason before he did. Something slithered beneath Ralph's chair. Following my gaze, he screamed. It was the opportunity I'd been waiting for. Grabbing Marma Lee's Skarie Sculpture beside the fireplace, I brought it down on Ralph's head with a crash. Ralph toppled to the floor. Something cold touched my ankle. I wasn't sure which snake it was, but I high tailed it out the back door directly into Boomer. Finding it perfectly suitable for the moment, I screamed bloody murder.

From my mad gesturing, Boomer ran to the front room. If he was the least bit astonished at finding a man who was supposed to be dead, he didn't let on. Of course, I shook so badly, I wasn't sure of his reaction. There was a perfectly good scream working its way up my throat. A figure raced across the field at top speed. I ran to meet him.

Blubbering is not attractive. Neither is hiccupping. Yet I did both. Mick assured me it was okay. If I'd started howling at the moon, he no doubt would have joined in so I wouldn't feel alone. Finally, I pulled away and pointed toward the store.

"Boomer. Ralph. Snake. Ernesto Skarie. Scary." He nodded and led me back to the shop.

Standing at the threshold, we peered inside.

"Boomer," Mick yelled. "Is everything okay?"

"Yeah, but we need some lights in here. Go check the fuse box in Mary Clare's office, will ya?"

So that was what Ralph had been doing in my office. We

hadn't had a power outage. He'd turned them off so no one could turn them on.

Mick turned to me. "Do you want to come with me or go to the cottage?"

"With you," I blurted. He squeezed my hand and led me through the dark. He wove around and dodged stray pieces of furniture. I looked for stray snakes.

"There's a snake somewhere in here," I warned Boomer. "Under Ralph's chair maybe."

"Mary Clare, it's too cold for snakes. Why don't you go on back to the cottage and rest? Get Lilly to make you a nice cup of cocoa or, Lilly. Where is Lilly?" His raised voice bounced from ceiling to floor and echoed throughout the building.

"Calm down. She's spending the night at Rennie's house."

Mick hurried to the office. I went with him, showing him the fuse box. Within minutes, lights were blazing in the main room. Mick and I rushed to Boomer's side. Ralph lay on his back, mouth wide open. Either he was out cold or really dead. I prayed I hadn't killed him. Boomer felt Ralph's neck for a pulse and pronounced him still among the living. Placing cuffs on his wrists, he shook his head with disgust. Ralph's knife was in front of the chair where he'd dropped it. Boomer told me not to touch it.

"Don't worry." I stepped back and stuck both hands in the air. Seeing the knife reminded me of the tie used to kill Smitty. I mentioned it to Boomer. He nodded solemnly.

"Now, we know the murder weapon. Forensics can do a lot with this." He pulled it carefully from around Ralph's neck and bagged it.

He hurried to the phone, but it wasn't working. It seemed Mother Nature, not Ralph, messed that up. Mick pulled his cell phone out of his pocket and called Clarence as well as an ambulance.

"How did you know to come, Boomer?"

"I parked the squad car at Mutt's and came to patrol on foot. I walked around to the window first. When I saw the cardboard gone, I knew someone was here."

I looked at the puddle on my beautiful new floor. "May I clean up the water?"

"Sorry. Stand where you are. We'll work as fast as we can." Within fifteen minutes, Clarence came in the front door. The EMT crew wasn't far behind.

Ralph lay perfectly still. The paramedics checked him over and deemed him unconscious but fine. I told them about Ethel. Up until that point, their faces remained impassive. Knowing a woman could be buried alive or starving to death altered their composure. Boomer instructed Clarence to contact Newton.

"Ask him for all their listings, Clarence. I want to know which ones are vacant. Tell him I need them within the hour." Boomer was quite impressive when barking orders. Clarence went to the cruiser to make the call. He was back in moments.

"Newton said he could give us that information without going through the listings. The only one is the old Weatherly house out on Highway 412. You want me to check it out?"

"Yes, but take a backup." He nodded at the EMTs. "Ralph's in no immediate danger. Ethel is. Radio back and let me know something."

"Yes, sir." He hurried out the door.

"Boomer." I stood far away from the chair Ralph had just vacated. "What are we going to do about the snake?"

"Honey." He ran his hand over his face. "You've suffered a trauma. The lights were out, and you probably mistook a sock or something for a snake."

"I don't leave socks in the shop. The snake was under that chair." I pointed to the one vacated by Ralph.

"If it will make you feel better, we'll take a look." He strode to the chair and lifted it with ease. "You see, Mary Clare, there's nothing…"

"It's a snake!" I hollered. "I told you so. Do something."

"Wait a minute." Mick scrambled over to the chair. "That's a king snake. They're harmless." He turned to me. "They get rid of predators."

I stared at the creature that looked almost as startled as I did. "He certainly helped get rid of one tonight. How did he get in here? Where's the rest of his family?" We searched for a point of entry. The broken window seemed unlikely for a snake. Raccoons, maybe. Snakes, no.

I spotted the ficus tree Mick had carried in and remembered the rustling sound coming from it just before I'd heard the soft thud. I thought Ralph ran into the tree. It was the snake coming out of the planter to rescue me. It had no doubt crawled into the pot before leaving the nursery. Pansy said they would look for a warm place. It slithered under Ralph's chair when I lit the fire.

"We can't leave him here." I nibbled on my lip. "We can't turn him out, either. Let's find a box to put him in. Will you take him with you?"

"Yes, I will." Boomer pulled at his ear. "I sure thought you were hallucinating."

We rounded up a nice, tall box from the storage room and placed the snake inside. Mick salvaged a generous stash of hay from the front porch and put it in with him. By the time Boomer finished with the preliminaries, the snake had a temporary name: Boo.

"I need to let Mama know what happened, Boomer."

"I'll get her. I'll have Rennie ride with us, and I'll explain everything on the way over. In the meantime, you get off your feet. I've never seen you so pale."

"I'm fine."

"I'll make sure she gets off her feet." In one fluid movement, Mick cradled me in his arms. "I'm carrying her back to the cottage."

Sounds from the heap on the floor alerted us Ralph was

gaining consciousness. He stayed conscious long enough for Boomer to read him his rights. Then, I stood on tiptoe to whisper in Mick's ear. Quickly, he went to the box. Ralph's eyes were flicking open when Mick stuck the snake in his face. One glance at the menacing-looking snake, and he was out again. We each bragged on it for a job well done, and Mick returned him to his comfy, warm box.

Boomer deposited a handcuffed Ralph into the patrol car. He sat in the back seat with Boo to keep him company. The formalities would be taken care of at the police station. Once that took place, Boomer could pick up Mama.

As we neared the cottage, we heard the yapping of two concerned greyhounds before we opened the door. I settled on the couch. Mick raced upstairs and soon had me bundled in blankets. As he tucked and fretted, he whispered the dearest, sweetest things in my ear. Things that made me blush…then ask him to repeat them. When he ran out of whisper material, he stroked my hair and held me. Safe, warm, and exhausted, I dozed off. The next thing I knew, Mama held my head and bawled. Rennie did the same at my feet. Groggily, I thought this must be what it's like to be loved from head to toe. I sat up with an effort and looked at the four concerned faces. Boomer and Mick stood back and let us have a good cry.

It took an hour to explain everything. I started with the bracelet Uncle Ardmore found and ended with the snake's perfect timing. "Have they found Ethel yet?"

"Yes, honey." Mama smoothed my hair. "Clarence radioed Boomer as he brought us over. They found her. She's in pretty bad shape, but they were taking her to the hospital."

"She and Saige will have plenty to talk about. He's out of his coma. He came out of it while we were there." Rennie looked at Mama, and her whole face lit up.

"What?" I demanded.

"Well," Mama started, "you know how we all wondered why

he wanted to talk to Marma Lee while he was in the hospital? It seems he thought Marma Lee was the one who clobbered him for giving her the brush off. He smelled a strong perfume and thought of Marma Lee and that horrible stuff she wore the night of the meeting. He wanted her to know he intended to press charges."

Boomer left to go back to the station, and Rennie went home to shower and change. Mama, Flash, and Blur were only a few feet away. Life was good again. I had a long thank you list to send to God. I looked at Mick. No more Etch-A-Sketch guys. I drifted to sleep in the arms of the real deal.

CHAPTER TWENTY-TWO

After church, Mama and I devised a plan. It would involve a trip to Jonesboro, some quick phone calls, and balloons. We didn't stop for hot chocolate, nor did we shop for clothes. Blue light specials did not beckon to us. We were on a mission.

Six o'clock arrived, and Mama and I put the last-minute touches on our plan. A huge sheet cake sat atop the replacement dining room table. Brightly colored balloons floated all over the store. The once despised Skarie Sculpture now held a place of distinction on the mantle where it would remain. The prominent sign beside it read Not For Sale.

The first person arrived shortly before six-thirty p.m.. With his usual aplomb, Richard handed Mama a bouquet of red roses and listened as we filled him in on the plan. Rennie, Marma Lee, and Mick arrived shortly after and heard the same version. At seven, the men in blue arrived.

Boomer rushed in the front door. "Are you all right?" Clarence followed him. I had instructed the dispatcher to send both and that it was urgent. It wasn't a lie. We urgently needed to thank the men who saved our lives.

"Looks like a party." Clarence's observation skills improved daily.

Boomer scanned the room, hand on his revolver and confusion wrinkling his face. "We were told you had an intruder on the premises."

"My exact words were 'something is sniffing around the property.'" I smiled.

He cocked his head and looked at Mama. She took up the reins.

"Gentlemen, please sit." She gestured toward the easy chairs. They obliged, looking at one another. Clarence, in particular, appeared ready to jump.

"This past week was horrible for all of us. There's no way to sugarcoat it. In one week's time, we've had a murder, an arson, a kidnapping, and I nearly lost Mary Clare. The only reason we're all safe tonight is because very brave men took care of us." She stopped and swallowed. "You'll never understand how much respect and admiration you hold in our hearts."

Mama blushed. I sat beside Boomer on the couch and patted his hand. He opened his mouth to say something when a scratching sound stopped him. Clarence visually cordoned off the room.

"Relax," I reassured him. "I wasn't lying when I told the dispatcher something was sniffing around." I stood and walked the few steps to the old steamer trunk in front of the fireplace. Lifting the lid, I withdrew a puppy and handed it to Boomer.

"Where did this come from?"

"Mama and I talked the Humane Society supervisor in Jonesboro into opening for us today." I scratched the puppy behind the ears. "I saw an advertisement on the news the other night. The director is a sweetheart and has heard about you. She's quite intrigued." I wiggled my eyebrows.

Boomer stroked the pudgy black lab. He grinned like a little kid. "He looks a lot like Luke. Maybe I should call him Luke Junior." He studied the dog's soulful eyes.

"Nope. That won't work. He already has a name," I explained.

"Oh. Well, what is it?" Boomer inquired.

"Milo. The lady at the shelter said he and his brother came from police dog lineage."

Milo howled.

"I think he just said yes. He's grown fond of this old trunk, so we'd like to give it to him. He'll need a place to sleep, you know. He prefers the lid up." I grinned.

A scratching noise came from the office.

"What's that?" asked Mick. "You didn't have a racoon get in here somewhere, did you?"

"No racoons, thank goodness, but you remember I said Milo had a brother. We brought him and the mother home too. Ethel wants to keep Raven. She's the mama. We're giving the puppy to someone special as a sort of welcome to the neighborhood gift." I cut my eyes at Mick. Ah, there were those pearly whites again.

"You got a puppy for me?" He all but bounded to the office. He looked like a proud papa as he carried another wiggly pup into the room. Trailing behind was an anxious blonde lab. It nudged Mick. He reached down.

"Does this one have a name?" Mick asked, grinning as the pup licked his face.

"His name's Bear," Mama answered. "Raven only had two puppies, and he was so tiny they didn't expect him to make it. They thought it would help if they gave him a good, strong name."

Clarence looked proud. "I've got a new pet too."

"You do?" Mama looked thrilled.

"I kept the snake. I've permanently named it Skarie. I've got it a real fine place fixed in my living room. King snakes make great pets, you know."

"It's also a proven fact that pet owners live longer, happier lives," Marma Lee added and crossed her legs.

Mama turned her attention back to Clarence and smiled. "I'm glad you'll be taking care of Skarie. He certainly took care of Mary Clare." Rising, she hurried to the office and returned carrying a book which she handed to Clarence.

"I hear snakes like to be read to periodically. Maybe he'll enjoy this." Clarence unwrapped the book. He held in his hands a first edition of Sir Arthur Conan Doyle's *Sherlock Holmes*. He was speechless.

"You know," Boomer said, clearing his throat, "lawmen aren't supposed to accept gifts. It's against regulations."

Mama waved her hands in front of her. "Oh, these aren't gifts. All of these are lost items. We don't know where they came from. We're turning them over to the authorities until their rightful owners come to claim them. Of course, that book is well over a hundred years old. I'm fairly certain their owners are pushing up daisies by now, and Raven, Milo and Bear might have ended up being put to sleep."

After that, the party got underway. Boomer called the dispatcher and told him they would be at Pocket Change for the next hour. That gave Raven and her puppies plenty of time to acquaint themselves with Flash and Blur while Boomer and Clarence had a chance to relax and nibble Mama's goodies.

"Boomer, did you ever find out why Ruby needed to see you?" I bit into an enormous slice of cake.

He nodded. "Sure did." Milo sat in his lap, licking icing from his finger. "She wanted to tell me she saw Ralph accompany Ethel into the bank. She thought they were probably conducting a real estate transaction and then became worried when she heard Ethel disappeared."

"Ruby's a sharp lady," Richard spoke up. "I wonder what she'll want to do about Cora Ann."

"She phoned me this morning and said she'd like to give her

a proper burial." I stroked Raven's silky head. "I told her we'd do whatever we could to help. You know, Smitty insisted the cottage be moved back fifteen feet. I'm sure now it was because of Cora Ann's body."

"You're probably right," Boomer agreed. "We'll get a team in here this week and exhume the remains if that's what Ruby wants."

"Did you find out where Barlow ran off to?" I gathered up saucers and placed them on a tray.

Boomer and Clarence exchanged sheepish looks. "He's visiting his mother in St. Louis," Boomer admitted. "I guess we figured him wrong, Mary Clare."

"I still wouldn't trust him to handle our money." I ambled over to the party table. Boomer came up beside me.

"Mary Clare." His voice had a soft quality one didn't often hear.

"Yes." I figured he wanted to thank me for Milo and the trunk. I was wrong.

"You remember the night of the fire?"

"I can honestly say I will never forget that night."

"Did you wonder why I wasn't on duty?"

"Clarence said you had an important meeting to attend."

"Thelma called from Jonesboro. She wants me back."

"Oh. What are you going to do?" The woman knocked the breath right out of him when she left.

"She finally admitted her boyfriend dumped her. She just needs me until she finds some other guy. That's the way it's always been with Thelma."

"You don't deserve to be treated like that. God's got a better plan for you. A better lady."

He nodded then took off after Milo as he scampered across the room. I clapped my hands. The assembled group looked startled.

"I know this has been an unusual week."

"That's putting it mildly, sweetheart." Oh, that voice. Creamy chocolate.

If God chose this moment to double my freckles, add twenty pounds, and make my ears bigger, I'd still be a happy woman. Mick Walker called me sweetheart. For a moment my heart was so full, there was no room for the words in my mouth. My gaze lingered on Mick as he leaned against the doorframe, striking that luscious pose I adore. He was even cuter with a puppy in his arms.

I turned to Mama. "Now, I have something for you." I walked to the office and retrieved the wrapped box I'd hidden. When I handed it to her, she carefully unwrapped the paper and gasped. It was a replica of the clock she'd seen in O'Hare's Antique Shop thirty years ago. Thank goodness for eBay.

"It's exactly like the one your daddy gave me when we married. I haven't seen one in years." She caressed the oak sides. "The night your daddy presented it to me, he was so happy. He said time would never stand still, and God wanted us to find joy in every minute of it."

Across the room, Mick's eyes found mine. I looked into those promising green depths. "He was right, Mama."

AMEN

Mary Clare's O.S.P. (Old Standby Prayer)
Lord, when I am feeling tired or strained,
help me not to take it out on other people.
Amen

ABOUT THE AUTHOR

Debbie writes contemporary fiction for both adults and middle grade audiences. Humor often shows up unexpectedly. She holds a Master's Degree in Library Science and a Bachelor's in Elementary Education. She lives in a small nestled-up part of Arkansas with her incredibly patient husband and a band of rescue animals.

Her professional affiliations include ALA, Society of Children's Book Writers and Illustrators, ACFW, Sisters in Crime, American Reading Association, and Romance Writers of America.

Among her favorite authors are John Grisham, Christine Lynxwiler, Miranda James, Joy Avery Melville, Tara Johnson, Talya Tate Boerner, Shannon Taylor Vannatter, Dr. Seuss, Sheila Turnage, Debbie Macomber, and Jan Karon.

Her compass verse is Philippians 4:8 *"Finally, brethren, whatever things are true, whatever things are noble, whatever things are just, whatever things are pure, whatever things are lovely, whatever things are of good report, if there is any virtue and if there is anything praiseworthy—meditate on these things."*

Go to www.debbiearcher.com to find out more about Debbie, her social media outlets, and her cast of characters.

Jerome, Arizona: the largest ghost town in America

Antiques expert Marty Greenlaw comes to Jerome to face the horror that haunts her dreams: Did she kill her little sister twenty-two years ago?

Historian Paul Russell is in Jerome to face his own horror: Was the car crash that killed his wife his fault?

Their lives become intertwined when an old lady dies on a long staircase in a vintage Victorian house. As Marty and Paul search the house for a small copper box Marty believes will unlock the mystery, accidents begin to happen.

Someone else wants the copper box—someone willing to commit murder to get it. As Marty and Paul face the shadows in the house and in their lives, they must learn to put the past behind them and run the race God is calling them to.

The Copper Box by Suzanne Bratcher

www.ingramcontent.com/pod-product-compliance
Lightning Source LLC
Chambersburg PA
CBHW070622100726

47907CB00007B/1830